Others Were Emeralds

Also by Lang Leav

Others Were Emeralds

A Novel

✳

Lang Leav

HARPER ⬤ PERENNIAL

NEW YORK • LONDON • TORONTO • SYDNEY • NEW DELHI • AUCKLAND

HARPER PERENNIAL

HarperCollins books may be purchased for educational, business, or sales promotional use. For information, please email the Special Markets Department at SPsales@harpercollins.com.

FIRST EDITION

Designed by Chloe Foster

Library of Congress Cataloging-in-Publication Data:

Names: Leav, Lang, author.
Title: Others were emeralds : a novel / Lang Leav.
Description: New York City : Harper Perennial, 2023. |
Identifiers: LCCN 2023009537 (print) | LCCN 2023009538 (ebook) | ISBN 9780063304024 (trade paperback) | ISBN 9780063304048 (ebook)
Subjects: LCGFT: Bildungsromans. | Novels.
Classification: LCC PR9619.4.L446 O85 2023 (print) | LCC PR9619.4.L446 (ebook) | DDC 823.92--dc23/eng/20230307
LC record available at https://lccn.loc.gov/2023009537
LC ebook record available at https://lccn.loc.gov/2023009538.

ISBN 978-0-06-330402-4 (pbk.)

23 24 25 26 27 LBC 6 5 4 3 2

For Mum & Dad

Others Were Emeralds

Prologue

Sydney, 2000

WHAT COMES FIRST, the photograph or the memory? At the tender age of twenty, I am at a loss to find myself one midday, sitting on a dull red bench in the loud, bustling plaza of my hometown, Whitlam, a place I thought I'd long since left behind. In my hand is a photograph I had never seen, only imagined, one I wasn't entirely sure existed until now. As my fingers trace the lonely seascape, a wave of nostalgia bears heavily down on me and I shut my eyes tight, trying to hold back the tide. But then comes the phantom roar of the ocean, seagulls bursting into frame, crying their mournful song, the sound of a shutter click like the start of an old black-and-white movie, my lips silently counting down the years, catapulting me back into that snapshot frozen in half-light, the sun just at the tip of the horizon, jutting into view.

It was the year 1997 and I was seventeen. We were coming to the end of November, having just completed our twelfth and final year at Whitlam High. Tin and I had spent the whole night cruising in my parents' butterfly-blue Cressida, drifting through fog and starlight, until the darkness gradually disintegrated into gray, and we stopped by a deserted beach. There we sat with my back pressed up against him, with his arms circling my waist, legs concertinaed around my hips. Our bodies stamped into history, gently rocking to the metronome of the waves lapping the shore. We were waiting for the sun. It didn't occur to me that time had us in her grip then. A man walking by paused to gawk at us, eyes glazed, mouth hanging open like a vagrant in a drunken stupor. He was a strange sight, scruffy and bearded—naked but for a pair of white, ill-fitting underwear resembling a loincloth—sharp shoulder bones protruding like bird wings. He seemed as mystified by our presence as we were with his. Perhaps it was the way we were dressed: Tin in a rented tux, me in a red strapless dress, a small silver Nikon cradled in my lap, lens pointed outward with a ready finger on the shutter. The contrast of two worlds, one anchored firmly in the present, the other almost primordial. It was as though we'd just landed shipwrecked on a new frontier, met with a civilization still untouched by time. Perhaps the man was a symbol of rebirth. After all, new beginnings were often heralded by great tragedy.

Under my breath, I began to hum a tune from *The Sound of Music*. As kids, Dad never let my brother, Yan, and me stay up past ten. It was only days ago I had seen the ending to that movie. Before that, there were no spiderlike insignias popping up like weeds, no Nazi flags polluting the proud Austrian vista, no desperate escape in the dark of night. Rolfe never betrayed Liesl. Like me, she had been sixteen going on seventeen, waiting for life to start. Maria and the captain were falling in love. As we patiently waited for them to discover what we already knew, their happily ever after was just as much ours. How could it end with the family on the run, scaling a perilous mountain with nothing but the clothes on their backs?

Stories of war were passed around so casually at our dinner table, along with the thousand-year-old eggs and fermented bean curd. The furtive whispers between my parents of buried gold and photographs left behind in the dead of night, as though someone were still listening in. This was the familiar, well-worn narrative of peasants and farmers caught in the crossfire of war. Surely the same fate couldn't possibly befall the Von Trapp family, with their angelic, unattainable beauty and absurd wealth. How could the will of the outside world turn them out of the charmed lives they lived in their cavernous mansion— one grand enough to accommodate a ballroom that could easily swallow a block of flats like the ramshackle one where I lived. As I thought of all this, I felt myself tremble with the new and profound knowledge that everything could change in an instant, no matter who you were or how much you had. That luck or misfortune could strike at any given moment with the same cold indifference. I sensed something then that would take me years to put into words.

"What's that tune you're humming?" Tin had asked, gently coaxing me from my reverie.

Turning to nuzzle his neck, I said, "'Something Good' from *The Sound of Music*. By the glass house, Maria sings it to the captain right after he confesses his love to her. I've always thought that's the way the movie should have ended. Why didn't the director just yell '*Cut!*' and be done with it?"

"Because it's inauthentic."

"But it's meant to be fiction—isn't it? Not a documentary."

"Maybe it's a mixture of both."

"Do you think so?"

"Aren't the best stories told that way?"

Part One

One

February 1997

SINCE FRIDAY, WHEN it became official, the words had been fizzing on the tip of my tongue like popping candy. *I have a boyfriend.* The notion, novel and extraordinary, surfaced unexpectedly at times, bursting to the forefront of my consciousness, or went in a loop that kept circling back. At times it ended in a question: *I have a boyfriend?* Swinging wildly between wonder and disbelief. Yet here he was, arm slung casually around my shoulder, walking me to school. Like it was the most ordinary thing in the world. As we continued in our shy, awkward shuffle—I'd never walked with a boy's arm around my shoulder before—we snuck looks at each other, trying our best not to smile. There was the occasional "What?" And then one of us would laugh a little.

Farther along, we came upon two workmen in bright orange vests and hard hats, smoothing out freshly laid cement with their loud, circular machinery. All down the street were yellow plastic barriers set up to form a loose perimeter around their work.

Seeing how the men were distracted, I crouched down, picking up a twig by my feet.

"What are you doing, Ai?"

"Cover me." I tossed a furtive glance over my shoulder to check on the workmen again. Then, twig firm in hand, I etched in our names.

Later I recounted this thrilling act of vandalism to my friends during lunch break as we sat under our big tree. Aysum and I thought of it as ours from the moment we had staked our claim on this spot all the way back in the seventh grade, when all the newly formed groups were in their migratory phase. We could have just as easily ended up by the school canteen, with its noisy rush of foot traffic, or the back paddock, which offered little protection from the elements. Instead, we were safely tucked away in our cozy nook, sandwiched between the library and language block. During the hot, sticky summers, our tree provided us with plenty of shade. When it rained, we simply moved from the tree to the library steps, to shelter under its generous awning while swapping our packed lunches. I would trade my leftover chive cakes for Aysum's stuffed vine leaves. We were best friends up until the eleventh grade when Nadine came along and the two became inseparable. Around the same time, I became close with Brigitte, who was at this moment reminiscing about when she was caught red-handed drawing a giant penis on the chalkboard before Mr. Muni's science class. We all pitched in with our versions of the event that had immediately earned Brigitte a week's detention and cemented her place as the coolest girl in school.

Sying, the fifth and last member of our small girl-group, asked whether I put an ampersand or a plus between the names, and Brigitte gave her an odd look and said, "That's awfully specific, Sying."

I said, "To be honest, I don't remember."

Sying had joined our group after being ostracized by a clique we dubbed the Welcoming Committee on account of their overly studious, teacher's-pet personas. The rift had something to do with the forty-hour famine project they ran the previous year and a misappropriation of funds. After an intense period of finger pointing, the blame landed squarely on Sying, though it was unclear whether she was at fault or just a convenient scapegoat. The Welcoming Committee were known for their ruthless, cutthroat approach to dealing with conflict. Which is why no one was surprised when they threw Sying under the bus the way they had once done to another kid, who wound up having to leave our school for a neighboring one. Since defecting to us, Sying found it hard to shake the characterization of her previous group, and I wondered if it was because of her behavior or our own preconceptions. Either way, she acted as a kind of fifth wheel, constantly seeking our approval or trading alliances whenever it suited. She pressed, "Or was it a love heart?"

"Definitely not a love heart. I would have remembered that."

"I wonder if it had a chance to set before the workmen got to it."

I shrugged. "We can go and see after school."

• • •

It was there, next to someone's initials and a wonky yin and yang symbol.

Nadine squealed with delight. She'd just started dating a guy in our year named Trevor and was still in that lovey-dovey stage. Aysum was her usual calm self, surveying the scene with a beatific expression on her face. Brigitte remarked that, even with a twig, my penmanship was second to none.

Sying crouched down to get a closer look. "An ampersand after all."

"What difference does that make?" I asked.

She shrugged. "It's just interesting, that's all."

Brigitte and I exchanged a look. Sying could be finicky about things that most people wouldn't give a second thought.

"What was his reaction?" asked Nadine.

"It freaked him out a bit, but he was kind of impressed as well."

"You guys are going to have to stay together forever now, right?"

I traced the hastily scrawled words with the tip of my Converse sneakers. *Ai & Bowie.* "Yes." The word rang with all the conviction I held in my adolescent heart.

Bowie was the last person for whom I expected to fall. He was always on the periphery, like so many of the kids who never made a lasting impression. Brigitte had dated him the summer before eleventh grade, but that was before she and I were friends. Bowie and I shared a couple of classes but sat several rows apart. I guess it wasn't a single event or moment but an accumulation of small things that all happened on the first day of our final year at Whitlam High: seeing his name written on the library slip of a book I had borrowed, eyes meeting unexpectedly across the classroom after someone told a particularly funny joke, letting me go ahead of him in line at the school canteen. All these instances were like a line of dominoes that collapsed in one big crescendo, and suddenly there he was. My Bowie. With his floppy, jet-black hair, impossibly long lashes, and tawny skin. He was at least a head taller than most of the guys in our year, thin and reedy, backpack slung one-sided over his shoulder. Everything about him was casual and uncomplicated. He got good grades and played basketball. He patted the backs of his opponents when he was on the losing team.

Always at his side was his best friend, Tin, a boy who was Bowie's polar opposite. Where Bowie was sunshine and warmth, Tin was remote and reticent, with his hooded eyes and cheeks lightly pockmarked, tiny half-moon grooves that deepened depending on the time of day, at times vanishing altogether. The two had been best friends since primary school, without once falling out. Their friendship was viewed as something of an institution, one which I was wary of disrupting.

During my first few weeks as Bowie's girlfriend, Tin barely said a word to me. He would on occasion tag along on our dates to the movies or bowling alley. We would mainly converse through Bowie, our words passing through him like a satellite signal before reaching its intended recipient.

Soon, the four of us started hanging out at Brigitte's house, because her mother, Lucille, was hardly home. Brigitte and I would whip up plates of bánh xèo (Bowie's favorite) or croque monsieur with a side of hand-cut fries. Brigitte loved playing house and was an exceptionally good cook, taking after Lucille, who owned a popular French Vietnamese bakery named Paris, a hole-in-the-wall type of establishment opposite the railway station. At first, the arrival of a young, single mother in our conservative town had caused much consternation, and the rumor mill went into overdrive, spouting wild speculations about her past. One moment Lucille was rumored to be the mistress of a diplomat, and next the daughter of a revolutionist with ties to the Viet Cong. Some said she was a high-class hooker or a teenage runaway. In truth, she was a just a girl from Hanoi sent to live with her wealthy aunt in Paris where she fell pregnant at sixteen. After having baby Brigitte, Lucille was put through one of the best culinary schools in France. With Lucille being so young, the girls were raised more like sisters than mother and daughter. So the truth, though salacious in parts, could hardly be described as scandalous, and gradually she wore down the gossipmongers, even falling into their good graces. It also helped that Lucille was gregarious in nature, fluent in several languages, and quick to build rapport with her regulars. Besides, she hadn't stolen anyone's husband as initially predicted.

Lucille's bakery offered an array of pastries never before seen in Whitlam, ranging from pain au chocolat to dan taat (Chinese egg tarts) to pistachio-flavored éclairs—all as delicious as they were well presented. But where her talent shone brightest was in traditional French Vietnamese fare: pandan waffles, pâté chaud (Vietnamese puff pastry containing a variety of fillings), and bánh mì sandwiches stuffed with a medley of pork cuts, pickled vegetables, and coriander, finished with fresh chilies and condiments. Although there were several established bánh mì vendors, Lucille's were the best in town. I think the care and attention she put into each ingredient is what gave her an edge over her competitors. The baguettes were baked fresh each morning with crackling, paper-thin crust giving way to the fluffy, light-as-air interior. The steamed pork liberally seasoned with char siu was tightly rolled in Saran Wrap, then fixed with rubber bands to prevent a single drop of moisture from seeping through. Then there was the pâté, made from scratch with a specific mix of herbs, chicken livers, and brandy, chilled several days in advance, not to mention the melt-in-your-mouth, hand-whipped butter. You'd often see a line of people waiting to pick something up before their early-morning commute.

Paris was the one semblance of sophistication we had in Whitlam, a town littered with dingy eateries, one-hour photo labs, and junk shops crammed with toys and other plastic paraphernalia, fabric emporiums where rolls of organza and embroidered silk spilled past the store's threshold and onto the dirty pavement. Early on in our friendship, Brigitte introduced me to the gourmet world, taught me how to crack an egg with one hand, and how to pronounce the word "Camembert." She wasn't a snob because she was kind to everyone, and she always made you feel like you were on her level. But, like Lucille, she did appreciate the finer things in life. For instance, even though Whitlam was a comfortable stroll from one end to the other, you'd never catch Brigitte walking. She would drive her beat-up

Nissan everywhere, even if it was only down the street to pick up a chocolate bar from the corner store. Even though we'd been best friends for just over a year, it was hard to imagine my life without her.

Brigitte had transferred to Whitlam High toward the tail end of the tenth grade. She'd moved from the Blue Mountains, where she'd been the only Asian kid in school. The Blue Mountains was a region outside of Sydney frequented by tourists for its rural charm and small, picturesque towns, like Leura, where Lucille was previously employed as a baker. Leura was famous for its sweeping mountain views, enchanting gardens, and cherry blossom trees, a stark contrast to Whitlam with its chain-link fences and overgrown lawns strewn with junk and burnt-out cars. It was a bold move for Lucille to uproot the life she'd established in Leura, but she'd always dreamed of owning her own bakery, and here in Whitlam she had a handful of relatives who were happy to pitch in and help.

From the start, everyone could tell Brigitte was different. Sure, she was pretty, but no more so than a half dozen other girls at our school. Maybe it was her long, glossy hair and dancer's limbs, the way she was constantly in motion, like water reflecting the sunlight. Or it could have been her devil-may-care attitude, the knack she possessed for ending any conflict, minor or otherwise, with a shrug of her shoulders.

The day Brigitte started at our school, her presence seemed to shift things in a small but significant way. I'm sure I wasn't the only one who sensed this as I watched people around her behave in ways they normally wouldn't. The change was subtle: someone's laughter sounding slightly off-key or a furtive look that swiftly changed to one of feigned nonchalance—little things like that. Sying, then still a member of the Welcoming Committee, was tasked with showing her around our school and took the job seriously, as though she were escorting around a visiting dignitary. Aysum had said something like "Oh, there's the new girl everyone's talking about," pointing past my shoulder as I'd turned to look.

Whenever I recall that moment, Brigitte is in freeze frame by the basketball courts where Bowie had just sunk a ball and his team were being particularly loud and raucous, more for Brigitte's benefit than his, her eyes roaming methodically over the unruly boys before coming to rest on the tallest one. They started dating a couple weeks before we broke for summer. Usually when a couple got together, the rumor mill would go into overdrive, with every detail about the new relationship dissected and discussed. Everyone knew the quickest route to instant popularity was to hook up with someone else. But then the school year ended and by the time we started year eleven, Bowie and Brigitte were already over. It wasn't until then that I began hanging out with Brigitte.

Even though we'd seen each other around school, I don't remember us having a conversation until we were put in the same art class. That day, I had settled myself in during the lunch break to work on a personal bookbinding project. By the time class started, I was sitting in a quiet corner, sewing up the pages of my book with red string. Curious, Brigitte came over to me and asked, "What are you making?"

I paused, needle in midair, then tucked it into the binding. Handing the half-stitched book to her, I said, "I'm making a journal."

She traced her fingers over the red thread. "Is there a name for this style of binding?"

"Coptic," I said, straightening. Although we'd spoken before, this was our first real conversation, and I felt a strange urge to impress her. When she didn't respond right away, I quickly added, "It looks complicated but it's really not. I can show you sometime." To my ears, I sounded overeager and cringed inwardly.

She looked at me coolly, not seeming to notice the effect she had. "And what do you use the journals for? Do you give them away as gifts?"

"Sometimes, but mainly I just use them myself." Reaching into my backpack, I pulled out an old journal that I had bound using the saddle stitch method and the fur from an old teddy bear. She looked at it with genuine wonder. "Gosh, this is amazing. Can I look inside?"

"Sure," I said.

She must have caught a slight hesitation in my voice because she asked, "Are you sure? It's not private or anything, is it?"

I shook my head. "Go on, it's fine."

She flicked through, eyes widening slightly. Inside the book were pages of poems and sketches along with the odd pressed flower. She turned the book around to a sketch I had done of my mother sitting at her Singer. "Is this your mum?"

"Yeah, she's a seamstress."

She examined the sketch again, head slightly tilted. "That's probably my favorite in the journal. It's her eyes, I think. They're so expressive; she has the eyes of someone with stories to tell."

I nodded, pleased with her appraisal.

"Hey, did you mean what you said earlier?"

I looked at her blankly. "Earlier?"

"That you'd show me how to make a book using this binding technique."

"Sure." I smiled. "I don't have all the tools here, but you can come over to my place after school if you're free."

At home, we ran into my brother, Yan, in the hallway. I introduced them quickly, eager to get Brigitte into my room before he said anything embarrassing. But I didn't have to worry because she was keen to know all about the economics degree he was studying at Sydney U. I watched his eyes light up as she lavished him with praise and attention, wanting to know every small detail about campus life.

After she left, Yan said, "She's cute."

"Cradle snatcher," I teased him, even though he was only a few years older.

Later, Mum called out to us from the kitchen to set the table. Yan and I scrambled obediently out of our respective rooms and carried out the nightly pantomime. First, we grasped each end of the square foldout table with its chipped pale-wood veneer, kicking out the metal legs and positioning it in the middle of our small lounge room. Then I laid out the transparent table-cloth with a garish pattern of yellow chrysanthemums before scooping bowls of rice from the cooker and organizing the chopsticks. Next, Yan unstacked and arranged the metal-framed chairs with red vinyl seats. Finally, we took turns coaxing Dad from my parents' bedroom, where he would be working away diligently at his rickety desk almost buckling with the sheer weight of his heavy textbooks stacked haphazardly across the surface alongside calligraphy pens and inkwells, rolls of rice paper, spiral-bound notebooks, and dictionaries used to translate between Mandarin and Khmer. We carried out the same ritual every night. During dinner, Yan brought up Brigitte.

"Your friend—what was her name again?"

"What friend?" I feigned nonchalance as I spooned chicken and wood ear mushroom into my bowl of rice.

"Aw, come on, Ai."

"Is it Brigitte?" asked Mum in Teochew, blowing on a spoon-ful of her bone broth. She spoke to us in a patchwork of dialects, switching mid-sentence between Teochew, Mandarin, and broken English. Khmer, the language of her motherland, she spoke only with Dad, like a secret they had kept for themselves.

"Is it her mother, just open bread shop?" asked Dad, who mainly stuck to Teochew.

Then Mum said there were rumors about Brigitte's mother, Lucille. When I asked her what they were, she said she didn't like to gossip but it was best I don't hang around Brigitte too often. Then, addressing Yan and me, she said, "Careful: pretty girl trouble."

. . .

Despite her initial misgivings about Brigitte, Mum was easily won over with the odd treat from Paris Bakery and impromptu shoulder massages. Soon my new friend was a regular fixture at the dinner table, cracking jokes and showering Mum with compliments. "Auntie, this char kway teow is so tasty! What's your secret ingredient?"

"Salt duck egg," Mum would beam.

Chewing thoughtfully, Brigitte would say, "Oh, I see. Yes, that's why it tastes so good."

My tiny bedroom, sorely lacking in floor space, shrank even further with the futon almost permanently rolled out for the times Brigitte slept over, sandwiched between my bed and the tallboy. On those evenings our voices in the dark, strangely disembodied, seemed to melt away the walls around us. Our conversations flowed long into the night, our laughter low and conspiratorial. We talked about books—Brigitte loved period dramas and I had a weakness for fantasy—though we were willing to cross genres at the other's recommendation. It was the same for music, with Brigitte's fevered obsession with Tori Amos spilling into my love of grungy bands like Garbage and Hole.

But when it came to boys, we were hardly ever in agreement, as was evidenced by our favorite TV show, *Beverly Hills 90210*. Between the two leading men, Brigitte preferred Brandon, while I would passionately argue to the contrary why Dylan was the sexier of the two. From our preferences, we were able to ascertain that she liked jocks, while I preferred the quiet, brooding type.

Sometimes I'd hang out with Brigitte at Paris Bakery during the school holidays and weekends, when it was her turn to man the store. In between serving customers, we made crank calls to our friends or passed the time playing word games like I Spy. I never got paid, but every now and then she'd press a five-dollar bill into my hand.

Brigitte was one of those kids who always seemed to have money, which meant we were able to afford small luxuries, such as the latest issue of *Dolly* magazine, tubes of strawberry lip gloss, and packets of M&M's. I couldn't pinpoint the source of her funds but suspected she sometimes swiped from the till. Not that Lucille would have minded. They seemed to adore and loathe each other in equal measure. One moment they were screaming blue murder; the next Brigitte would be planting butterfly kisses across her mother's beaming face. I was jealous of their warm if sometimes volatile relationship. My mother seemed ancient in comparison, in the way her mouth drooped at the corners or in the crow's-feet that exploded like starbursts when she smiled. Despite her sporadic attempts at learning English, her accent remained thick and clunky with disordered syntax and improper pronouns, the kind of pidgin English that was widely mocked in popular culture. Lucille was fluent in both English and French, lending her an air of sophistication that set her worlds apart from the other mums in Whitlam. She would lavish me with gifts and attention, plaiting my hair or making up platefuls of my favorite spring rolls when I was over. But when I praised Lucille to Brigitte, she'd retorted, "She's only that way around you."

"What do you mean?"

"She just loves to play the perfect mum around my friends."

Still, I never sensed anything disingenuous about Lucille until the night Brigitte threw a surprise party for my seventeenth birthday. But I'll get to that later on.

Two

WHEN I FIRST realized my feelings for Bowie, I went straight to Brigitte. "Do you mind?" I asked.

She laughed. "Please, Ai, it was hardly even a thing."

My mind ventured back to the summer they dated. At the time, I was still working the odd shift at Pepe's, the local pizzeria, before quitting to focus solely on my studies. One night Brigitte stopped by with Bowie in tow. I was in the kitchen, and from there could see Bowie with his arm around Brigitte, looking as though he couldn't believe his luck. It was obvious to anyone that she wasn't nearly as enthused about him, especially since she was openly flirting with the manager, who everyone knew had a thing for her. Thinking of that night now, I said, "I know you weren't exactly crazy about Bowie, but I still feel kind of weird, though, because of the girl code."

"Well, I went on a couple dates with Yan."

"He's my brother!"

"You weren't thrilled when you found out."

"Only because you didn't tell me for ages. But it's different with Bowie: he was your actual boyfriend."

"For all of five seconds," she said, rolling her eyes. "Now, you know it would be a different story if you said it was Alex." She spoke her ex's name without the usual reverence, which suggested to me if she was no longer concerned with the supposed great love of her life, then Bowie was way down the chain. She'd met Alex while she was still dating Bowie and for a time, was seeing them both—a truth that she once confided to me. Other than that specific detail, I don't recall much else about their relationship. As far as I knew, Bowie was just another face in her long line of ex-boyfriends. Even so, I wouldn't have pursued it further if I'd sensed the slightest reservation on her part.

"Don't worry about it." She stamped her palm on my forehead. "You have my blessing."

Just being in Brigitte's proximity meant Bowie, at the very least, was aware of my existence. To me, that was a good start. As far as I knew, Bowie remained blissfully unaware that Brigitte had cheated on him. Given their amicable breakup and the fact that they remained good friends, she was now in an ideal position to gauge his interest, hopefully without him being all the wiser. Brigitte had a knack for covertly extracting information. For example, our English teacher, Mr. Carraway, once hinted that our next exam would be an essay question from a past paper. Brigitte then asked him a series of seemingly innocuous questions and from his answers was able to pinpoint exactly which paper he was referencing. Of course, I wanted her to use this same method to find out if I had a chance with Bowie, although I didn't want to straight-out ask. But the way things went, I didn't have to, because during the next lunch break, when I told the girls about my crush, Nadine said to Brigitte, "You're pretty chummy with Bowie: Do you think Ai's got a shot?"

"I wouldn't say 'chummy,' but we do have the odd chat when he stops by the bakery."

"Why don't you casually mention Ai next time he visits and see how he reacts?"

Brigitte poked me in the ribs. "What do you think, Ai?"

"Say a word to him and I will kill you!"

Aysum giggled. "Guys, check out Ai's face. She wants you to ask him so bad."

I bit down hard on my lip to stop the smile tugging at the corners of my mouth. Then, to my horror, Sying said, "What if I asked him for you, Ai? Bowie and I are distant cousins, after all."

"Absolutely not, Sying!" My tone stressing there was no room for discussion. Sying did not possess the subtlety of Brigitte, and I knew she would botch it horribly.

"Best leave it to the experts, huh?" Nadine nudged Brigitte conspiratorially.

Brigitte grinned my way, all dimples and mischief. "I promise to be subtle: he won't even know you like him. Boys are stupid like that. I'll suss it out for you next time he stops by."

I groaned and buried my head in my lap. But secretly I was pleased.

The next couple of weeks were excruciating as I wondered if Brigitte had spoken to Bowie. But I had to pretend I didn't care either way. I was in limbo, waiting for something that I wasn't sure would eventuate. My heart was like a ticking clock, set to an alarm that could go off at any given moment. As a consequence, my feelings were being blown way out of proportion, seemingly spurred on by all the uncertainty. Then one day, when I thought Brigitte had dropped the whole thing altogether, she came to me after first period. Tapping my arm, she said, "Ai, I spoke to Bowie."

"Oh . . ." I tried my best to look complacent, as though I had forgotten all about it. "And?"

"At first, I just asked him how he was and all that. Sussed out what was going on with his love life and so forth." She paused, and the look on her face made my stomach drop. "Look, I have some bad news. Turns out he's just started seeing this girl from Mary MacKillop. They have to keep it real quiet because her parents are strict."

"Oh, well," I said, struggling to keep the disappointment from registering on my face.

She gave me a quick hug. "It was only a crush, right? No big deal?"

"No big deal."

"That's okay, then. Plenty of fish in the sea."

My feelings for Bowie only intensified after that, even though I tried my best not to show it. I fell into a kind of restless despondency, spending hours scrawling tirelessly in my journal. At school, when I saw Bowie walking toward me, I would swiftly change direction or pretend I'd forgotten something and turn around to walk back the other way. If my friends mentioned him, I would brush it off with a laugh or a comment such as "What was I thinking?"

But the more I tried to dismiss my feelings for Bowie, the more they seemed to grow. Sure, I'd had crushes before, but this felt like something else entirely. Up until this point, I'd always been able to keep a firm grip on things, no matter what I was going through. My thoughts, usually consistently calm like the gentle swing of a pendulum, now veered wildly like a wrecking ball on a chain. In a bid to make sense of it all, I began pouring my angst into long, tedious poems that delved into the depths of my emotional state, finding a strange comfort in capturing fragments of my inner turmoil and constricting them into verse. In this way I was able to bring a sense of order to the chaos.

One day I suspected my façade was perhaps not as convincing as I had imagined when Sying, who was the least perceptive in our group, asked me, "Everything okay with you, Ai?"

For some reason I didn't feel like confiding in her, but I did seek out Aysum during a free period. We were sitting under the awning of the school library, sharing a pack of Skittles.

"You know I still have feelings for Bowie, don't you?" I broached.

"I kind of figured," said Aysum.

"Is it that obvious?"

"It is to me, but that's probably because of how well I know you. Why are you acting like you don't care?"

I relayed to her what Brigitte had told me about Bowie's secret girlfriend. She hesitated.

"You're not joking, are you, Ai?"

I shook my head no.

"But I thought—" She stopped, frowning.

"What is it?"

"Never mind."

"Hey, you can't begin something and not tell me the rest."

"It's probably nothing. I saw Brigitte talking to Bowie this morning, and for some reason thought it was about you."

"Why would you think that?"

"I don't know, Ai, just something about the way they were talking. Like I said, it's probably nothing."

When Valentine's Day arrived, all I could think about was whether Bowie would be spending the day with his mystery girl. It was hard to conjure an image of her, based off the tiny fragment of information I'd gleaned so far. Not that I didn't try, but, to be honest, I just kept picturing someone who looked just like Brigitte, probably because she was the only girl I knew of that he'd dated. Mary MacKillop was a private school, so it was likely the mystery girl had wealthy parents. Either that or she was there on a scholarship, which meant she could be some kind of brainiac. This made me feel woefully inadequate.

All these thoughts were circling around in my head during Modern History when two prefects walked in, each carrying a wicker basket full of red roses. A hush fell over the classroom, followed by some good-natured banter between the prefects and our teacher. Then the atmosphere became one of tense anticipation when the Rose Giving began.

The Rose Giving was a yearly tradition at Whitlam High.

A couple weeks before Valentine's Day, a trestle table was set up over by the school office on which was placed a slot box. Next to it sat a pile of slips and pens to fill in the name and year of the person to whom you wished to send a rose. The cost was two dollars per rose, which was a significant amount, especially if you purchased more than one.

The table itself was like a center of gravity leading up to the big day, with gossipmongers keeping a keen eye on the comings and goings. The bulk of the orders were girls buying roses for their friends, which meant most girls would get at least one. One year, no one got a rose for Sying—I think there may have been a miscommunication between Aysum and me—and we felt wretched about it. Since then, we'd made sure never to make the same mistake again. Sying was sitting beside me now, craning her neck in a vain attempt to read the tiny print on the name tags that were attached to each rose. But she needn't have worried because her name was called shortly before mine and we got one each.

A commotion broke out toward the back of the room, and we turned to see that Bowie had received a rose. Boys rarely sent them to each other, so when one did receive a rose, it was likely to have come from a genuine admirer. Everyone in the classroom made juvenile oohing noises. You would think he was the only person in the class to get one. Sying leaned in close and said quietly, "Are you the one who sent him that rose, Ai?"

I looked around, panic-stricken, praying no one had heard.

"Sying!" I hissed angrily, and she looked crestfallen. I immediately felt bad and softened my tone. "No, it wasn't me."

"Oh. I wonder who it could be."

• • •

I thought nothing of it when, after school, Brigitte suggested we go roller-skating at the park near her house. The afternoon brought a cool change, a welcome break from the stifling February heat. I hadn't had a chance to speak to Brigitte since morning and was eager to process the day's events with her. Now we were rolling down the concrete path in our gym shorts and I was telling her a little huffily about Sying's gaffe earlier in Modern History. "That girl has absolutely no tact."

"Oh, you know Sying," said Brigitte breezily.

"I know I shouldn't have snapped at her, but sometimes she says the most idiotic things. What if someone had heard her? It would be all over the school! I swear, I will never tell her anything from now on."

"I kind of feel sorry for her. You know how sensitive she can be."

"Anyway, I wonder who sent Bowie the rose."

"Probably the girl he's seeing."

"But she doesn't go to our school."

"Maybe she got someone to buy it for her. Remember how Alex sent me a dozen last year?" Her expression was suddenly wistful.

"Isn't that the same number of times he's cheated on you?" I said, snapping my fingers at her. As her best friend, I felt it was my duty to point out this fact whenever nostalgia threatened to cloud her judgment.

She gave me an impish grin. "Okay, smack me if I ever mention his name again. I mean it this time!"

The hum of cicadas erupted through the still air, reaching fever pitch as we passed by the sports field where a team of boys in white jerseys was playing a game of soccer. A ball was kicked in our direction and two guys chased after it. As they got closer, I noticed one was kind of cute. "Hey, beautiful," he called. We slowed to a stop.

"Which one are you talking to?" his friend asked.

"The hot one," he replied, eyes shining hopefully at Brigitte.

"She's single," I said with a wink.

Brigitte elbowed me. "I'm not interested. Sorry."

He clutched his chest as though in pain. "But it's Valentine's Day!"

His teammates who had been watching the scene were calling to him now, waving their arms impatiently, eager to get back to their game.

He gave Brigitte one last questioning look and she shook her head. With a grin, he shrugged good-naturedly and turned away, passing the ball to his friend as they jogged back up the field.

"You should have got his number," I said as we continued our way. "But I guess you can afford to be picky, can't you? I bet you got a ton of roses today."

"Not this year. I just got one—from Sying." She stuck her bottom lip out in mock disappointment.

"For real?"

"Uh-huh. How many did you get?"

"I only got one as well, but mine was from a 'secret admirer.' I'm guessing that was you?"

"Nope, I only sent one rose to Sying."

"Then mine must be from Nadine or Aysum."

"They got one for each other, so yours must have come from Sying as well."

"I asked Sying, and she said it wasn't her."

Brigitte winked at me. "I guess you have a secret admirer."

"Don't be silly," I laughed, trying not to look too pleased.

We were now approaching the tunnel, after which the path suddenly curved to a sharp right, ending abruptly at a gritty, heavily graffitied brick wall. Brigitte turned to me and grinned. "Race you to the end?"

"You're on!"

I fired up, grinding my wheels against the concrete, all my focus channeled into propelling myself forward. When I rounded the corner, a figure flashed suddenly into my line of sight, and in that split second I realized it was too late to avoid a collision. Everything was a blur then as the impact sent me and the person tumbling onto the grass. I gasped in pain, grabbing my knee, which had taken the bulk of the shock.

"Jesus," groaned a familiar voice, jolting me to my feet. I stood with my mouth agape, staring down at the boy sitting bent over on the grass, arms wrapped around his stomach. Raising his head slowly, his eyes met mine and the grimace on his face transitioned into a slow, shaky grin. "Hey, Ai."

"Bowie?"

He stood up, gingerly rubbing the back of his neck. "Man, I didn't expect you to come barreling into me like that."

I stared, speechless. Then, glancing past his shoulder, I noticed a table setting that looked like it had been taken from a fancy French restaurant and transplanted over by the brick wall. White tablecloth, red roses in a vase, a large silver cloche between two white china plates, fluted champagne glasses, and a bucket of ice cradling a couple of bright cans of cherry cola. Tied to one of two foldable stools was a red, heart-shaped helium balloon. I figured he was on a date with the mystery girl, and I eagerly scanned the area, hoping to catch a glimpse of her. Taking in the scene, I thought with a kind of perverse glee, *Wait until Brigitte sees this.* I turned to the tunnel expectantly, waiting for her to burst through, but it remained empty. Confused, I whipped my head back around to Bowie, whose eyes were fixed on my injured knee.

"Hey, that bump looks bad, Ai." He led me over to one of the stools and sat me down. In one smooth motion he took a handful of ice from the bucket and wrapped it in a napkin. Crouching down on his haunches, he pressed the makeshift cold pack to my knee, looking up at me. "Is that better?"

I nodded, tossing another glance at the tunnel, still mystified by Brigitte's absence. Of course, when I look back now, it was dead obvious, but when you're confronted with something so unexpected, it really messes with your sense of reality. "What happened to Brigitte?" I asked dumbly.

Bowie's face grew serious, like he had something important

to say. Then, in an action that felt strangely formal, he put down the ice and, still crouching on the ground, took both my hands in his.

"Ai," he began as I flinched involuntarily from the touch of his cold, damp fingers. He dropped my hands immediately and they fell limply onto my knees.

That's when it began to dawn on me that Brigitte and Bowie had organized this surprise date, and they had planned it all for me. As I let the realization sink in, I expected to feel a sweep of elation. After all, wasn't this what I had been dreaming of for weeks now? But instead I had the sense you got when someone seems keen on telling you a joke but halfway through it it's obvious to them you had heard it before.

This must have shown on my face because the recognition of that fact was plainly visible on his. As though to confirm this, Bowie said in a tone that bordered on cynical, "Well, it's pretty obvious what this is—isn't it?"

When I didn't say anything, he continued in a rush, almost like it was something painful he had to get over with. "A couple of weeks ago, Brigitte somehow got me to admit I liked you, then she suggested I wait for Valentine's Day to ask you out. It was supposed to be a small thing, you know—a bunch of flowers at school or whatever—but somehow it turned into this." He gestured at the table.

"That sounds like Brigitte all right," I mumbled.

"She even made up a fake girlfriend to throw you off."

"The one from Mary MacKillop?"

He nodded. "It seems so stupid now, doesn't it?"

"No, no . . . it's great. I'm flattered you went to all this trouble for me. It's just a lot to take in, that's all. I'm not used to stuff like this."

"Exactly!" He groaned, sinking into the stool across from me. "This feels too staged. I thought girls liked all this soppy stuff, but it's not really you . . . is it, Ai?"

A cool wind swept by, causing the heart-shaped balloon emblazoned with the words *Be My Valentine* to bob comically above Bowie's head. I noticed the contrast between the neatly printed script on the balloon and crude graffiti on the wall, when a word taught in art class sprang to mind: "juxtapose." If you knew Brigitte like I did, you would understand this was her trademark. No matter what task she undertook, you could count on her going the extra mile to ensure everything was picture-perfect. For example, if she were to serve you breakfast, it wouldn't be your ordinary jam on toast. She would instead present you with a silver tray of homemade bread and marmalade, a warm stick of butter, and an ornamental rose she'd shaped from an apple peel. Everything she did felt curated, and for me this was as much the appeal of our friendship as it was at times a drawback. Which explained why this scene, which looked straight out of a teen romance movie, had Brigitte written all over it. And it was hard for me to understand why I felt how I did when by all accounts I should have been swooning. Instead, it was as though, mistaken for the wrong actor, I was suddenly pushed onto the stage to face the glaring spotlight, not having rehearsed a single line.

An uncomfortable silence fell between Bowie and me that seemed to grow bigger by the second. He picked morosely at the baguette, pulling out bits of crumb, rolling it between his thumb and forefinger into a ball. I peeked under the silver cloche to see a beautifully laid-out fruit-and-cheese platter when my attention was drawn by a dark shadow suddenly appearing in my periphery. I looked up in time to see a magpie smacking against the side of Bowie's head. His expression of shock mirrored my own as our eyes darted skyward, where the offending bird was now ominously circling. Since grade school, teachers had warned us about swooping magpies, sharing their wisdom on how to evade their indiscriminate attacks. One teacher advised us to wear sunglasses on the backs of our heads, to trick the magpies into thinking we had an extra pair of eyes.

As though stuck in a trance, I followed the flight path of the magpie, gasping when it suddenly plunged into a sharp dive, my forehead appearing to be its target. Bowie snapped into action then, pulling me up into standing position, holding me steady as I wobbled on my skates. We raced toward the tunnel with the crazed bird trailing closely behind. When we were safely undercover, I collapsed against the side of the wall, straining to catch my breath. Then, straightening, I tilted up my chin to get a better look at his injury. In my skates, we were almost eye to eye. Reaching over, I touched the apple of his cheek, which was already showing a bruise. He placed his palm over my hand and we smiled at each other. And, just like that, it stopped being awkward.

Three

I LOOK BACK on this memory, not only because of my fondness for it, but to establish how, in the latter part of the year, things got to where they were. In hindsight, I could plainly see how my Valentine's Day date with Bowie was the first in a series of compounding events that ultimately led to the one on which my story pivots. But before we get that far along, I want to explain how things were at the start.

Movies always have a certain way of showcasing the beginning of a relationship. You know: those cheesy scenes strung together like a television advertisement, designed to give you a warm, fuzzy glow. I'm not saying there wasn't any of that, but overall I would describe that period as more like settling into a new pair of jeans. There was an initial adjustment and then things seemed to assume their natural order. But in that short time I was constantly mindful of how my relationship with Bowie was impacting those around us—Brigitte and Tin in particular. The first time we went out as a foursome, I found myself being hyperaware of everyone's feelings, putting aside my own to ensure the evening would go smoothly.

It was a Saturday night and I had just spent the day at the mall with Brigitte. Autumn was approaching, and we each needed a new sweater. We ended up buying the same one at Sportsgirl, where they had a two-for-one special. Brigitte chose a plain white while I opted for a royal blue. Shopping bags in hand, we made our way to the cinema located on the rooftop and waited by the entrance for the boys. When I caught sight of Bowie, I felt a swell of emotion that took me by surprise. My feelings tended to fluctuate wildly around him, sometimes barely registering, other times so intense it was almost unbearable. He looked particularly handsome that night in his baby-blue polo top and jeans. Cheeks lightly bronzed, sun-kissed from a fishing trip with his dad earlier that day. Our eyes connected across the crowd and he sauntered over, Tin in tow.

"You're late!" Brigitte declared, a hint of tension in her voice.

"Sorry." Bowie grinned. At this stage, everything for me was still rosy, and I didn't know how his penchant for tardiness would soon get on my nerves. Of course, Brigitte was already familiar with this flaw in his character and was less forgiving.

Looking at the session times, Brigitte suggested we see *Jerry Maguire*.

"Nah, that looks boring," said Bowie, who wanted to watch *Scream*.

"There is so much hype about *Jerry Maguire*," Brigitte insisted. "Besides, if we watch *Scream*, we have to wait until the next showing, which is ages away." I felt this was a slight dig at Bowie's lateness, but it seemed to go over his head.

"Then let's get something to eat while we're waiting."

"I'm not hungry," Brigitte countered.

"Why don't we go to the arcade, then."

Brigitte ignored him and turned to Tin. "What do you want to watch?"

Tin shrugged. "I don't really have a preference."

"Ai?" Brigitte pressed.

"Why don't the two of you decide."

Brigitte sighed loudly, making a show of looking at her watch. "Well, *Jerry Maguire* is starting soon, so we need to make a group decision. No sitting on the fence here, guys."

"*Scream*, I guess," said Tin.

They all turned to me, and it felt like a test.

"*Scream*?" I said uncertainly.

"Okay," said Brigitte. "I guess that's settled, then."

I thought about that interaction a lot over the next few days. At the time, I had thought choosing *Scream* would bring about a quick resolution. If Tin had chosen *Jerry Maguire*, I probably would have gone along with that. But a small part of me wondered whether I had made my decision to please Bowie, even if it was on an unconscious level, and whether this was an indication of where my loyalty truly resided. I brought this up with Brigitte when we were hanging out at her house after school.

She burst out laughing. "Ai, you honestly overthink these things!"

"I've been feeling bad about it for days," I admitted.

Poking my left cheek affectionately, she said, "You're starting to sound as neurotic as Sying."

"But you did seem a bit peeved that night."

"Only at the beginning, but that's because Bowie was half an hour late. It's so frustrating how he expects everyone to wait around for him—so damn inconsiderate! You'll see what I mean when you get to know him better. But as for the movie, it wasn't a big deal. It's not like I didn't want to watch *Scream*, and I ended up liking it way more than I expected. Anyway, I remember it being a fun night overall."

"I suppose . . ."

Brigitte's eyes widened a fraction. "Didn't you have a nice time?"

I nodded quickly to reassure her I had. "It's just that Tin seemed a little quiet, that's all."

"Isn't that just the way he is?"

"I hope he doesn't feel I'm encroaching on his friendship with Bowie."

"Why would you think that?"

"He hasn't been all too friendly toward me—has he?"

"Maybe Tin's just shy. If you give him time, he might come around."

Even though Brigitte's words had alleviated some of my anxiety, I was still plagued by doubt. With their shared history to lean on, Bowie and Brigitte got along fine. I would watch them chatting animatedly and wish I could emulate the same rapport with Tin. I couldn't quite work out if his indifference to me was shyness or carefully concealed animosity. I would often try to coax him into conversation, only to get back single-word answers or a barely audible mumble. Then, after feeling like I was getting nowhere, there was finally a light at the end of the tunnel.

We were now well into March, and at this stage I'd been with Bowie for over a month. It was a rainy Tuesday afternoon and the four of us were in chem. Our teacher was away sick, so we essentially had a free period. I was sitting on top of the desk with Bowie standing behind me, arms wrapped around my waist. Brigitte was perched on the chair to my left, and Tin was leaning against a workbench where a Bunsen burner had been left out from the previous class. We were just mucking around when Brigitte brought up the topic of the major project we were expected to complete as part of our visual arts class. Toward the end of our final year, we were required to submit a finished work to be graded and then considered for the annual Art Express Exhibition. For any dedicated art student, getting into Art Express was a big deal. Not only was your work shown at the Art Gallery of New South Wales but students who got in were often photographed for the local newspaper. Only the very best works in the state were selected and just a handful from Whitlam High had ever been chosen to go on display. A component of the project was your Visual Arts Process Diary—VAPD for short. This was usually a large spiral-bound sketchbook that we used to document our ideas and experimental processes. It was a way for the markers at Art Express to see how we arrived at our final work and whether it was worthy of being included in their exhibit.

Brigitte fished her VAPD from her school bag, balancing it on her lap while she went into detail about her project.

"I'm thinking of doing a series of photographs titled 'The

Articulation of Love.' Or something along those lines. What I want to do is find and capture visual cues of love—you know, those moments when it's hard to deny. For example, love can be visible in an expression or a gesture. Culturally, Asian parents don't express love through words but through actions, such as cutting up a plate of fruit or buying their children designer shoes they can't afford. There was a time when I was obsessed with lamb chops, but Mum couldn't stand to have the smell going through her kitchen, so she'd take the portable cooker to the farthest corner of our backyard and cook up a batch for me there."

"Mum did stuff like that for us all the time," I said, welling up with sentimentality. "I grew up thinking Mum loved pizza crust, like it was her favorite thing in the whole world. For her last birthday, Yan and I gave her a box of crusts we'd cut from a whole pizza, and she was so confused. 'Why would you do this?' she asked us. Turns out, as kids we could barely afford pizza, so she pretended to like crusts just so we wouldn't feel bad about her eating our leftovers."

"Once Dad asked me what I wanted for my birthday." Bowie grinned. "And I said, 'A little brother,' so he had sex with Mum to make my birthday wish come true."

"Yuck, Bowie!" I laughed, playfully elbowing his ribs.

Tin winced, stuffing his hands into his pockets. To invite him into the conversation, I said, "What about you, Tin? Did your parents ever do anything like that?"

Tin looked visibly uncomfortable, and I instantly regretted my question. I hadn't meant to put him on the spot and was about to change the subject when, after clearing his throat, he said, "Mum died in the war when I was a kid, but, yeah, there is something I do remember."

I held my breath and waited for him to continue.

"Everywhere she went, Mum would always have a slingshot tucked into the waistband of her pants. I always thought it made her invincible, that sling. As long as she had it within reach, Mum said no one could ever hurt me. Once, we were on our way to the market, where we'd go by a large mango tree. Usually the mangoes were a dull, faded green but that day, it was as though they had ripened overnight. The tree looked like it was on fire. Even now, the colors are so vivid in my mind—blushing pinks and reds seeped into sunshine yellow. 'Which one do you want?' Mum asked me. I pointed to the biggest one, and without the slightest hesitation she whipped out her slingshot and shot it right out the tree. Then I remember us crouched on the side of the street, the noise of the foot traffic going past, Mum laughing at how the mango was almost the size of my head. I can still taste the sweetness of the fruit now, how the juice running down my chin made me feel rich beyond my wildest dreams. It was my last good memory of her, I think."

We were silent, mesmerized by the scene that Tin had so vividly painted. I had no idea his mum had died in the war. It was the first time I could recall him mentioning anyone in his family.

Bowie shook his head. "That sure beats the hell out of my story."

Brigitte, whose eyes had filled with tears, said, "That's beautiful, Tin. Do you mind if I write it down as research for my art project? I've started documenting stories by refugees."

"Not at all," said Tin.

Tin's story had taken us by surprise, sending an unexpected wave of emotion crashing through us, and I think we weren't quite sure how to react.

To defuse the tension, Bowie made another joke about something unrelated while Brigitte busied herself by scribbling down the main parts of Tin's story. When she was done, she turned her attention to me.

"How's your major work going, Ai?"

"I don't even have a solid concept yet—but I'm thinking of doing something with books."

"Have you got your VAPD on you?"

Rummaging through my backpack, I said, "Sure do. Here it is."

Brigitte leafed through my diary with interest, stopping at a page I had filled with rambling prose. Pointing at a line, she read out loud, "'This is the part in the story where someone I love would only appear again in flashbacks.' That's real pretty, Ai."

"It's a loose translation from what Mum said once when she saw the Khmer Rouge dragging her best friend away while she hid in the bushes. It was then she was hit with the realization that someone she loved would now only be a memory."

With a shudder, Brigitte said, "Horrible . . . I can't even imagine . . ." Reading further, she added, "Your writing is getting so good, Ai, especially your poems. I know you want to be an artist, but I think there's something special about your words."

"Aw, Brigitte." I ducked my head, feeling self-conscious. For me, writing was simply a means to an end, the method I used to process my thoughts and emotions. It never occurred to me that my words could possess any real artistic value.

"There's something in that line about flashbacks, I think. I'm not sure what, but it really grabbed me. And this poem you've written, 'Doors,' fits in nicely with the theme." She read it aloud:

"'The first door was my mother, where I passed through, into the world of others. The second a funeral wreath and a word silently mouthed, and then a tiny mound of baby teeth. The third a stuck-on gold star, I thought was the sky—only it was a lie. After that I lost count because anything, anything at all, can be a door. What is that jittery sound? Is it the minute hand of a clock or a time bomb ticking by? What sparkles on the other side? A birthday surprise or a firing squad. You cannot know until at the threshold, you raise a cautious hand to knock.'"

Tin raised his eyebrows at me. "That's really good, Ai."

I grinned, genuinely pleased that he liked it. "Thanks, Tin."

Bowie gave me a quick squeeze to show his appreciation and I reached behind to give his cheek a playful pat.

Brigitte snapped the visual diary shut and handed it back to me. "I like the sentiment 'anything can be a door.' It makes me think back to all those defining moments that have led me here, like a Choose Your Own Adventure book. It's weird, because you never really notice the significance at the time; it's only when something occurs in your present that it prompts you to look back and think, 'This is happening to me now because of a decision I made back then.' I always used to visualize these moments as points on an axis, but I think doors are more poetic."

"Do you know what else can be a door?" asked Bowie before answering his own question. "A door."

"Hilarious, Bowie," I said, rolling my eyes.

"A book can be a door," Tin suggested.

Surprised, I turned to him, and our eyes met briefly before he looked away.

"Visually, yes, a book is very much like a door," I agreed. "Metaphorically speaking too."

"There could be something in that," said Brigitte. "Right now, I'm envisioning a bookshelf lined with tiny doors, a whole world behind each one. I'm in awe of the way authors can bring these worlds to life the way they do. Like Wonderland for example. It's so detailed, it feels just like a real place to me—as real as any other."

"There's such a fine line between memory and imagination, isn't there? Like you said, Wonderland feels like a place I've physically been to. Yet, unlike a real place, I don't have any means to commemorate my visit, not a single photograph or memento . . ." I stopped as an idea began to take shape in my mind. "But suppose that were possible . . ."

"Oh?" Brigitte said curiously.

"What if I were to create a set of 'souvenirs' collected from my literary travels?"

Brigitte straightened up. "Yes! What a great idea!"

"Hey, that sounds cool," said Bowie.

Enthused, I continued. "And what if I made a passport filled with notary stamps from places like Wonderland or Oz? I can even keep a travel journal of what I did, who I met, what I ate. Just like in real life."

"Oh, gosh, Ai—imagine a pack of Turkish Delight with the Snow Queen illustrated on the box. It will be like a piece of installation art."

"Yes, I love that!" I beamed at her, my mind churning with ideas, already keen to get started.

"Well, there you have it." Brigitte grinned. "You just never know when an idea will find you."

"Speaking of ideas, did Sying tell you about her project? I was so impressed with the concept. She's going to sew high-fashion logos onto traditional dresses like the sarong or cheong-sam to highlight the fashion industry's exploitation of Asian immigrants."

Brigitte looked sheepish. "Actually, I kind of helped her with that. She wanted to do something with fashion, and I suggested the idea to her."

"Really? I thought she'd come up with it all on her own. I mean, that's the kind of stuff that gets you into Art Express."

"Only if Sying does the idea justice," Bowie said cynically.

"Don't be mean," I chastised him.

Brigitte tossed her hair back. "Anyway, it's mainly private school kids who get into Art Express."

"That's not true! They also pick out artworks by public school students."

"Next week, when we go on our school excursion to see the

Art Express exhibit, take note of the private versus public students. You'll be surprised."

We started up a discussion on the disparities between public and private schools. Tin pointed out that the motto for Sydney Grammar was *Laus Deo*, which translated from Latin meant Praise Be to God, whereas at Whitlam, ours was Striving & Serving. "Their motto implies a charmed existence, one that suggests their close proximity to the big man himself. Ours, on the other hand, is a picture of struggle and subservience."

In response to this, I jokingly said, "Mottos aside, my biggest gripe is not having a locker big enough to store my art materials."

I didn't think further of this conversation until the next morning, when I found a note someone had slotted into my locker. I ran my eyes over the words and read, *I have extra space in my locker if you ever need it.* Taped to the note was a small silver key. It wasn't signed, but I recognized the distinctive slope in the *r*'s of Tin's stilted script.

This wasn't the only example. That weekend we were hanging out at Brigitte's house, slouched around her floral-print L-shaped couch, passing around a large bowl of nachos. It was a warm, still day and Bowie was strumming lightly on Brigitte's guitar, playing the same three chords on repeat. Brigitte was telling us in exalted tones how Lucille had promised her a kitten after graduation, and we began suggesting potential names.

"What about Kiki? From *Kiki's Delivery Service*." That was Bowie's suggestion.

I chimed in with Easter, which Brigitte liked because it ref-erenced a line from a Tori Amos song, an artist whom Brigitte worshipped.

"Maybe I should call her Ai," said Brigitte jokingly.

I played along, rubbing the back of my hand against my cheek to mimic a cat. Then the conversation moved on to name meanings.

"Do you know Ai means 'love' in Chinese?" Brigitte slow blinked at me.

"Actually," said Tin to Brigitte, careful not to look directly at me, "Ai's name can be made into a whole sentence; that's if you think about it laterally."

She titled her head, curious. "Oh? How?"

"In Vietnamese, the meaning of Ai is 'whom.' Phonetically, in English, it sounds like the pronoun 'I.' And you guys already know what it means in Chinese."

"'Whom I love.'" Brigitte strung together the phrase, clapping her hands with delight. "That's so clever! You're great with words, Tin. Do you know that? You must think about them a whole lot."

He grinned at her, flattered. "Maybe if I didn't think about words so much, I'd have an easier time saying them."

Four

WE WERE ON excursion to see the Art Express exhibition at the Art Gallery of New South Wales, strolling leisurely from wall to wall, assessing the works on display. Following on from the conversation we had back in chem class the previous week, Brigitte said, "See? Most of the works here are by private school kids."

I frowned. "I wouldn't say 'most.' Looking around, I can see plenty of public school ones who got in this year."

"Well, I'd say it's nowhere near an even split: the numbers clearly skew in favor of private. But even with all things being equal, there are more than twice as many public schools as private, which puts a spin on the numbers. Without question, you're more likely to be selected if you're a private school kid."

"That's true, but you can apply that to anything. If you live in an affluent area, there will always be better access to resources. But I still believe if your work is good enough, you've got every chance of getting in."

Tilting her head, Brigitte said, "You're right about us having less resources. Art is all about experimentation, after all. Supplies can get expensive. At Whitlam High, they have us painting over the old canvases left by past students. When it comes to the arts, materials can sometimes make all the difference. Yes, talent accounts for a lot, but for people like us, getting our hands on quality materials can be tough."

Nodding, I said, "I suppose, but with some imagination, you can do extraordinary things with so little. Remember when that kid made a sculpture of the Opera House using only tooth-picks?"

"That was pretty impressive," she admitted. "And I'm not saying it's impossible to make headway in the art world if you're underprivileged. It's just more of an uphill battle if you're strug-gling to make ends meet. There was that time I applied for an internship at the Modern Art Gallery. I couldn't believe my luck when I scored an interview. Hundreds must have applied, and they only call in a handful. That morning, me and Mum were tearing the house apart, looking for my best shoes. You know those patent leather ones? At that point in the day, the internship still seemed within my reach. Anyway, I got there just as one of the interviewers walked out the last candidate—a girl who looked to be my age. I watched as they shared a quick hug and then I heard the interviewer say to the girl, 'Tell your mum I said hi.' And I knew right away I wouldn't get it. I still went through the motions of course, although I just knew it wouldn't amount to anything."

"Oh, Brigitte," I said, giving her arm a sympathetic squeeze. I couldn't imagine any candidate with a better portfolio than hers. But I knew her talent would one day get the recognition it deserved. "They saw something special in you, Brigitte. Even if it was rigged, they still wanted to see you. And you only make that effort if you see something special in someone."

Outside on the expansive lawn, kids from Fairfield High were scattered, standing around in animated conversation or jostling. When I spotted Alex, I moved to steer Brigitte away, but the two turned their heads almost in tandem and caught sight of each other. I groaned inwardly as Alex grinned and strolled over.

Eyeing Brigitte, he said in his lazy drawl, "Long time no see."

Like Brigitte, Alex was French Vietnamese, with dark, brooding eyes and inky, waist-long hair pulled into a tight bun. Tattooed down the length of one arm was a pair of Japanese-style koi writhing against a rogue wave, spitting up sea foam. There was a tattoo parlor a train stop away from Whitlam that never asked for ID and consequently had a robust clientele of underage kids.

He squinted at me. "Um, you're Ai—right?"

I rolled my eyes. "Hi, Alex."

With the tip of his foot, he tapped Brigitte lightly on the shin and this seemed to sway her composure. "I found the T-shirt you were looking for, Bridge."

Something seemed to pass between them, perhaps the spark of a shared memory.

In a tentative voice Brigitte asked, "Do you mean the Chicago Bulls one?"

With a smirk he answered, "You want to come over and pick it up?"

"No, you keep it."

"Okay. If you want it, you know where to find me."

When Alex left to join his classmates, I gave Brigitte a pointed look. "You're not going to fall for this again . . . are you?"

Brigitte shook her head, "I won't. I'm not."

There was a hesitancy to her voice, and I let out a frustrated sigh. "Seriously, Brigitte, the guy's a real jerk. Don't you remember what happened with the kitten?"

Alex had shown up to her house one day with a Ragdoll kitten just when I happened to be there. Brigitte had been ignoring his calls and I guess he was getting desperate. The kitten came adorned with a diamanté collar. After Alex left, I wondered out loud how he could afford such an extravagant gift, but Brigitte was so smitten, she didn't question it. Lucille, on seeing how happy the kitten made her daughter, agreed to let her keep it. A week later, we spotted a poster tacked to a lamppost, pleading for information about a missing Ragdoll, along with a recent photograph. Recognizing the diamanté collar, Brigitte tore the poster from the pole, eyes tearing up. She hadn't settled on a name yet but had spent most of her savings on a cat bed and toys.

Seeing the pained look now on Brigitte's face, I said, "Look, I don't mean to dredge up bad memories, but I don't want you to forget what kind of a guy he is."

She reached over and gave my hand a squeeze. In a quiet

voice she said, "I'm glad you reminded me, Ai. It's easy to overlook all the bad stuff sometimes."

Over the next few days, I watched Brigitte closely to make sure she was sticking to her promise. She had shed way too many tears over Alex, and I didn't want her to get caught up again in all his drama. But soon I was distracted by the lead-up to my seventeenth birthday and forgot all about it. I don't usually get all worked up about my birthday, but this was my first one where I was in a relationship and somehow that made it special. Better still, it fell on a Saturday, which meant I could sleep in that morning.

It turned out Bowie had a different plan in mind. He showed up bright and early that morning with a McDonald's breakfast laid out on a tray: hash browns, sausage, Egg McMuffins, and hotcakes. As I happily wolfed down my meal, he said, "Wait until you see what we have planned for you today."

After breakfast, we went to the mall to pick out my birthday present. I had just finished trying on some outfits in Dotti when the shopgirl told me Bowie had left to make a phone call. Outside the store, I spotted him just up ahead, so I followed behind at a safe distance planning to pounce on his shoulders and say "Boo!" But then he kept looking back in a way that aroused my suspicion. I tailed him until he got to a row of pay phones and then I hid partially behind a pillar. From my vantage point, I watched Bowie pull a coin from his pocket and slot it into the machine. After punching a number into the keypad, he waited a moment before asking for Brigitte. I heard him say things like

"Yeah, she's trying stuff on. Okay, sure. Yeah, I can do that. Okay, see you soon, then."

I jumped out at him from behind the pillar, grinning, and he hastily put the phone down. "Jeez, Ai, you scared me."

"Who was that?" I teased, sensing he and Brigitte were again up to something. It was my birthday, so this was no surprise, but I still wanted to suss out as many details as possible.

"Uh, just had to let Mum know I couldn't pick up my baby brother, Tai, from Chinese school today. Did you see anything you liked?"

I shook my head, pouting.

"My God, woman," he joked. "We've been shopping for hours."

Around six that night, Bowie came to pick me up. He was wearing a brand-new linen shirt, light gray speckled with tiny white flecks. When he kissed me hello, I caught a whiff of expensive cologne on his skin, a mix of tobacco and flowers. "We must be going somewhere fancy," I joked, and he just shrugged and smiled in response.

First up, we had to pick up Brigitte, but when we arrived, the house was completely dark. "It looks like no one's home, Bowie. Are you sure she's not with Tin?"

"Hmmm, you wait here, birthday girl, and I'll go and check."

Exiting the car, he walked up the short drive to her front door and rang the bell. When no one answered, he turned to me and raised both hands in a shrug. Then he gestured sideways to indicate he was going round the back to check. I nodded, waiting.

For a long while, nothing happened, and I drummed my fingers on the dashboard, wondering why Bowie was taking so long. Reaching over, I gave the horn a couple of sharp, impatient beeps. When there was still no sight of him or Brigitte, I clicked open the car door and stepped out. Almost as though it were perfectly timed, the entire house was suddenly ablaze as though every light had been switched on at the same time. I gasped, standing back in astonishment. A drumroll sounded in the crisp cool air and then a crowd emerged from the side of Brigitte's house, advancing toward me. As I watched in genuine surprise, they burst into song. Tin was holding a toy drum with Lucille marching alongside him, both smiling widely. Among the faces in the crowd, I spotted Sying, then Nadine with her boyfriend, Trevor, along with some other kids from school. The group was led by Brigitte, who was holding a cake made of profiteroles arranged in the number seventeen, topped with more than a dozen sparkling candles. Instead of the typical birthday song, they were singing Dean Martin's "That's Amore" in loud, boisterous tones. Next to Brigitte stood Bowie, strumming the tune on guitar. I clapped my hands and laughed as neighbors came out onto their front porches and cheered along with the rest of us. After blowing out the candles and thanking everyone, I said to Bowie, "I didn't know you played guitar."

"I taught him the chords and he practiced like crazy," said Brigitte, gathering me into a hug. "Happy Birthday, Ai Spy."

"Thanks, Brigitte the Baguette."

Taking my hand, she led me to the patio out back, which was decorated with strung-up fairy lights twinkling and a foil banner that read *Happy Birthday*. Piñatas in the shape of pineapples and bananas hung from the awning, framed with streamers and balloons. A large table was laden with all my favorite foods: Lucille's spring rolls, Chinese sausage fried rice, platters of sliced cucumber, pork belly, vermicelli noodles, and jars of nước chấm sauce ready to assemble into bowls of bánh hỏi by a stack of paper plates and napkins. Bottles of Diet Coke and Fanta were placed on the table next to a glass bowl filled with ice. Someone said, "Where's the music?" and on came "I'll Never Break Your Heart" by the Backstreet Boys. I loaded my plate with spring rolls, popping one into my mouth.

"You happy?" Asked Bowie, smiling down at me.

Cupping a hand over my mouth, I swallowed, nodding.

Reaching into his pocket, he pulled out a small gift box.

"But you already got me a present," I protested. By the end of our shopping trip that morning, I had settled on a white crochet top, which I was currently wearing.

"That was a decoy. This is your real present."

Inside the box was a silver necklace with a small bird charm attached. I held it up to the light, squinting.

Bowie said, "It's a magpie—you know, from our Valentine's Day date? They had it in gold as well, but I could only afford the sterling silver."

"I love it, Bowie!" I cried, throwing my arms around him.

He helped me fasten it around my neck, working the clasp

with some difficulty. When it was finally secured, he stepped back, grinning at the necklace. "It suits you," he said, as I touched the cool of the silver.

"I promise never to take it off—not even when I shower," I gushed. We'd only been dating for just over a month, so in no way did I expect such an elaborate and meaningful gift. Right away, I went around showing it off, relaying the story of when a magpie chased me and Bowie into a tunnel.

When I got to Nadine she said, "Did you know they drove all the way to the mountains for that? Brigitte knows a jewelry artist in Leura who makes these cute Australiana birds like kookaburras and things."

Sying, who had appeared at her side, quipped, "So, not only did Brigitte teach Bowie the chords to 'That's Amore,' she also told him where to get Ai's present. Bowie does whatever Brigitte tells him, doesn't he?"

"Sying!" Nadine snapped, then rolled her eyes at me as if to say, *Just ignore her.*

Trevor said, "Shit, that's fancy. You've got to put out now, don't you, Ai?" to which Nadine retorted with "Yeah? Where's my necklace, then?"

Later, Brigitte got us all to gather around the lounge room, where she sat me down in front of the television. She popped a video into the recorder and dimmed the lights. Everyone fell silent as footage began playing on the screen. The camera was focused on our big tree in the schoolyard, then panned to the right, where Nadine was dressed as a reporter, complete with a microphone in her hand. There were titters all around the room as a crawl appeared at the bottom of the screen read, *Breaking news! Ai turns seventeen*. I smiled, toying with my new necklace, fingers tracing the cool of the silver. It would soon become a nervous habit of mine.

Nadine said in a serious tone, "First, we cross over to Aysum and Sying, longtime friends of Ai. They know her best—or do they? Let's test their knowledge, shall we?"

The camera zoomed out to show Aysum and Sying standing in their school uniforms with matching party hats. The light was a soft, golden hue, so Brigitte must have filmed it either early morning or late afternoon.

Pointing the microphone at Aysum, Nadine quizzed, "What's Ai's favorite color?"

With a faraway look, Aysum answered, "Ai's favorite color is the ocean just before a storm, or something along those lines."

"No, no," Sying interjected. "Ai's favorite color is the blush of a lotus flower just as the first petal falls."

"Actually, I reckon it's more like the tinge of a rose quartz touched by the light of the sun during the peak of its summit."

"Very funny," I laughed.

Turning to the camera, Aysum said, "Hey, Ai. Sorry I can't be at your party but I'm always there in spirit. Happy birthday and love ya, girlie!" She blew kisses as the camera zoomed in on Sying, who cried, "Happy birthday, Ai. See you on the big night!," then blew on a party streamer.

The scene cut to Aysum, Sying, and Nadine standing in a line, pulling party poppers in succession before cheering wildly.

Then there was Trevor lying side-on in the grass, blowing on a dandelion seed head and saying in a sultry tone, "Happy Birthday, Ai. May all your wishes come true tonight," as the room erupted into laughter.

Nadine appeared again. "Now we go to Bowie, Ai's new and shiny boyfriend. Describe the moment you fell in love with the birthday girl . . ."

I nudged Bowie, grinning. On screen, he looked bashful, running a hand through his hair. "Ahhh . . . well it all began when I had this serious craving for a pandan waffle, so I set out on a mission to Paris Bakery. Ai just happened to be manning the store when I put in my order. She curled a finger above her top lip like a mustache and then, in a shockingly bad French accent, proceeded to tell me they were out of pandan waffles and 'if monsieur would please consider a croissant instead?' She looked so cute grinning at me with her braces, which I never noticed before. I know it sounds weird, but I have a thing for braces. Anyway, I knew I was in big trouble then."

"Aw," I said, ruffling his hair and planting a kiss on his cheek.

When I turned back to the television, Tin's face filled the screen. From behind the camera, Nadine said, "Now we go to the man of few words. Do you think you can spare a couple for your best friend's girl?"

With a shy smile, he said, "Sure."

"You guys have all been hanging out together, haven't you? Getting to know each other?"

"Yeah, that's right."

"Making memories and all of that."

"Ah-huh."

"And what's your favorite memory of Ai so far?"

Tin blinked. "Uh, favorite memory? Do you mean . . . Ah, okay . . . Well let me think . . . Right, so every morning at school, I'd walk past Ai sitting under the big tree, totally immersed in a book. That's the only image I previously had in my mind, which is why I assumed she was mostly quiet. But that changed when we went on a class excursion to see *Twister* last year. After the movie, we were all hanging out by the Queen Victoria Building and Ai and Brigitte were throwing stale bread at the pigeons. The birds crowded around the two of them in a frenzy, fighting for scraps, and Ai looked totally enthralled. One particularly brave pigeon came right by her feet, and to my surprise Ai reached down and grabbed it, laughing maniacally as it fluttered crazily in her cupped hands. I guess out of all the memories I have so far of Ai, that's the one that sticks out to me the most."

It was sometime during the evening when I made my way to the kitchen for a glass of water. Brigitte was talking quietly with her mum while they rinsed the dishes. I was just about to announce my presence when something in Brigitte's tone stopped me. They didn't notice me as I stood in the archway, eyes fixed on the neat apron bows that rested on the smalls of their backs.

Brigitte sounded upset when she said, "It's just hard, Mum, seeing him with her. But don't tell Ai about this, okay? She doesn't know I still have feelings for him and the last thing I want to do is ruin her birthday."

"You're the pretty one, you know." Lucille's words were like ice in my veins. Were they talking about me and Bowie? In relation to me, Brigitte had always been labeled the "hot" one. Just like the cute soccer guy had pointed out on Valentine's Day.

I continued to listen as Brigitte said something that was partly obscured by the dishes clinking in the sink. "—it's not that I want him back or anything."

"Of course not, honey. I'm just saying if you ever did"—she clicked her fingers—"You could have him."

Five

IT WAS THE late '90s and the world was on the cusp of a digital revolution. Dial-up modems had now reached 56k in speed; the internet was moving at a pace unlike anything we'd ever seen. It felt as though a collective revolution was brewing among my generation, who were now connected in ways that our parents found baffling. I was thrilled with this new, largely text-based universe where, for the first time in my life, the color of my skin was inconsequential. Every night I sat at our clunky PC computer, multiple chat windows open on mIRC, talking to strangers around the world. That's where I met my internet friend Pedro, an eighteen-year-old from Spain who lived by the ocean in a rambling stone cottage with his parents and five sisters. He described each of his siblings so vividly, I felt as though I knew them. There was the parole officer, the dancer, the hairdresser, the aspiring human rights lawyer, and the incandescent bride-to-be. I told him about my seamstress mother who had once slaved away for pennies a garment. Dresses that ended up in the shop windows of upmarket boutiques sold for outrageous amounts of money. The end customer turning a blind eye to the exploitative nature of the industry.

Growing tired of the abuse, Mum attempted to open a bridal shop on the main shopping strip in Whitlam but was turned down for a loan. It was just as well, since we began hearing stories about gangs terrorizing shopkeepers for a cut of their earnings, which they justified as a "protection tax." As an alternative, Mum began peddling made-to-order wedding dresses from our garage downstairs. Pedro loved hearing about the sequins I helped hand-stitch onto silk, one at a time, and the hours Mum and I spent sorting out jumbo bags of buttons bought at discount while under the watchful gaze of the blue-eyed, caramel-haired women with their dazzling white teeth and tiaras, torn from the covers of bridal magazines to grace the concrete walls of my mother's workshop. I often wondered what they thought of our small, shabby space. What they would make of my mother's busy, bulky Singer, the rolls of fabric stacked up against the back wall. The single mattress tucked into the corner for those long nights when a demanding bride insisted on the finished product earlier than was previously agreed on. A rusty silver kettle and tin can of jasmine leaves on a rickety old side table, given a second life after Mum had found it dumped on the side of the street. A folding screen where her customers could change and check their reflections in the full-length mirror, crudely patinated before it was trendy. Then there was the altar displaying a composition of black-and-white photographs salvaged from the war, wreathed by red ribbons stamped with gold Chinese lettering, a silver urn stuck hedgehog-like with burnt incense, where we laid offerings of fruit, fake gold ingots, and bowls of rice. I shared these glimpses of my life with Pedro, who aspired to be a fashion designer someday and was fluent in the language of dressmaking. Words such as "patterns," "seams," and "wadding" ping-ponged on the screen between us. But Pedro was a romantic at heart, and our main topic of conversation always circled back to Bowie. We even discussed the incident at my birthday when I had overheard Lucille comparing me unfavorably to Brigitte. It was a conversation I found deeply unsettling, as it felt completely out of character for Lucille. What's more, it seemed implausible to me that Brigitte could still harbor feelings toward Bowie. With the memory of that exchange growing hazy over the passing weeks, I decided that I must have misheard somehow. Pedro was less sympathetic: his words on our chat screen cautioned me to "keep an eye on my man."

The dawn of the internet age also coincided with the rise of right-wing politics in Australia, placing a hot, glaring spotlight on Whitlam and its Asian immigrant population. On the nightly news, we saw ourselves reflected in a rolling montage of drugs, chronic unemployment, and gang violence. It was hard to fathom that the White Australia Policy had only been abolished a few shorts years before my family's arrival in Sydney in 1981.

The White Australia Policy was a set of laws established mainly to exclude Chinese immigrants—a prejudice that went as far back as the 1880s, when the Chinese were competing with the English settlers on the goldfields. As a fiercely proud and homogeneous nation, Australia welcomed its first significant wave of immigrants from Southeast Asia with a degree of wariness. Families from war-torn countries, shell-shocked and bewildered, were thrown into settlements like Whitlam and largely left to their own devices. There was no counseling or support provided, no period of adjustment or talk of mental illness. It is no surprise how in the subsequent years our town came to be plagued with its many problems.

By then, it had become my daily ritual to step over junkies that loitered on the stairs outside our door as I left for school. They were slumped like rag dolls, eyes half-closed, heads lolling weakly, off their faces on heroin. From behind the counter at Paris Bakery, Brigitte and I watched more of them step off the trains, touted as the Junkie Express. It was like a slow-moving zombie apocalypse. Kids with bleached hair, pale faces, and vacant expressions wearing baggy, unwashed clothes, speaking in their slow, stupid drawls. They were regarded by our community with a mixture of apathy and disdain. It was the dealers and their shady bosses we loathed and feared.

Used needles with their trademark orange tips began to appear by rubbish bins, shop fronts, and playgrounds, casually tossed like cigarette butts. A child was found playing with one, and the story became a cautionary tale, encapsulating the fear of every white middle-class suburban household.

The maelstrom of hate and bigotry shadowed much of my adolescence, but I lacked the knowledge or means to improve my situation. As though the immediate threat of gang violence wasn't enough, their behavior led to the stigmatization of Whitlam and its residents, casting us all in the same light. By then, racism had become so normalized in our society, it infiltrated all aspects of my life. Printed in a school textbook were statistics showing how television shows dropped in ratings if an Asian actor joined the cast. On an English exam that came back, an angry red scrawl warned me that essays on racism were usually marked down and to bear this in mind with my HSC exams on the horizon. Nazi symbols graffitied on buildings and fences were accompanied by discriminatory phrases such as *Gooks Go Home* or *Stop the Asian Invasion*. In the school library, I stumbled on a page in a popular joke book depicting an illustration of a burly Caucasian man exiting a Chinese eatery with a panicked schoolgirl slung over his shoulder while her slanty-eyed, bucktoothed parents looked on in horror. Underneath the picture was the catchphrase "Chinese Takeaway." By the only pub in Whitlam, white middle-aged men who reeked of cigarettes and stale beer stood outside, jeering at Brigitte and me as we walked past in our school uniforms, pitching racist slurs with full impunity when we ignored their advances. When I was older, I asked Mum why we had tolerated it back then. Why we didn't stand up for ourselves. She answered, "Yes, they say to us bad things. They spit on us. But, my daughter, what can we do? In Mum's country, my people try to kill us."

Soon after my birthday, Sying developed a keen interest in politics that rapidly escalated to militant. The first instance when this became apparent was after she and Brigitte participated in a debate that was held at a nearby school. That day I didn't see either one of them until the lunch bell rang and I headed over to the big tree, catching up with Nadine and Aysum along the way.

In the distance, we saw Brigitte and Sying, who appeared to be in the middle of an argument. As we got within hearing distance, Nadine jokingly said to them, "Girls, I thought the debate was over?"

Brigitte sucked in a deep breath as though she was struggling to stay calm.

"What happened?" Aysum asked.

Gesturing at Sying, Brigitte said, "She sabotaged our debate."

"I was just taking a political stance, Brigitte," Sying countered, emphasizing the word "stance." Her tone came off as patronizing, and this riled up Brigitte further.

"What do you mean she sabotaged your debate?" asked Nadine, looking from Sying to Brigitte.

Brigitte threw up her hands in a gesture of frustration. "The topic was whether multiculturism was a good thing for our society. Our team had to argue against the ideology, which was a lot trickier than you think. But against the odds, we managed to build a strong case and were feeling pretty damn good about ourselves when the time came to present. When it was her turn to speak, Sying just stood there, not saying a word."

"I was making a point, Brigitte. With all this backlash against Asian immigrants, you'd think this was something you'd be concerned about too."

"Who the hell says I'm not?"

"Well, I don't see you putting yourself out there like I did today."

"And did your little stunt make one iota of difference, Sying? Did all the TV vans pull up outside and commend you for your bravery? And what about the rest of your team that you completely blindsided? If you were going to pull something like that, it would have been nice to let us all know beforehand. We wouldn't have bothered doing all that work."

"Oh, Sying," said Nadine, shaking her head. "Brigitte's right, you know. You should have warned everyone if that's what you were planning to do."

"I thought my silence would be more impactful if it came as a surprise, even to my own team members."

"How do you figure that, Sying?" Brigitte retorted.

Aysum shook her head. "I'm sorry, Sying, but Brigitte's right: you've got to pick your battles."

Sying looked to me, eyes imploring. "What do you think, Ai? You've been awfully quiet."

I swallowed, thinking carefully about my response, as I didn't want to upset Sying. "I think your heart was in the right place but maybe you should have discussed it with the rest of the team first. Like Brigitte said, everyone worked so hard, and maybe you should have considered their feelings."

"Oh, really, now!" Sying said in a harsh, mocking tone. "Well, why aren't I surprised? You always take Brigitte's side over mine."

"That's not fair," I said, taken aback by the accusation.

Aysum rushed to my defense. "Ai's just trying to be diplomatic, Sying. She's not attacking you or anything. There's nothing wrong with having principles, but you have to think carefully about how your actions might affect others."

"I'm so disappointed in all of you, but especially you, Ai. There's so much hatred being directed our way right now, and you're happy to sit back and do nothing? Just be frogs in a pot like our parents were back in Cambodia?"

Rolling her eyes, Brigitte said, "Sying, give it a rest. We're all very much aware of the political climate right now, and there are ways we can address it. But how you went about it was all wrong. If you don't get that, I don't know what else to say."

Later that afternoon, Brigitte came over to my place to see how my major artwork was progressing. In my room, I showed her a small, antique-style suitcase found in a junk shop. "I'm going to line it with this red velvet fabric Mum gave me and display the literary 'souvenirs' inside. Some of the items will be found objects: I saw a pair of silver heels in the window of St. Vinnies which would be perfect as Dorothy's slippers. Other things I'll make from scratch, like the box of 'square sweets that look round' from Willy Wonka's shop."

Squeezing my chin, she kissed me lightly on the cheek. "I can already visualize it, Ai. It's going to be great." Flopping down on my bed, she began flipping through a magazine while I sat at my chair and went to work lining the suitcase. A calm silence fell between us and remained for a while as I focused on my task and Brigitte was engrossed in her magazine. Then she made a "huh" sound and I looked up. "What is it?" I asked.

"Just reading the 'Ask Betty' section where people send in for advice. This girl described here sounds so much like Sying . . ." She paused, then read from the segment: "'Dear Betty, I have a suspicion that my friend is trying to undermine me. I don't have solid proof but there have been times where she's made me look bad in front of other people. When I confront her about it, she always has an excuse ready. A few of our mutual friends seem to be turning against me and I suspect it could be because of her. She's really good at playing the victim and making everyone feel sorry for her. What should I do?'"

I raised an eyebrow at Brigitte. "What's Betty's advice?"

Brigitte continued, "'You know the old saying, "Keep your friends close and your enemies closer." Establishing whether you're dealing with a friend or foe may take a little detective work on your part. Try having an open discussion with your circle of friends and get their feedback. If that fails, then I would suggest setting boundaries between you and this person. For example, if they say or do anything that upsets you, let them know immediately. If they continue with this behavior, it could mean that your instincts were correct in the first place. Best of luck.'"

Our eyes met over the magazine, and I shrugged. "Well, Sying hasn't really said anything to me so far—about you, I mean. Besides, we were all on your side earlier today, remember? She's hardly turned anyone against you."

"I guess so," Brigitte sighed. "Maybe I'm just being paranoid. I should smooth things over with her, maybe tomorrow when we've both calmed down."

"Do you think it's true what she said—about how I always take your side?"

Brigitte put down the magazine, a thoughtful expression on

her face. "No one can deny you have a natural bias because we're best friends. But in this case she was clearly in the wrong. You'd see that even if you didn't know either one of us. The truth is she let the team down, which means we only have one chance left to make it to state and, thanks to her, that's now highly unlikely. So, in answer to your question, I don't believe you always take my side. You try your best to be diplomatic—sometimes to the point of being ridiculous. Look at Tin, for example: you keep seeking his approval. You're always looking for assurance that he's okay with your relationship when it shouldn't matter what he thinks."

I groaned, burying my face in my hands. "Oh, great. I had no idea it was that obvious until now."

"Relax, Ai. I doubt anyone other than me has noticed, and that's because I know you better than most."

"Then why do you think I am so concerned with Tin in the first place?"

She shrugged. "Maybe it's just your way of trying to keep everyone happy. Unless . . ." She frowned, tilting her head. "Unless there's another reason."

I swallowed. "What do you mean?"

"Well, another way to look at it—now, don't take this the wrong way, Ai—maybe you're jealous of Tin?"

"Me, jealous of Tin? That's crazy."

"It kind of makes sense though, doesn't it? To be honest, I remember feeling twinges of this when I was dating Bowie, even though I knew I was being irrational. The boys are super close and go back a long way. It's hard to compete with that. Which could explain why you're going out of your way to include Tin in everything. You're overcompensating for your guilt."

"Do you really think so?"

"It's just a theory, Ai."

What Brigitte said about me being jealous of Tin stuck in my mind over the next few weeks. I couldn't deny she was onto something. After all, I always felt the need to check with Tin before making plans with Bowie. Neither of them had given any indication this was necessary, and we spent most of our time hanging out as a foursome anyway. Yet the impulse to consider Tin's feelings remained stubbornly fixed at the forefront of my mind. For example, there was the time when they tagged along with me to a routine appointment to get my braces tightened. The dentist was situated on the main strip of Whitlam, a short walk from our school, where we had just finished up for the day. On the way there, I was wondering aloud what color bands I should get this time round, which led to a robust but friendly argument between Bowie and Brigitte. He thought I should get blue, while Brigitte was adamant it should be hot pink. Then she said something like "Who do you love more, Ai? Is it me or Bowie?"

She said it in a joking way, but it was enough to put me into a spin. Especially when it occurred to me that I was mainly interested in Tin's input. When he still hadn't weighed in, I prompted, "Okay, guys, it's either pink or blue. Should we all vote on it?"

Tin said, "I'll go with the pink, then," as Brigitte gave a hoot of delight.

When my dentist asked me which color I wanted, I immediately chose the hot pink. And then at once I realized Brigitte's neat summation of my feelings toward Tin may have been on point. You could argue it was two against one and I was merely being democratic, but secretly I had wanted the blue bands to go with my new sweater. I knew I was overthinking this and I had no idea why I was placing myself under such intense scrutiny, only that it was tied to that very specific time in my life when revelations were shooting up to the surface, one after another. I treasured each new epiphany like a jewel in my palm, something shiny and glittering to be admired and examined from every angle and then stored away with the others. Some jewels were more like polished stones. Some were semiprecious. Others were emeralds. At times I felt as though I was unearthing something that was better left buried. But I couldn't help myself.

When my feelings toward Tin still felt unresolved, I sought out Aysum's advice. I found her in the back paddock, a large, grassy expanse where our school ran themed carnivals and running marathons. Once, the founder of a chain of electronics stores landed his helicopter right on the field. It was the area of our school least policed by teachers, where the cool kids could smoke or blast rap music in peace. At present, Nadine was feverishly making out with Trevor, lost in her own world. Aysum was sharing a cigarette with a couple of his friends when she turned and caught sight of me. Getting up, she brushed the grass from her pants and made her way over.

"Everything okay, Ai?"

"I just wanted to go over something with you."

We found a patch of grass and sat ourselves down. It was a warm, sunny day, even though we were already heading into June. Aysum could always tell when I had something on my mind, almost like she had a sixth sense about these things. She had a special way of seeing right through to the heart of something. Brigitte once said Aysum was wise beyond her years, and I felt that about her whenever we got into a serious conversation.

When we were settled, she asked, "So what's on your mind, Ai?"

"Tell me the truth, Aysum: Do you think I've changed since dating Bowie?"

Aysum frowned, thinking. "Sure you have, Ai; it would be weird otherwise. That's what happens when you get into a relationship, right?"

"Have you noticed anything specific, though? Anything you can think of, even if it's negative?"

"Wait: Why are you asking me this? Has Sying said something to you?"

"Actually, no—it was Brigitte who brought this up."

She seemed surprised by this. "Brigitte? What did she say?"

"Well, I've been walking on eggshells around Tin because I'm afraid of encroaching on him and Bowie. Brigitte suggested the reason I'm so anxious about this is because, deep down, I'm jealous of Tin. Do you think that's true?"

"Now that you've mentioned it, I do see how you go out of your way to include Tin. You're like that naturally, but with Tin it's more obvious. Brigitte could be right about you being jealous of Tin, although"—she shook her head, thinking—"for some reason that doesn't seem to fit. I think there's something else going on that you haven't considered."

"What do you think that is?"

"Suppose . . ." Aysum stopped and seemed to choose her words carefully. "Suppose it's not Tin but Brigitte who you're jealous of? And you can't bear that thought, so you've projected that guilt onto Tin instead."

I bristled at this and then, on noting my own reaction, knew there could be something to it. As usual, Aysum had a way of cutting right through to the bone.

"But Brigitte's my best friend. You know how much I love her. If it ever came down to it, I'd choose her over Bowie for sure."

"I'm not doubting your loyalty to Brigitte. But it's totally natural to have these feelings. Brigitte and Bowie were an item, after all."

"But Brigitte keeps saying it wasn't a big deal."

"Of course she'd say that: she just wants you to be happy. But there was a period when she did like him enough to date him and that only changed because Alex came along. If he hadn't come into the picture, who knows if she'd still be with Bowie?"

My stomach tightened at the thought. "It's weird because I wasn't even friends with Brigitte back when she was dating Bowie."

"You weren't?"

"No. They dated the summer holidays before Brigitte and I became friends, remember? Maybe that's why it seems like it happened in a different universe."

"Oh, that's right. I suppose that does make it harder for you to think of Bowie as Brigitte's ex—but that's exactly what he is, Ai. Whether you like it or not, they were an item."

"It's not as though I've just brushed their relationship aside," I insisted. "We all talk about it openly; no one's trying to hide the fact they used to date."

"Does Brigitte ever talk about Bowie?"

"I think she goes out of her way to downplay it, maybe to spare my feelings," I admitted.

"So maybe that's the real story here, Ai. You're jealous of Brigitte and that makes you uncomfortable, so you'd rather divert that guilt onto Tin. And the four of you have gotten so close anyway that it's easy to get everything mixed up."

I thought about the time when Tin shared the story about the mango tree. How the four of us got swept up in the same emotional tide.

"What's it been like for you, with Nadine getting together with Trevor?"

She rolled her eyes. "I think he's a bit of a dickhead, to be honest, but he makes her laugh. If she's happy, I'm happy. But it's different for me because I don't feel the need to get along with her boyfriend. I might hang out with them for a bit during lunch, but that's it. You know how strict my parents are, so I don't see them outside of school anyway. It's different with the four of you. You're always together and feelings don't have clearly defined boundaries. That's why these things can sometimes jump from one person to another."

After my conversation with Aysum, I briefly considered getting Sying's take on the whole thing but then quickly thought better of it. Her relationship with Brigitte was rocky at best, and I suspected she might lack objectivity when it came to my situation. Besides, she was constantly rambling on about her anti-racism campaign to the point where you could hardly get a word in. She printed off flyers at the school library and stuck them up wherever she could. Headlines like *Stop Racism Now!* and *Asians are Australians too* beamed at us from noticeboards and school lockers. Aysum and Nadine rallied behind Sying out of their own juvenile sense of injustice and their reality of living day-to-day in Whitlam polarized with the media stories that were dramatized versions of the truth.

Sying appeared to be well and truly in her element. She spent all her free time scurrying from group to group, preaching fear and hysteria, the way she once did with idle gossip, her signature phrase "Hush-hush" when she revealed something particularly salacious, stubby finger held to her lips while her body bristled with self-importance.

I was cynical about her motives, which came across as self-serving. All the same, I helped stick up some flyers, even if they were to the tune of her incessant rants. I had to admit, it did get tiresome at times, and I would roll my eyes like any teenager would in the presence of overenthusiasm.

"Do you really think it's as bad as what you're saying, Sying?" I asked her once after English as we headed toward our next class. She had been in an intense monologue about a popular talk radio show from the previous night. "Sure, people can be cruel, but it's mainly just name-calling and stuff. I've never felt as though my life was in danger or anything."

"What about that time on the train when those scary men were throwing racist slurs at you?"

I thought back to that incident the past December. I had gotten a casual job at a gift-wrapping booth in a busy city mall. With only a week left until Christmas, there was a manic pace to everything. I'd ended up working an eight-hour shift and was exhausted by the time I stepped onto the busy train, grateful for a seat. I closed my eyes and tipped my head back as the rocking motion of the train lulled me into a deep sleep. I woke with a start, looking around to find the train was now almost empty. I realized I had missed my stop.

A few seats up from me sat a pair of ruddy-faced men, one sporting a thick, wiry beard and clutching a can of beer. There was a looseness to his posture, a slackening of his jaw that made it obvious he was inebriated. To my dismay, the two were glaring directly at me as I quickly assessed my situation. To my relief, there were a handful of other people in the carriage. Still, I quietly slipped my hand into my bag, where I happened to have a pair of scissors. The ones they provide at the gift-wrapping booth did a terrible job at curling ribbon, which was why I had brought my own pair from home that morning.

"She's awake," said the one holding the beer can. "Hey, do you speak English?"

Terrified, I looked to the other passengers for help, but they were doing their best to ignore me, looking out the window or down at their laps.

"Hey, slanty eyes," the man called out again. "Answer me."

I stiffened, hands tightening around the scissors.

The man stood up, one hand gripping the top of the seat to steady himself. Taking a swig of his beer, he slurred, "Oi, what are you doing in our country? Why don't you go back to China?"

I dropped my head to avert his gaze, cheeks burning.

"She can't understand you," his companion drawled.

The men continued to goad me until the train arrived at their stop and they got up to leave, still hurling abuse at me on their way out. I stayed on board, waiting until there was a busy station before alighting. Then I found a pay phone and called Yan to pick me up.

Thinking back on that now, I said to Sying, "I told you there were people around, so it was no big deal."

"Yet no one stood up for you. Which means every individual riding in that carriage felt it was perfectly acceptable for two grown men to verbally abuse a young teenage girl. Don't you think that's really messed up?"

"I just don't think the men would have done anything, Sying, not with people watching."

"And what about when there's no one watching? What then? Seriously, Ai, you should tune in next time the radio show comes on. You are going to be shocked at what the callers are saying. There is so much anger in their voices. It didn't help that the host was whipping it all up, giving these xenophobic jerks a platform to voice their sick anti-Asian views."

"But it's only rhetoric, right? Surely it will blow over."

"Rhetoric," Sying scoffed. "That's how it started with Pol Pot in Cambodia, and look how that turned out."

At home, I found Mum in the garage, bent over her Singer as it bumped along noisily in the small, arid space. English lessons were playing on her old tape deck. Asinine phrases the listener is instructed to repeat, parrot-like, in the pause between each proposition. *"Ask me: Do you like to ski? Tell me: Yes, I like to ski."*

I asked Mum about the war and if there was a defining moment when she knew her old life was irretrievable.

She stopped and looked up, her expression one of mild bemusement. "When I steal fish."

"You stole a fish?"

"Khmer Rouge make us work in camp. Daddy very, very sick. We scared they take Daddy away. The men—they alway take away. Kill. Yan just a little boy, and you in mum's belly. I see someone cleaning many fish on table and them throw"— she pauses, thinking—"you know all the yucky things take from fish?" She made a motion to simulate scaling a fish.

"You mean guts?"

"Guts," she says, taking a moment to absorb the word. She continued. "Them throw *guts* in bucket. I look and wait. I watching. When no one there, I go look inside bucket, maybe got something okay to eat. I can't believe! Inside many, many *guts* but mum saw one fish—one fish, nothing wrong with! I want to cry. Must be from God, I think. I take fish. If they catch mum, they kill whole family. But they not see. Me and Daddy make fish salty, put in plastic and hide. We hide rice too. Next day Vietnamese fighting Khmer Rouge. We run away. Mum, Daddy, Yan running for long time. Only have fish and rice. Nothing to eat in jungle. We make soup with little fish and rice. If we don't have this one, we die for sure. Fish save our life."

"And you walked all the way to the Thai border with me in your belly?"

"I carry Yan on back."

"The whole way?"

"Whole way. Daddy very sick."

"Mum . . . are you worried about what's going on right now, with all the talk about immigrants?"

She frowned. "No, I not worry."

"But isn't this the way it started in Cambodia?"

"Not same, Ai. We in Australia now. This good country. We safe here." She went back to her work.

"But what if the same thing happens again?"

Without looking up, she answered, "Stop asking many question and make rice for mum."

Mum changed her tune when we got a call from the police requesting us to pick up Yan from the station. When he appeared trailing behind a stocky officer with a ginger mustache, it was all I could do not to cry. My brother's skinny frame seemed somehow diminished as his eyes met mine, bottom lip trembling. We had to bring his driver's license, which Mum clutched tightly in one hand, along with a clipping of our local paper where Yan was featured for winning a statewide science competition.

Accompanying us was the local mailman, Roger, whom my parents had befriended. He was a brawny, heavyset man dressed in stubby shorts and a white Bonds undershirt stretched tightly across his considerable gut. Still, it helped to have a Caucasian man with us in these situations, even one of questionable repute.

"He's a good kid, this one," said Roger to the officer, placing a hand on Yan's shoulder.

Mum, with her head bowed and eyes averted, apologized to the officer in her stilted, broken English. Then she made a vain attempt at pushing the article about Yan into his hand. The officer looked past her, past the both of us, eyes fixed squarely on Roger. "Make sure the kid stays out of trouble."

My dad, always so soft-spoken, berated Yan when we were back home. They got into an argument, and I came to my brother's defense even though I knew Dad was more scared than angry. Mum cried and told Yan to be more cautious from then on, even though she knew his actions had little to do with the arrest. For my parents, it must have brought back terrible memories of the war.

After things had calmed down, I went to Yan's room, where he was doing sit-ups on the light gray carpet. I sat cross-legged on his bed and waited for him to finish. His room was neat and orderly to the point of being clinical. Other than a tacked-up poster of the periodic table above his bed, there was little else to look at. In contrast, mine was plastered wall-to-wall with boy bands and movie posters, clothes and unfinished craft projects strewn across every surface.

"Are you okay?" I asked.

Yan did another set of sit-ups, then stopped to catch his breath. "Yeah."

"What happened?"

He reached for the glass of water on his bedside table and gulped it down before answering. "I'd just finished a game of squash at the Police Boys' Club. I was waiting for a friend on the front steps outside. Two cops came and asked me what I was doing. Then they wanted to check my gym bag, which they had no right to do, but they went ahead anyway. All they found was a squash racquet and other exercise gear. I think they were disappointed. They even tore apart my pack of gum. By then they knew they had nothing and were starting to look stupid in front of the people who'd gathered to see all the commotion. They said they wanted to check my pockets. I told them they had no right to touch me. One went to put his hand in my shorts pocket and I grabbed his wrist to stop him. That's when they pounced on me."

I felt a burst of anger. "Such jerks! I've been hearing similar stories about random kids getting picked up for no reason."

"You better be careful, Ai."

"Me?"

"The cops are hassling girls, too, even though it doesn't take a rocket scientist to tell the difference between a drug mule and a high school student. I think they're under a lot of pressure to make arrests. When you get these young, ego-driven cops in a heavily politicized town like Whitlam"—he shrugged—"it's not a good combination."

"I'll be careful," I promised.

"When you're walking around Whitlam to school or whatever, make sure you're carrying books with you so you look like a student. Move as though you're trying to get somewhere. Don't loiter: it makes you less of a target for cops. Oh, and you know those costume glasses of yours—the clear ones you sometimes wear for fun? It wouldn't hurt to put those on too."

I rolled my eyes. "Ironic, isn't it? The Khmer Rouge were going after people with glasses because they were a symbol of intelligence. Mum and Dad had to pretend they were illiterate to stay out of danger, and now we have to go around acting like scholars."

He stood up, toweling his neck. "Totally nuts."

"Do you recall much about the war?"

Yan frowned. "Just flashes here and there. Mainly, I remember how hungry I was. It's hard to describe what the sensation is like. You start drooling uncontrollably. I put pebbles in my mouth to stop it, but Mum yelled at me because she was afraid I'd choke. She kept checking my mouth obsessively. And you know the story of what happened when we got across the border."

"Dad swapped gold for candy."

"My uni friends are mainly kids from the North Shore, and they have this almost perverse appetite for my war stories. I think it's because they've never had to struggle, so it fascinates them. But I would trade my life with theirs in a heartbeat. Private schooling, tennis lessons, holidays in far-off places . . . what a dream."

"Who cares about all that stuff, Yan? You've worked hard to

get to where you are, and that counts for something. It's not a fair race, but at least you're getting somewhere."

When I told Brigitte about Yan's arrest, she threw herself behind Sying's cause with a vengeance. At first, she lent her skills in graphic design to give Sying's posters a professional touch; then she helped edit the copy. Often you would catch them butting heads over the tonality of the material. Sying insisted on using harsh, confrontational language for dramatic effect, whereas Brigitte preferred a gentler approach.

By the end of June, Sying's campaign had gained considerable traction, thanks to Brigitte's help. This was around the time when Brigitte shared an idea with our girl group that could take their campaign even further.

This idea came about one Thursday when all five of us happened to share a free period that backed onto the lunch break. During this almost two-hour-long interval, we made the trek into town, stopping at BKK, an international food court by the main plaza. Inside, we ordered an avocado shake each, along with a couple takeaway containers of bok lahong, a green papaya salad garnished with cherry tomatoes, dried baby shrimp, and tiny pickled crabs. The whole journey over, Sying had been harping on her anti-racism campaign. We didn't interrupt her on the off chance she'd take offense, but I think, like me, the girls had tuned out. Finally, Sying stopped when we were all busy scouring the jam-packed hall for a free table. We were about to give up, when Nadine spotted a family of four vacating their seats.

We settled ourselves into the hard plastic chairs, and Brigitte set about dispersing the papaya salad on paper plates, dishing out the napkins and plastic forks she'd grabbed earlier from a nearby condiment stand. As we got started on our lunch, Sying, who was sucking on the end of a tiny crab leg, continued her running dialogue. "I know my posters are getting the word out there, but I'm thinking much bigger than that now. I want the whole of Australia to sit up and take notice, for all the politicians and media to pay attention. I want everyone to know we're human beings, that we shouldn't be treated as second-class citizens in our own country or labeled as 'New Australians' when some of us—including me—were born here. I just feel stuck and don't know what to do next. Do you guys have any ideas?"

We fell quiet for a few moments, thinking. Then Aysum said, "Brigitte, you're the ideas lady. Have you got anything?"

Rubbing her hands together, Nadine joked, "Our Brigitte always has something good up her sleeve."

"No pressure, Brigitte," said Sying. It was obvious she'd meant to keep her tone lighthearted, but I caught a contemptuous ring to it.

Brigitte took a sip of her avocado shake and nodded. "Actually, I do." When she launched into her idea, she seemed to be addressing everyone at the table and not just Sying. "As you know, I've been photographing Asian refugees for my major art project and am blown away by some of the stories in our community. The thing is this country gets fed the same old narrative about Whitlam: gangs, crime, drugs, and unemployment. These are the buzzwords that are splashed across the daily newspaper or nightly news the moment someone turns on their television. They don't know about all the people who went through hell to get here and despite all the adversity are making something of their lives. But if we can somehow bring more visibility to this section of our community, then maybe we can start to shift their opinion. Ai, do you remember that anecdote Tin shared about his mother—the time she shot the mango out of the tree?"

I nodded, relaying the details of Tin's story as best as I could. It was so visually rich and poignant that, even secondhand, it had the desired effect. Everyone listened, transfixed, even Sying. When I finished, a quiet hush fell over the table as we each absorbed the emotional impact of the scene.

Sying was the first to break the spell by shoving a forkful of shredded papaya into her mouth. After swallowing, she said, "That's a nice story, Ai, but how do we turn that into a protest? What do mangoes have to do with anything?"

I shrugged and looked to Brigitte, who said, "Well, Sying, this goes back to my idea for your campaign. I thought you could curate an exhibition here in Whitlam. I'll be glad to help, of course. Together, we could interview refugees with stories like Tin's and we can show what they've made of their lives here in Australia. I'll bet the Whitlam Library would be keen to host it."

"That's a gorgeous idea, Brigitte," Aysum breathed. "I was mesmerized just now by Tin's story, and I think it would capture the imagination of others like me."

"Yeah, and it would definitely humanize refugees, show another side that most people don't often see," Nadine added.

Sying frowned. "It's a nice idea, Brigitte, maybe for an art project, but I'm thinking much bigger than that. I'm just not convinced Australians would be interested in hearing about a bunch of refugees. What I had in mind was something huge, like maybe we can organize a protest in the city where we can really make some noise. No one will pay attention to a puny exhibition here in Whitlam."

"I think you're crazy to rule it out, Sying," Nadine said, and Aysum nodded in agreement.

Sying shot me a questioning look and I said with a degree of wariness, "It's up to you, Sying, but I also think it's a great idea. Like the girls said, I think it could help to shift the narrative."

By now Sying seemed to be taking our points of view as a personal attack. She had the tendency to lash out like this, leaving us all on eggshells. In a wounded voice, she said, "Of course you'd all say that. But not everything Brigitte comes up with is brilliant, okay?"

"Hey," said Brigitte sharply. "You asked for my help, Sying."

"I was asking everyone, Brigitte. But as usual you had to make it all about you."

"Sying!" Nadine snapped. "That's uncalled for. You asked us all for help, including Brigitte. The truth is she's helped you lots on your campaign. You can't expect everyone to agree with everything you say; we have minds of our own, you know."

Brigitte looked tired suddenly. "Oh, forget it, Nadine. I don't really care to be honest. I'm getting sick of Sying's attitude anyway."

Sying looked at Brigitte as though she were weighing something up in her head. Then, softening her tone, she said, "Look, I'm grateful for all your help, Brigitte, and I'm sorry if I've offended you. It's just not the kind of thing I was looking for, that's all. I wanted an idea that is revolutionary—one guaranteed to make a splash—not a castoff from some art project you're doing. I'm sorry, but that's just the way I feel."

Brigitte sighed. "That's fine, Sying. Like I said, I don't really care."

Even though Sying hadn't been keen on the exhibition, Brigitte decided to go ahead with it on her own. Whenever Brigitte was on a mission, things tended to move at lightning speed. Almost overnight, she got funding and approval from the council. As she predicted, the Whitlam Library were thrilled to host the exhibition, especially after seeing samples of her photography portfolio. With their backing, Brigitte set out into the community with her Nikon and notepad. The first person she interviewed was my mother, who shared anecdotes of the time my family were on the run from the Khmer Rouge. One evening, after they had spent the entire day trudging through forest, they stumbled on an old, dilapidated farmhouse. Mum said she was exhausted in a way she'd never known. She collapsed on the field, her head resting on something warm and luxurious, before falling into a deep sleep. It wasn't until morning that she realized she had been laying her head on a pillow of cow dung.

As the weeks wore on, the spotlight shifted predictably away from Sying to rest squarely on Brigitte. I thought it was a good thing, as Brigitte's influence helped to temper the growing viciousness of Sying's campaign. After many complaints from students, one of her more controversial posters was taken down. Above a picture of the First Fleet, Sying had placed the title: *Boat People?*—a play on the terminology to describe the Vietnamese diaspora that was also used as a slur against anyone of Asian origin. The poster then went into graphic detail about the horrors of colonialism: the rape, murder, and enslavement of our indigenous population. It was a poster that called for revenge rather than reconciliation. I echoed the sentiment of others who thought she'd gone too far, and secretly favored Brigitte's approach of celebrating diversity.

During that time, Sying seemed to diminish somehow. Before Brigitte's involvement, she'd walked with her nose practically in the air, but now her shoulders bore a noticeable stoop. It was as though she was being slowly drained of something vital. It came to a head one day during lunch break. We were all sitting cross-legged under the big tree and Brigitte was talking about the exhibition. It was to be held the same week as our school formal toward the end of the year. Even though that was ages away, Aysum was lamenting about missing out on both events on account of her strict parents while Nadine questioned whether she should wear the same dress twice. There was a palpable excitement about the exhibition, and Brigitte was telling us how the organizer said she had a great eye for photography. Sying stood up, body trembling with a pressure cooker–like fury, fists clenched tightly at her sides. "Shut up!" she screamed down at Brigitte, her face screwed up like she was going to cry. "Shut up! Shut up!"

We all watched in horror, waiting with bated breath for Brigitte's response. "Sying?" she said softly, an expression of mild bewilderment on her face.

"Don't you 'Sying' me! You weren't even interested in all this to begin with. But you saw how much attention I was getting and you couldn't stand it. You always need to be the center of everything. This movement was mine, and you just came waltzing in like you always do."

"What the heck?" Brigitte sputtered. "You seemed pretty damn happy to accept my help at the time, Sying. You can't just gloss over that fact now things haven't gone exactly the way you wanted."

"I didn't expect you to muscle in on my campaign, even though I should have known better. And now, with this exhibition, you've squeezed me out completely."

"That's not fair, Sying: I gave you the idea for this exhibition, but you brushed me off. Remember our lunch at BKK? We were all there . . ."

"Oh, great." Sying's eyes roamed over us, blazing with fury. "So now you're all going to gang up on me, is that right? Typical."

"Don't bring the girls into it, Sying. Despite you turning your back on the exhibition, I've still tried to include you, and you know it. I've asked you to come along with me to the interviews and help me write up profiles."

"As your underling?"

"No—of course not! It's a lot of work and I could really use some help."

"Don't you get it, Brigitte? You should be the one helping me, not the other way around!"

Nadine looked from Brigitte to Sying, eyes wide. "But the exhibition was Brigitte's idea in the first place. We were all there with you at BKK. You can't just turn down an opportunity and then get upset when it works out for someone else. That's not fair, Sying."

Sying glared at Nadine. "But I was the one who started all this! She wouldn't have gone down this road if it hadn't been for me."

"Nadine's right," said Aysum. "You had every chance of running this project with Brigitte's help. Anyone could see what a great idea it was, so none of us are surprised it's getting all this attention. But it's not Brigitte's fault she came up with it. And it's going to do some real good, which is what I thought this was all about. Your entire campaign was built on creating a counternarrative and this seems to be working. Does it matter if you're not the one who achieves it—so long as someone does?" As usual, Aysum had a way of cutting right to the heart of the matter, and Sying stared at her, speechless.

Standing up, Brigitte reached out a hand to Sying. "How about we start over—put our differences aside and work together as equal partners—"

"Equal partners?" Sying scoffed, slapping Brigitte's hand away. "Do you think I believe for a second that you would give me the credit I deserve?"

"Of course I'll give you credit," Brigitte insisted. "Everyone knows you started this anti-racism campaign; everyone knows that. I've never tried to take that away from you, Sying, not once."

Brigitte's attempt to reason with Sying seemed to fall on deaf ears. Pointing a shaky finger at Brigitte, Sying continued her tirade. "You can pretend all you want, but I see who you really are and how you've manipulated this situation to your benefit. Soon the others will see things from my perspective too. You can't keep this façade up forever. One day you'll slip: someone else will see the real you, if only for a second, but that's all it'll take. That day will come, and it will come much sooner than you think." We watched open-mouthed as Sying roughly grabbed her schoolbag and stormed off. After a moment's pause, I went to look for her.

I found Sying at the library, in the back rows where no one ever went. She was sitting on the carpet, knees drawn in, crying softly. I crouched down and peered at her.

"Sying?"

"Brigitte always does this," she sobbed, slapping away at her tears. "She takes anything she wants and she makes everyone else think you're the crazy one. The other day Nadine was telling me that I'm overreacting. She doesn't get it. This was my thing—mine! I started it, and now she's going to make it all about her." She thumped at the ground.

My eyes widened in surprise. "Come on, Sying, there's no need for that. I really don't think Brigitte has it in for you or anything. I'd be the first one to know, wouldn't I? She's never said a bad word about you to me, not even once. In fact, she's always the first to defend you. And you did ask for her help, Sying. It's not Brigitte's fault she has great ideas."

"Have you ever wondered who sent the rose to Bowie on Valentine's Day?"

The change in subject was so swift, it almost gave me whiplash. "The rose?"

"Remember when someone sent Bowie a Valentine's rose?"

I threw up my hands. "It could have been anyone, Sying. It doesn't matter now because he's with me."

"How do you know it wasn't Brigitte who sent him the rose?"

I frowned, considering the possibility. "I guess it could have been Brigitte. If that's the case, she would have sent it as a diversion."

"You don't think it's weird she was so heavily involved in planning that date, along with your surprise birthday party?"

"I think it was nice of her to do those things for me."

"You have no idea what she's doing, do you? It's because she's pretty, she can get away with it."

I looked at Sying's round, earnest face and felt tremendously sorry for her. As though she knew and felt repelled by my pity, she spat, "You'll find out the hard way, Ai. Just you wait and see."

During chem the next morning, Brigitte and I heard our names broadcast over the school loudspeaker, instructing us to make our way to the common room. By the door, we were greeted by our year adviser, Mrs. Parker. As we entered the room, we saw

Sying seated on the yellow U-shaped couch. She was pale faced and teary, twisting a used tissue in her hands.

We all took seats facing each other. Mrs. Parker drew in a breath and said to Brigitte, "Sying claims you've been bullying her."

Brigitte balked at the word. "Bullying?"

"You've hijacked my campaign!" Sying cried.

"I have not!" Brigitte protested.

"Sying, apart from your view that Brigitte has muscled in on your anti-racism campaign, are there any other specific incidents of bullying you'd like to share with us?" asked Mrs. Parker.

"She told me once that wide-legged pants don't suit me because I'm too short."

"You asked for my help to pick out a new outfit. I thought bootlegs are better for your shape, that's all."

"Is there anything else you can think of, Sying?" Mrs. Parker coaxed.

Sying screwed up her face, thinking hard. "Look, there's a ton of stuff, but it's hard to think of anything specific, okay? It's just a bunch of stupid little things."

"What are your thoughts, Ai? Have you witnessed acts of bullying by Brigitte?" Mrs. Parker asked me.

"Not that I can recall," I said, fingering the silver magpie chain around my neck. Sying shot me a wounded look, but I continued. "Sure, everyone knows Sying started this anti-racism thing, but it was only after Brigitte had the idea for the exhibition that it really took off. And I don't know if anyone can really own a movement."

"That's a good point, Ai," said Mrs. Parker.

Sying seemed like she was struggling to compose herself for a moment; then, taking a deep breath, she looked intently at me. "What about the rose, Ai? The one you think Brigitte may have sent Bowie on Valentine's Day."

I reddened, stammering. "What? I didn't . . ."

Brigitte shot me a look. "What's she talking about, Ai?"

"Sying brought it up yesterday and I admitted there was a possibility you sent the rose. But I did say it was probably just part of the plan to throw me off. It's no big deal."

"If it's no big deal, why didn't you just ask me?"

"I didn't ask you because it wasn't a big deal. If it had bothered me in the slightest, of course I would have asked."

"But you discussed it with Sying?"

"It wasn't a discussion or anything. Like I said, it just came up in conversation."

Brigitte blinked at me, a hurt expression on her face. "Well, the truth is, I did send him that rose. You were right, though, about it being part of the plan to throw you off. There's nothing more to it and I don't even know why you'd think otherwise."

In a thin, wobbly voice, Sying asked, "What did you write on the note, Brigitte?"

"What?" Brigitte looked confused.

"Did you write, 'From your secret admirer,' or was it 'With *love* from your secret admirer'? Which one was it?"

"What difference does it make?"

"You don't think the word 'love' makes a difference in that sentence?" Sying straightened, her sudden change in posture suggesting a growing confidence. "If I was sending Bowie a rose just for the sake of it and felt no emotional attachment, I would have written, 'From your secret admirer.' Personally, that's what I would have written if it had been me."

With a shrug Brigitte said, "Well, if that's the case, then it's probably what I wrote."

Sying's eyes narrowed sharply. "Liar."

"Sying!" snapped Mrs. Parker. "It's not helpful to call each other names."

Ignoring her, Sying continued in a cold, brittle voice, "On our way out of class that day, I deliberately went by Bowie's desk where the rose was sitting. I could clearly see what was written on the note and I can assure you, it read: 'With *love* from your secret admirer.' What's more, Brigitte had put not one but two *x*'s after that very telling sentence. I don't know about you, Ai, but to me that note seems kind of intimate for a prop. If I were to guess, Brigitte sent the rose to Bowie for real because she still carries a torch for him."

I stared at Sying agape, shaking my head. And yet her words had tugged at something that lurked in the dark recesses of my mind.

Calmly, Brigitte said, "That's ludicrous and Ai knows that."

I felt the sudden impulse to end this discussion before it went somewhere for which I was not prepared. In a tone more forceful than usual, I said, "You've got it all backward, Sying. It doesn't make a scrap of difference what Brigitte wrote on the note. If I thought there was any possibility she had feelings for Bowie, I wouldn't have gone out with him in the first place. So just drop it, okay? You're taking an innocent comment I made and blow-ing it up into one big drama."

"But, Ai," she said, gesturing at Brigitte as though she weren't sitting right there, "surely you can see through that 'little Miss Perfect' act she puts on. You can see what she's trying to do."

I shook my head, making my position crystal clear.

Sying looked deflated, as though for a moment she almost had me convinced of Brigitte's treachery. By now the tissue in her hand was shredded into tiny pieces, bits of white dandruff-like fluff pooling on her lap. "It's so unfair. It's just so unfair. Bri-gitte always gets everything handed to her on a silver platter, but it's never enough for her. She had to take away the only thing I cared about."

With a sigh Brigitte said, "I give up, Sying. If you feel this strongly about my involvement, then I quit. You can take full control of the exhibition from now on. I will let the organizer at Whitlam Library know and hand over all the material that's been gathered so far. I have taken about seven portraits and writ-ten up half a dozen profiles. We're aiming for fifteen all told. I was going to incorporate this exhibition into my major artwork, but I'm moving in a different direction anyway. Does that work for you, Sying?"

All eyes were on Sying, who was still looking down at her lap. Slowly, she nodded.

"Do you have a camera for the portraits?"

Sying shook her head and Mrs. Parker said the art depart-ment could provide one for her to use. Then she stood up and said, "I think that's a fair resolution," just as the bell rang to announce the next period.

When we left the common room, Sying broke away from us and stumbled off in a daze. It was as though she'd gotten what she wanted, but somehow it had fallen short of her expectations.

"Sying—wait up!" Brigitte ran over to her.

I stopped and watched them at a distance. Brigitte's demeanor seemed friendly, and I guessed her intention was to offer words of comfort to Sying. The two girls spoke quietly for a few moments before moving into an awkward embrace. And then I watched as Brigitte tipped her head to align her lips perfectly with Sying's ear. I saw her mouth move just a fraction. I don't know what she said, but Sying's expression switched from one of resigned misery to pure, wide-eyed terror.

Six

THE MODERATING SESSION had unearthed some trou-
bling thoughts, which I was still trying to process while at
Bowie's that afternoon. We were in his room, and I was waiting
for him to finish up what he was doing on his giant, custom-
made PC computer. To this day, that's how I see Bowie in my
mind's eye: sitting at his desk, forehead creased in concentration,
tapping away at the monolithic contraption he had created, my
constant reminder of the hours spent trailing him at computer
fairs while he bargained for bits of hardware bought with money
saved from working at his uncle's fruit shop. His computer
reminded me of a miniaturized industrial plant with its attach-
ments and cords, puttering away contentedly by his single bed,
where I'm lying belly down with the fan spinning overhead, the
cool wind on the backs of my thighs. Looking at Bowie, I felt
something bittersweet stirring within. I wished I could tell him
everything that had happened that day and he'd understand the
complexity of what I was feeling. I practiced the words in my
head, but even there they didn't sit right.

"How much longer?" I asked, after sensing enough time had lapsed since I last hassled him.

"Just five more minutes," he promised, keys clicking furiously under his fingers.

"You said that five minutes ago."

"Sorry, but there's a guy here saying Macs are better than PCs and I'm using cold, hard facts to prove him wrong."

"Who cares what some random guy on an internet forum thinks? Besides, I prefer Macs. They're cuter."

"That's because you're a girl," he teased.

I threw a pillow at him.

"Hey!" he laughed, batting it to the floor. "You've got a pretty strong arm there—*for a girl*."

Soon we were on his bed, wrestling playfully, gasping with laughter. We paused, thinking we'd heard footsteps outside his room, and braced ourselves for the door being flung wide open, his little brother, Tai, bursting in to show off a new toy or his mother standing at the threshold with a basket of laundry. But it remained shut and he pulled me in close to him. "You're so cozy."

Eyes closed, I murmured something low and sweet.

With a contented sigh, he wrapped his arms tighter around me. Then, giving my waist a gentle squeeze, he said, "Ai?"

"Mmm?" I shifted on my back to face him. He had a nervous look on his face, and for a moment I was worried. "What is it?"

Then he grinned, sheepish. "You know, I've got some Chinese New Year money set aside. I was thinking . . ."

He was a quiet for a moment and I prompted, "You were thinking . . . ?"

His hand inched below my naval and I felt waves of pleasure radiating out from where he was touching me. "What if we booked a hotel room the night of our school formal?"

I burst into laughter, burying my head beneath his pillow. "That's so cliché, Bowie," I mumbled.

"I know," he conceded, pulling the pillow away as I playfully hid my face behind my hands. He gently peeled my fingers one at a time, but I kept my eyes firmly shut. "But what do you think?" I could hear in his voice that he was still grinning.

Slowly, I opened one eye and then another. "I think . . ." After a long dramatic pause, I blurted, "I think it's the best idea."

His grin widened. "Really?"

"I have to lose my virginity at some point—don't I?"

"Jeez, Ai, you don't have to put it that bluntly. You know we don't need to have sex. We could just cuddle. I don't want you to feel pressured or anything."

"Oh, come on, it's not like I would be doing you a huge favor, you know. I want this too."

He stroked my cheek. "Yeah?"

I rolled on my side to face him and for a while we just stared into each other's eyes, taking everything in.

"Or we could just do it now, get it over with," I joked, partly to relieve the emotional intensity of the moment.

He groaned, pulling away from me and lying on his back. "Don't tempt me—I want the first time to be special for you."

"Bowie"—I put my hand on his cheek—"it will be special because it's with you."

"Have you been thinking about it, Ai?" He was looking at me with that intense expression again, the one that made me giddy and light-headed. His bed was as soft as a cloud, and I wanted to sink in deeper until it swallowed us whole. To always stay with him like this.

"Of course I've been thinking about it . . . ," I finally answered him.

"What do you think about?"

I elbowed him, laughing. "I'm not going to tell you that."

"Aw, why not?"

"Anyway, you'll find out on the night of our formal."

He squeezed me hard, clearly jubilant. "Okay, I'll start organizing it. Leave it all to me."

"As long as you're the one organizing it." I meant it as a joke, but there was an undertone to my voice that betrayed my true feelings.

I felt Bowie tense up. "What do you mean?"

"Well, it would be weird if Brigitte helped you out this time, wouldn't it?"

"I don't need her help to book a hotel room, Ai." He sounded defensive.

"I was just joking, Bowie," I said with a small, nervous laugh. "Honestly, I didn't mean anything by it."

"Well, for the record, this is just between you and me. It's not the first time I've booked a room before, you know."

"Oh, really," I teased. "I guess the last time would have been for Brigitte. Unless there was another, secret girlfriend I don't know about."

"Um, no, silly. I booked a room at the Hyatt for my cousin's bachelor party. It cost a bomb, but everyone invited pitched in."

"You and Brigitte never did it, then?"

"Isn't that something you girls would have discussed?"

"I wasn't friends with her when you guys were dating, remember?"

"Oh, yeah, that's right. I keep forgetting."

"And besides, we don't discuss every minor detail about our lives, you know."

"Okay, well, yeah, we came kind of close, but, no, we didn't go all the way."

I let out a quiet breath of relief. I was sure Brigitte would have mentioned it to me at some point, but I couldn't remember for sure. I could have asked her directly but didn't feel comfortable going down that road now that Bowie and I were an item. It shouldn't have made a difference either way. It wasn't as though I was keeping score.

Bowie nudged me, drawing me back to the present. "Anyway, speaking of Brigitte, don't you think it would be great if she started dating Tin?"

It seemed obvious Bowie wanted to steer the conversation away from his past with Brigitte. I wondered if this was something he'd always done and I just never noticed. After a moment's pause, I said, "Brigitte's out of his league, don't you think?"

"You can never tell with her. She's been with some real weirdos."

"Like you, for example."

"Ha-ha. I was probably the only non-weird one."

"Then why did you let her get away?"

"I don't know. A girlfriend seemed like a lot of hard work back then."

"Do you mean a girlfriend in general or one like Brigitte?" I was fishing.

"Hey!" He lightly thumped my arm. "We're meant to be talking about Tin, not me. Seriously, what do you think, Ai? Would Brigitte go for it?"

I thought about his question. The idea of her dating Tin had never occurred to me, but I suddenly warmed to it, realizing it would bring a nice equilibrium to the group. "It would be so cool, right?" said Bowie, as though he'd been reading my mind.

"Not if one likes the other and the other one doesn't feel the same way. Then it could get awkward. Do you think Tin is interested?"

"A few days ago he made a comment about her. We were walking down Railway Parade and I thought I saw her ahead of us. But Tin said it wasn't her and it turned out he was right. When I asked how he knew, he said, 'Because Brigitte has nicer legs.'"

"Oh," I said as a stab of jealousy went right through me, clean as a knife. That was when I knew without a doubt that Aysum had been right about my true feelings toward Brigitte. Even though Bowie was only relaying a secondhand comment made by Tin, it affected me in the way it would have if he'd made the comment himself. My mind went back to the moderating session and what Sying had said about the rose. Then the image of Brigitte whispering in Sying's ear flashed into my head.

Cutting into my thoughts, Bowie said, "That's the first time Tin's said anything about a girl—a real one, anyway."

"What do you mean by 'real'?"

"The only crush I know of is some character from *Final Fantasy*."

"All right, I will ask Brigitte what she thinks, then."

"In that case, I'll see if Tin is interested."

"I'm sure it will be an easy sell for you: we're talking about Brigitte, after all. I think most guys would be gagging to go out with her."

"Not all guys," Bowie said pointedly. He drew me into him again, squeezing me so hard, his chin dug painfully into my shoulder. I loved being held like this, to the point where it hurt, and arched my back like a cat to luxuriate in the moment. We lay like that for a while when I decided to bring up the thing that had been at the forefront of my mind since the moderating session. Turning to face him, I said, "Hey, Bowie, do you remember the rose you got on Valentine's Day?"

"Yeah, what about it?"

"Did you keep it by any chance?"

"Why would I keep a dead rose? It would have made a mess and Mum would have had a fit."

"I meant the note, dummy. Did you keep the note?"

"Why would I keep the note?"

"Do you remember what was written on it?"

"Um, I think it said, 'From your secret admirer,' or something like that."

"Did it say, 'From your secret admirer,' or 'With *love* from your secret admirer'?"

He paused. "Jeez, Ai, how could I remember something like that? I was thinking about you all that day, wondering if the big, elaborate thing I planned would work. I didn't care about the rose, to be honest. I just threw it in the trash."

"Do you remember if it had *x*'s on it—as in kisses?"

"Jeez, maybe, but I can't say for sure. What's the point of this? Why are you asking me these weird questions?"

"Oh, just something Brigitte said earlier today. You remember how in the middle of chem our names were broadcasted on the loudspeaker?"

"Brigitte said that Sying called a moderating session or something."

"Well, Sying accused Brigitte of bullying her."

"Brigitte?" Bowie scoffed. "Sying's the bully, if anything."

"Why do you say that?"

"Ah, I don't know. It's not my business, really, but if you ask me, she's a troublemaker, that one."

"And Brigitte is an angel, right?"

"Hey," he exclaimed, sitting upright, "you're being weird, Ai. What have you got against Brigitte suddenly?"

Frowning, I said, "I saw something kind of strange after the moderating session between Sying and Brigitte—something I wasn't supposed to see. But maybe I'm reading too much into things."

Bowie sighed. "Don't let Sying get in your head, Ai. That's my advice."

Brigitte brushed away my suggestion of her dating Tin and the idea dissipated like summer rain. When I told Bowie our matchmaking plans had gone awry, he just shrugged and said, "Oh, well, it was worth a try."

He was over for dinner that night, and at the table Yan was telling Bowie about a TV show we recently watched about coins. In the show, a man unknowingly had in his possession a fifty-cent coin worth a small fortune. The show had given examples of several other such coins and the hallmarks to look for. For example, there was the humble five-cent coin where an error had been made during the minting process and the head and tail weren't exactly aligned. "A coin like that could fetch over a hundred dollars," Yan explained.

"Wow," said Bowie, pulling a handful of coins out of his pocket and separating the five-cent pieces. The two examined them closely; then, with a shake of his head, Yan said, "Sorry, dude."

Mum asked me, "Where Brigitte? She know I making char kway teow?"

"I think she's busy studying," I said.

Bowie raised his eyebrows at me, looking doubtful. "Brigitte . . . studying?"

With a shrug I said, "Well, I think she mentioned something along those lines . . ."

Yan laughed, shaking his head. "Since when does Brigitte need to study? That girl's got a photographic memory. Studying is for regular people like you and me, Ai."

"That's not true," I said. "Brigitte does study. We've crammed for stacks of exams together."

"More like she was tutoring you, sis," Yan teased.

Bowie laughed along good-naturedly and I bristled. It was true Brigitte made everything seem effortless, but they didn't have to turn it into a comparison.

"All week, not see Brigitte," Dad mused. "You fighting?" It was rare for Dad to comment on my friends, but I suppose Brigitte was the type of person whose presence you missed.

"Oh, come on, it's obvious, isn't it? Ai doesn't want a pretty girl like that hanging around her boyfriend," Yan joked without realizing he'd struck a sore spot.

"Shut up, Yan," I snapped.

His eyes widened, taken aback by my outburst.

Bowie, always the diplomat, reached over, squeezing my shoulder. "Ai's got nothing to worry about. Kate Moss could walk in right now and I wouldn't even notice . . ."

Blinking back tears, I made a fuss of picking up my bowl of half-eaten noodles. "I'm going to finish this in my room."

Bowie came to find me sitting on the floor, back against the tall-boy, chopsticks stabbing at my noodles. "Hey, you okay? You're kind of taking out your anger on those noodles. They didn't do anything wrong."

I smiled in spite of myself.

He joined me on the floor, bumping his shoulder gently into mine. "Don't listen to what your brother said; he's just messing with you. Isn't that what brothers are for? Normally, you'd be laughing along with us, wouldn't you? But lately you've been so sensitive about Brigitte."

"Don't you think it's weird she's dated both you and my brother? I mean, who's next? My dad?"

"Hey, that sounds awfully like something Sying would say." His voice, gently reproachful, caused me to immediately regret what I had said. But it wasn't the joke Yan had made that bothered me but what it signified. If it was that obvious to Yan, then everyone else must be thinking the same thing: Why would anyone choose me over Brigitte? Just like Lucille had said, Brigitte was the pretty one. Anyone with eyes could make that distinction. That had never been an issue for me—not until Bowie came into the picture.

"Come on, Ai, don't be upset." Bowie pinched my cheek playfully, bringing me out of my troubled thoughts. "Even though you are so damn cute when you're angry."

I wrinkled my nose at him and he grinned, sensing the lightening of my mood.

There was a knock on the door and Yan poked his head through. Looking straight at me, he said in a deadpan voice, "I'm going to pick up some donuts. Do you want some?"

It was his way of making peace.

• • •

Soon it reached a point where I had to acknowledge my feelings toward Brigitte were noticeably changing, although I couldn't think of anyone I could truly confide in about this. Bowie and Tin were always too quick to rush to her defense, and Aysum in her own considered way would probably do the same. As for my internet friend Pedro, he was a good sounding board but, having no real-world context of Brigitte, could only make generic assumptions about her.

Soon I began to look at Brigitte in a different light, becoming hyperaware of the interactions between her and Bowie, perhaps reading far too much into things that could have been perfectly innocent. One day, against my better judgment, I finally admitted to Sying my growing suspicion that Brigitte still had feelings for Bowie. She jumped on this right away. "She doesn't want Bowie, but she doesn't want anyone else to have him either. Especially not you. That's just how she is. I'm glad you're seeing it now."

"Do you know Bowie still has no idea she was cheating on him with Alex?"

"She goes through guys like underwear. No one stays with her because she's so high-maintenance. And what about that whole Valentine's Day fiasco? That was way over-the-top, don't you think? It was like she was planning her own fantasy date with Bowie. And that surprise party she organized for you—teaching Bowie how to play guitar. Going up for a long drive to the mountains to pick up your necklace, just the two of them. Notice how all this stuff she plans for you involves long lengths of time where she gets to have Bowie all to herself?"

A strange alliance formed between Sying and me, based on the suspicions we held about Brigitte. We spent hours dissecting everything she said to catch her out, but there was never anything we could hold up in a court of law. Sometimes the bitchy nature of Sying's comments made me uncomfortable, and I would attempt to defuse the conversation when I felt a line had been crossed. I sensed Brigitte noticed the distance growing between us, in the small comments she made every now and then. "Oh, you never told me that," she'd say when Sying referenced a conversation she'd shared with me. Then came the surprise drop-ins Brigitte would make to our flat, bearing a plateful of Lucille's spring rolls like a kind of peace offering, even though neither of us directly addressed what was going on. This changed late one afternoon when Brigitte stopped by our flat. I was at my desk felting, jabbing at a ball of wool to form the shape of a rabbit's foot, when I heard her in the hallway, greeting Mum. They spoke for a few moments before Mum said, "Ai in bedroom."

Shortly, there was a knock on my door, and I said, "Come in."

"Hey, you," Brigitte said brightly.

I swiveled my chair around to face her as she stood framed by the doorway.

"Hey," I said.

"What are you doing?" she asked.

"Just felting a rabbit's foot for my major artwork."

She came over to look. "That's coming along great, Ai, especially the box of square sweets that look round. So cute."

I smiled in spite of myself. "I found a candy box template in a packaging book and designed it around that. Then I got it professionally printed at a copy shop."

She picked up the box, peering through its plastic window. "There's so much detail here—it's like a tiny diorama. I love how the sweets looking back at you have different expressions. You've given them real personality, Ai."

Brigitte's assessment of my artwork made me realize how much I still craved her approval. My inherent need to impress her was something I immediately resolved to change. Abruptly switching the subject, I said, "How's your major work going?"

"Okay, I think," she said, taking a seat on the edge of my bed. "Dropping the exhibition has given me loads of extra time to experiment. I'm really excited about this new concept I'm working on."

"This late? What's it about?"

A soft smile played on her lips. "It's about the kind of love stories that unfold in plain sight, without anyone really noticing. But when you look back, the clues were all there . . ."

I looked at her, stunned, wondering how she could be so brazen. Was she trying to tell me her project was about her and Bowie? If that was the case, it wasn't as secret as she thought. I turned back to my work, struggling to level my breath.

"Ai," she said, tentatively, "I want to talk about what's going on with us."

I stiffened. "What do you mean?"

"You know what I mean. You've been shutting me out lately and I can't figure out why."

"That's not true: we're still hanging out all the time."

"Only at school or when we're with the boys. I can't remember the last time just the two of us did something together."

"We're together now, aren't we?"

She sighed, exasperated. "Why are you acting like this? Can't you just tell me what's the matter? What did I do wrong?" The frustration in her voice grew as she spoke. "Ai . . . can you at least look at me?"

I spun my chair around to face her, holding up the ball of wool. "Can't you see what I'm doing? I've been busy with my major work. You know I got started late and have so much left to do."

"I get it, Ai: you're busy. We're all busy. But you don't seem to have trouble making time for Sying. You've been acting so weird ever since the moderating session. You don't actually believe the things she said, do you? Because you should know me better than that."

I wasn't sure if she was aware of how her behavior around Bowie was affecting me. Surely she could sense why I was upset without me having to spell it out for her. She may not be overtly inviting Bowie's attention but neither did she try to discourage it. Avoiding her gaze, I said, "Look, I don't know what to tell you, Brigitte, I really don't."

From the corner of my eye, I caught a glimpse of her expression. It looked like she was going to cry. I felt myself well up, too, and swiftly turned my attention back to my work.

After a moment she said in small voice, "The worst thing about all this is not knowing. At the very least you can tell me what I did wrong. You used to tell me everything and now it's like you're a stranger."

As she turned to leave, I was hit with a powerful sense of déjà vu. It was as though I'd dreamt this exact moment, the ball of wool in my hand, Brigitte's back framed in the doorway, the late afternoon sun streaming through the open slats of my window. It felt like a distant memory that was playing out then and there. I had a powerful urge to stop her from leaving. I wanted to tell her about the feeling of déjà vu that had just gripped me. I knew she would understand its significance. She would be able to explain it in a way that made sense to me. Then the moment passed and Brigitte was gone, the door firmly shut behind her.

The ongoing issue I had with Brigitte reared its ugly head again the following weekend at Bowie's. It was early morning, and we were preparing for his brother Tai's birthday, sitting cross-legged on the floor of his bedroom, having spent the last hour blowing up balloons with a hand pump. The day started out fine with the two of us watching in awe at how quickly the balloons filled up the room, cocooning us in our own little world.

"Aren't they pretty?" I sighed, moving my hand through the balloons, agitating their movement as they bumped gently against each other.

"Not as pretty as you," said Bowie.

I fluttered my eyelashes at him, playfully biting on the mouth of a red balloon.

"Hey, why don't you blow me instead of that balloon," he joked.

Laughing, I said, "You wish, Bowie."

He made a lewd gesture with the hand pump and I snatched it off him, holding it high above my head. Spotting the opportunity, he reached under my arms, tickling me until I was rolling around in hysterics.

"You know, I've found a picture of the dress I want to wear in the latest issue of *Girlfriend*. It's a halter neck, with a long flowing skirt and slit that goes all the way up my thigh."

He grinned. "Sounds easy to get off." Every time we spoke about the school formal, Bowie would say something that alluded to our plans afterward. The night was still months away, but the anticipation was already building. The thought of spending an entire night alone seemed almost too good to be true.

"It's going to be real tight, so I'm not sure if I can even wear anything underneath."

He groaned at the thought and pulled me into him. "I love having you as my girlfriend."

Then we were kissing, and I wanted the moment to go on forever. The door flew open and I pulled away from him breathlessly, hoping the balloons had given us enough coverage. Tai's little face emerged, grinning. "Wow! How come so many?" he shrieked.

"They're for you, dummy," said Bowie, ruffling his brother's hair.

"Wow!" Tai shouted again, running around the room, batting

at them and watching open-mouthed as they danced onto the bed. Jumping up, he whacked the balloons against the ceiling with all the enthusiasm and zeal of a seven-year-old. "So many!" he exclaimed again before hopping off the bed and zooming out of the room, balloons spilling out after him. Then, as though he'd forgotten something, he dashed up to the door again, skidding to a stop. Addressing Bowie, he asked, "Is Brigitte coming today?"

"She wouldn't miss it for the world, buddy."

He leapt up, punching the air. "Yes!"

Bowie looked at me, shaking his head with a laugh. "That kid sure is crazy." Reaching for the pump, he went back to work.

"Brigitte's coming?" I asked, feeling myself tense up.

"Yeah. So's Tin. Why?"

I shook my head, grabbing a fresh pack of balloons and tearing it open with a loud crinkling sound.

After a few moments of awkward silence, Bowie said, "Ai, why are you being weird about Brigitte coming today?"

"Why do you have to invite her to everything?"

"You know how much my baby brother likes her. Besides, she's still your best friend, isn't she?"

I busied myself with the balloons, not wanting to give him an answer.

"What's going on with you and Brigitte?"

"Nothing's going on. Why do you ask?"

"You guys haven't been hanging out lately."

"We went to the drive-through just the other night."

"That's with the four of us. When was the last time just the two of you hung out? I mean, even Tin thinks something's up."

"So you've all been discussing this behind my back?"

He sighed, exasperated, attaching the mouth of a yellow balloon to the pump. "No, we're just trying to figure out what she did to upset you."

"Well, I wish she'd talk to me instead of running to you and Tin."

"She says she's tried but you gave her the brush-off."

"I'd hardly call it that. And what's it to you, anyway? People grow apart, you know. Maybe we're just getting to that age."

He looked sad about this. "We're talking about you and Brigitte here. You've been best friends for ages."

"Only for a year or so," I reminded him.

"Well, it seems way longer than that. Anyway, it's weird how you're always hanging out with Sying now."

"What's so bad about Sying?"

"Well, she's different to Brigitte, don't you think?"

"Different how?"

"I don't know. There's just something about Sying I don't like. She's shifty. My parents don't like her mum even though they're kind of related. Besides, you have way more in common with Brigitte, and she's a better friend to you—she's a better person in general. I'm sorry, but you can't compare someone like Brigitte with Sying."

I batted a balloon away from me to express my annoyance. "I'm so sick of hearing about how amazing Brigitte is. That's all I get from you these days. Brigitte this and Brigitte that. If you think she's so great, then why don't you just cut to the chase and get back with her?"

His expression darkened. "Look, I don't want to get into a fight about this right before my brother's party, okay?"

"Maybe I should go, then."

"Maybe you should."

I spent the afternoon chatting to Pedro, off-loading all my angst. He advised me to follow my gut instinct and not allow Bowie and Brigitte to get the better of me. Pedro said if Bowie really loved me, he wouldn't have let me leave the party so easily, which I thought was a good point. The conversation left me feeling vindicated, but that certainty began to dissipate when I was left alone again with my thoughts.

After dark, Bowie brought over a slice of cake, a sheepish look on his face. We sat on the top step just outside my front door as I picked at the sponge with a plastic fork. It was du-rian flavored—my favorite—with bits of fruit and cream, a sliver of Spider-Man's costume in blue-and-red jelly. I was sorry to have missed the party, even though I never felt truly welcome at Bowie's house. His mother was ready to cast doubt on my suitability as his future wife, pointing out my lack of interest in housework. Even though I laughed it off, part of me still found the comment hurtful.

After a long silence, Bowie said, "I don't know what's going on with you and Brigitte, and it's really none of my business. It just makes me sad to see the two of you growing apart, and I don't want it to be because of me."

"It's not," I said quickly. It was only a partial lie. I wasn't sure if my feelings toward Brigitte stemmed from Bowie or if he was merely the catalyst.

As though reading my mind, Bowie said, "I don't want you to ever doubt the way I feel about you, okay? I love you to pieces, you know. All I want to do is make you happy."

His words filled me with warmth, and I rested my head on his shoulder. He put his arm around me, squeezing gently.

"Anyway," he said, "I have my worries, too, you know. Things are going to be different next year. You're going to college for sure, but I'll be staying back here to help my uncle with the shop. You'll probably forget all about me when you're mixing with a whole new group of friends, some of them guys."

I'd been so caught up with my own issues that I didn't stop to think Bowie had his insecurities too. I straightened up and looked him squarely in the eyes. "Bowie, I will never, ever forget you for as long as I live. Besides, who knows if I'll get into college? I've been spending so much time on my art project, I'm falling behind in my other subjects."

"Then lucky for you they accept students based on their portfolios. When they see yours, you'll be guaranteed a spot for sure."

Bowie's confidence in me wasn't entirely unwarranted. A week later the College of Fine Arts were hosting student interviews at their leafy Paddington campus. Inside one of the rooms were three desks set up in a neat row where professors sat, reviewing portfolios. When it was my turn, I glanced quickly around the room to see a couple of other girls with identical leather-bound portfolios, wearing serene, placid expressions. I tried my best to convey this sense of nonchalance but already felt self-conscious about the cheap plastic case which housed a handmade booklet featuring photographs of my work.

My interviewer introduced herself to me as Sharon. She had red frizzy hair, her neck was adorned with a chunky necklace made of African beads, and she had thick glass bangles on her wrists. As she was leafing through my portfolio, she asked, "Have you decided on the course you'd like to enroll in?"

I examined her face, hoping to see some kind of indication of how she felt about my work. In a tentative voice, I said, "I really like the look of 'craft arts' or a 'bachelor of design majoring in textiles.'"

"Yes, I thought as much. There's a real tactile quality to your pieces, and I see you enjoy working with paper . . . Is this origami?"

I peered over at the work to which she was referring. It was an intricate paper swan, made by assembling hundreds of pieces of paper folded in triangular modules. "I suppose, technically, you can call it that . . ."

"It's a lot more complex than your average paper crane," she laughed. "Are you Japanese?"

Giving my head a quick shake, I said, "My parents are Cambodian with Chinese heritage. They immigrated to Australia after being driven out by the Khmer Rouge back in the late '70s."

"I see," she said, now scrutinizing my face the way she had my portfolio. "You must have been a baby when you arrived. That explains why your English is so good: I can't detect the slightest accent, and I'm not just saying that. If I closed my eyes, I wouldn't be able to tell you apart from any other Aussie in this room."

I shifted in my seat, unsure how to respond. It seemed she meant it as a compliment, so I mumbled a thanks.

Back to reviewing my portfolio, she reached the final page, which showed pictures of my recently completed box of square sweets that look round, taken at different angles. "Oh!" she said, sounding genuinely delighted. "I remember this from *Charlie and the Chocolate Factory*. So whimsical! How did you arrive at this idea?"

I began to feel more at ease as the conversation moved away from my ethnicity and toward my work. I launched into the concept I'd derived about documenting my literary travels while she cocked her head to one side, listening intently. Looking back at the photographs, she asked, "Have you studied typography at all?"

I laughed nervously. "Only in books from our local library,"

"You seem to have a natural talent for typesetting. In fact, this piece shows off a number of skills in creativity and making. It's obviously a passion you adopted early on."

Encouraged by her words, I said, "Absolutely. It's been that way all my life. I'm always in the middle of a creative project, sometimes several at once. My parents say as a little girl I always had a pair of scissors in my hands."

"Is that so?"

"When I was about five, I locked myself in my parents' room. They were frantic, banging on the door. When they finally managed to get in, they found me calmy sitting at my dad's work desk with a pair of scissors, snipping away at the family photos. 'What are you doing?' they cried. I told them I was giving Daddy a haircut."

She laughed, clapping her hands so her bangles clinked softly together. "What a charming story." Then, leaning in close, she said in a low voice, "Personally, Ai, I think you're a great fit for this college. And what's more, you'll be pleased to know we're quite diverse here. We host many international students on this campus, so you'll feel right at home." It was on the tip of my tongue to remind her I was an Australian but decided against it. With a wink, she added, "Hopefully we'll see you next year."

Outside in the main square, I spotted Bowie standing by the coffee cart. Our eyes locked, holding a silent conversation. He must have seen from my expression that the interview went well because his face suddenly lit up. We closed the distance between us and I grinned, nodding. "I think it went okay."

"Yeah?"

"The woman interviewing me was kind of weird but she really liked my work."

"Do you think you'll get in?"

"It's not a done deal, but she told me I would be a 'great fit' for the college. That's a good sign . . . right?"

"You bet it is." His face was shining with pride. "My girlfriend the college student. Wow."

• • •

Later, we walked down the treelined streets of Paddington, cobblestones underfoot. Down a lane we found a café and ordered a plate of fries to share.

"Did you see the portfolios the others were carrying?" I said, dunking my fries into a small bowl of ketchup. "They were fancy, weren't they? It looked as though they were bought from the same shop. I can't even imagine how much one would cost."

"Who cares? It's what's inside them that counts."

I knew Bowie was alluding to the success of my interview and I beamed, glowing with the first real acknowledgment of my talent from someone in a position to cast judgment on these things. Under the table, Bowie took my hand. "What do you think of the campus?"

"It's a lot smaller than I imagined, but I like that. It means I'll never be late for class. Also, I passed by some glass cabinets displaying artworks by students. I tried to figure out the techniques used in some of the pieces, and I couldn't. Imagine learning how to work with mediums like ceramics, wood, and metal. Imagine all the cool stuff I would be able to make."

A soft smile played on Bowie's lips as I continued, enthused. "And did you notice the ratio between girls and boys? It's way off, don't you think? There were hardly any guys."

"Good—I don't need the competition."

"As if you'd ever have to worry about that. Anyone can see you're way out of my league anyway."

"You got that right," he joked as I kicked him playfully under the table.

"And if I work over the summer, I may save up just enough to move out here. You can visit me anytime, even stay over . . ."

He grinned. "I like the idea of that."

"Do you know what the others are planning to do after school next year?"

"Tin's main priority is to get out of Whitlam, only he doesn't know how he's going to do it. Brigitte's going back to Paris. Her aunt knows a fashion photographer who is looking for an assistant."

I felt a jolt of sadness as my mind settled around the thought of Brigitte leaving. Bowie must have sensed the sudden dip in my mood because he said, "Ai, can I ask you something serious?"

"Sure."

"Do you want me to stop being friends with Brigitte?" His eyes were earnest as his hand reached across the table, searching for mine. "Would that make you happy?"

I gave my head a firm shake. "No, of course not. I like it when the four of us are hanging out. And I know how much it means to you."

"But you do know you're my main priority—right? Most likely Tin and Brigitte won't be here once this year is up, so you're my only sure thing. To be honest, I don't need anyone else."

"I know that, Bowie, and I feel the same way."

"But you're right. I do like it when the four of us are getting along. There's just no telling how long it would last, you know."

"Yeah, I get that."

"However you feel about Brigitte, just remember she won't be here for much longer."

I felt myself tearing up at this. The idea of her being that far away felt almost incomprehensible to me. And then something in Bowie's hopeful expression made me realize how much I valued what the four of us had—that feeling of camaraderie and belonging when we were all together. Suddenly I wanted it all back with a fierceness that took me by surprise.

I felt my body slump with the full weight of the day. The interview with Sharon had stirred up many conflicting emotions. It was the kind of encounter that I could only really talk about with Brigitte. Where Sying would have viciously branded Sharon a racist, Brigitte would have just chalked it up to a well-meaning individual who simply lacked awareness when it came to my unusual set of circumstances. She would nudge my attention back to the positive outcome of the meeting, ask me to describe again and again how impressed Sharon was with my work, allowing me to revel in the moment for as long as I wanted. On the other hand, Sying would zone in on the negative and ignore the rest. When I thought of the two scenarios, each felt like a pathway branching off in separate directions with me standing at the crossroad. This internal struggle must have shown on my face because Bowie said, "Ai, are you okay?"

"I'm okay," I said, giving him a weak smile. "I was just thinking about how much I wanted to share my news with Brigitte. Besides you, she's the only other person I know who would be truly happy for me."

"And what about Sying?" Bowie asked cautiously. "If you told her about your meeting today, would she be happy for you?"

I knew the answer to that question right away, we both did. Quietly, I said, "No, I don't think so." When it came to Sying, I would be downplaying parts of my story to compensate for her feelings, careful not to say anything that might upset her.

Bowie remained silent, as though allowing me time to grasp the significance of what I had just concluded. After a few moments he said, "Ai, why don't you call Brigitte, make things right with her?"

I shook my head. "I think it will take more than a phone call to set things right again . . ."

"It would be a start though, right?"

"What if it's too late, Bowie? What if I've ruined my friendship with Brigitte for good? Like you said, we're all going our separate ways."

He touched my arm. "There are certain friendships that you can't ruin, no matter how hard you try. That's how it is with me and Tin. If ten years were to go by without us speaking a word—I know the instant I call him, he would answer. That's what you have with Brigitte; that's what the four of us have with each other."

Until he put it in that way, I hadn't realized what it meant to me. "Okay, Bowie, I'm going to make a real effort with Brigitte, make amends for the way I've been treating her. You'll see, I'm going to set things right again."

I stayed true to my word, reaching out to Brigitte in small, earnest ways, leaving unexpected gifts for her, like handmade bookmarks quoting *The Little Prince*, "Language is the source of misunderstandings," alluding to our rift and hinting at my desire to make amends. I was surprised at how quickly we were able to acclimatize back to how we were—how such small acts of consideration could bridge a divide so vast.

By the week's end, there was a change in our group, a buoyancy that seemed to lift us all. I think that's why Brigitte suggested a picnic at The Royal National Park that weekend. The night before, we were at her place, gathered around the coffee table, playing a game of poker. We gambled with sweets that were evenly distributed before the start of the game: gummy worms, chocolate freckles, and White Rabbit candy. At the start of the evening, there was a strange vibe, almost somber, but I couldn't figure out why. Everyone looked as though they were tired, but I chalked it up to our upcoming exams, figured none of us were getting much sleep.

Soon the mood lifted as we played in pairs, girls against boys. Brigitte and I revealed our carefully concealed hand—a royal flush—shrieking with joy at the win. The boys groaned and handed over their stockpile of candy, which Brigitte scooped up with glee. Then she clamped my cheeks between her hands so my lips puckered, fishlike, and said, "Where have you been, Ai? I've missed you." She emphasized the word "missed" in an exaggerated tone, which I mirrored just as eagerly.

"I've missed you too." Throwing my arms around her and squeezing as though holding on for dear life, we tumbled onto the carpet, gasping with laughter. Over her shoulder, I caught Bowie looking at us, positively radiant.

Although things were going better than I had imagined, it wasn't a complete turnaround for me. The same old doubts still circulated in my mind, despite my best efforts to quash them.

But with the seed of mistrust already sown, I still found myself adding to the list of accusations accumulated against Brigitte: looks exchanged with Bowie that seemed imbued with meaning, a hand on his arm that lingered.

When Bowie volunteered to pick up the pizzas from Pepe's, Brigitte said she'd go with him because the manager always threw in extra garlic knots for her. Of course, once the combination was set, I couldn't change it. It would have been weird to say, "I'll tag along," because my motive would be painfully obvious. If I'd spoken up before Brigitte, that would have been fine, but usually in this situation the boys went together.

When Bowie and Brigitte left, an awkward silence hung between Tin and me. He seemed quieter than usual tonight, and when I looked closer, there were dark rings around his eyes. On the television, *Pretty Woman* was playing and had cut to a raunchy sex scene, making the tension between us almost unbearable.

On the L-shaped couch, we were sitting apart and perpendicular. He glanced at me and smiled. "What's up, Ai?"

"Nothing much."

"How is your major work going?"

"Good! I've been working on *Alice in Wonderland*. Want to see my VAPD diary?"

"Sure."

I located my bloated spiral sketch pad and passed it over to him. He flicked through it with interest, then, pausing at a page, asked, "What do you call this—with all the swirly paper?"

"Quilling," I answered.

"Oh. It looks really complicated."

"It's easy when you get the hang of it." I jumped to my feet. "Wait—let me show you!"

I went to gather a few supplies from Brigitte's room and stopped. On her bed were a pair of boy's shorts stitched with Whitlam's school insignia. My stomach tightened, wondering if they belonged to Bowie. I picked them up to get a closer look, patting the pockets. My heart skipped when I heard a rustle, but it was only a five-dollar note.

Back in the lounge room, I dumped all the supplies on the coffee table and began my demonstration, explaining the process as I went. "So you take a long strip of paper and curl it like this. Then you glue it down onto the card to make flowers and stuff."

"Hey, that's neat," said Tin.

"It's kind of like curling a ribbon. Want to try?"

"Sure." He was all thumbs and got his hands tangled up in the strip of colored paper, letting out a growl of exasperation. "You made it look really easy."

I stifled a chuckle.

He said, "You're really good at all this stuff, Ai."

The boy's shorts I'd found on Brigitte's bed were still niggling away at me when I heard Bowie's car pull up. I went to stand by the window in the kitchen overlooking the driveway, gently sliding it open. I heard a car door slam and caught the tail end of a conversation.

"Do you think she'll be okay?" Brigitte's voice was strained with worry.

"I don't know. I feel so bad about what's happened . . ."

"She doesn't deserve this, does she, Bowie? My heart breaks for her."

"Yeah . . . but at least she's got Tin."

Almost as an afterthought, Brigitte added, "And us: she's got us too."

My heart was racing, head reeling. By the time they arrived at the front door, I was a vicious animal, blind and seething, hands clawing at the silver chain that suddenly felt too tight around my neck. The clasp broke, coming loose in my hands. In a single motion, I threw the necklace at Bowie. "What do you feel bad about, huh? What did you do?" I yelled in his dumbstruck face.

"Ai," said Brigitte in a stunned voice.

I turned to face her, eyes blazing. "I heard you, Brigitte! I heard you talking about me just now. Tell me why, Brigitte. Why is your heart breaking for me? And what are Bowie's shorts doing on your bed?"

They had the nerve to look perplexed, as though they hadn't just been caught red-handed.

"Bowie's shorts?" said Brigitte, confused. I wanted to claw that stupid, bemused look from her face. Sying was right; she had been right all along. Brigitte took whatever she wanted because she could. She was the pretty one. Just like Lucille had said.

"The shorts! On your bed. They're Bowie's, aren't they?"

I was dissolving now. Tears spilling down my cheeks, gasping for air. I couldn't breathe.

"Look . . . I'm going to take her home," said Bowie.

• • •

In the car, I calmed down, my onslaught of tears now reduced to a trickle. I gulped, wiping my nose on the sleeve of my shirt, then looked Bowie in the eye. "Tell me, is there anything going on with you and Brigitte?"

"Of course not!"

"Then what were you two talking about?"

"It's got nothing to do with you, Ai, believe me."

"How can you say that when I was the subject of the conversation?"

He shook his head. "You weren't."

"Then who the hell were you talking about? Why can't you just tell me?"

"I just can't, okay? At least not yet."

"But you can tell Brigitte?"

"It's not like that, Ai. You've got this all wrong."

"Bowie," I said, my voice breaking at the apex of his name. I pushed an errant lock of hair behind his ear, feeling like I was losing him.

His eyes shone at me with so much sincerity, I felt my resolve weaken. "I love you, okay? God, Ai, I'm crazy about you, idiot. You seriously have nothing to worry about. How could you think otherwise?"

"Because . . . ," I gasped. "Because . . ."

I didn't have an answer for him.

After Bowie dropped me off that night, I logged online and was glad to see Sying. I knew she'd be little more than an echo chamber, but, in my present state of mind, validation was all I craved.

Yet the moment I told her about the incident at Brigitte's house, I immediately regretted it. I know she tried to come across as sympathetic, but even through lines of cold, hard text, I sensed an underlying glee. I withdrew from our conversation, and when she asked me if I was okay, I left the chat box unanswered. I was just about to log off when Pedro came on. When I relayed the entire story to him, he responded with, "Baby girl, are you blind? Dump him! You deserve so much better."

By dawn I was wide-awake and in two minds about attending the picnic. After the clash at Brigitte's, I had been adamant I wouldn't go, but in the light of day everything felt watered down, rendered shapeless. All I had to cling to were my fears and suspicions. I still needed hard evidence, irrefutable proof that I hadn't misread the situation.

With reluctance, I dragged myself out of bed, my body sluggish from a long night of tossing and turning. I felt a pang of guilt when I thought of how I had ignored Sying the night before. On impulse, I called and invited her along. In the bathroom, I scrubbed my face and grinned Cheshire cat–like at the mirror, my braces tracked across my teeth, silver with hot pink bands. My tongue bumped over the cold metal, back and forth, rubbing my skin raw. By the time I heard the blast of Brigitte's horn, I'd been ready for hours. Three short bursts, then one long.

"Brigitte here," said Mum unnecessarily. "Where are you go?"

"To the Royal National Park for a picnic."

At the door, she handed me a cardigan. "Take this one, Ai; mum worry you catch cold."

Seven

WE'D PLANNED FOR an early start but now had to pick up Sying, who had recently moved to a social housing development, a fair bit out of the way. Then Brigitte realized she'd left her Nikon on her dresser at home and we doubled back for it.

It was almost midday when we were finally on our way, bumping along the freeway in her beat-up Nissan, which rattled noisily every time she switched gears. I was riding shotgun while the boys and Sying were squeezed into the back. Brigitte was humming along to Frente!'s cover of "Bizarre Love Triangle" and I was flicking through her collection of burnt CDs, the album titles scrawled in black marker on the mirrored discs catching flashes of my reflection. I winced at my painfully ordinary face, teeth hemmed with braces, shoulder-length jet-black hair, an angry blemish forming on my chin. I'd put coverup on it that morning, but Brigitte said it looked worse on, so I rubbed it away. Now I was regretting my decision as I decided between *OK Computer* and *CrazySexyCool*. Brigitte used to date a guy who had excellent taste in music and could get her any album she wanted. Bowie and Tin were deep in discussion about the specs of Bowie's PC, and Sying was gazing out the window. Even though we all tried to make light of it, her unanticipated presence in the group seemed to cast a strange vibe.

We found a place by the wide-open lake, which extended all the way to the mountain ranges in the distance. We came to a large willow tree and decided it was the perfect spot to set ourselves up. It wasn't as crowded as we expected, with a few families throwing bread crumbs from public benches or gathered around brick barbecue ovens. The smell of burnt sausages and onions wafted over as Brigitte shook out the rug and we set down our gear: a picnic basket, a cooler box, and a portable radio set to Triple J. Bowie sat the way he always did, with his long legs pulled in, arms resting casually on his knees, Brigitte next to him in a pretty sundress, daisy yellow, legs tucked primly under her skirt. I bet if anyone were to guess, they would say Brigitte and Bowie were a couple. It was something about their loose, effortless limbs, the way they moved through the world as though nothing bad would ever happen.

Sying needed to use the bathroom, so Brigitte and I went with her. To get there, we had to walk through a narrow dirt path framed by thick shrubbery, where we spotted two Caucasian men who looked to be in their late teens to early twenties walking toward us. One had shaggy copper-colored hair and freckles; the other sported a buzz cut and wore a shark-tooth pendant on a length of black string. As they passed, the one with the buzz cut stuck out his teeth in an exaggerated overbite and pulled his eyes up at the sides. "Ching chong, ching chong," he chanted crudely as his friend broke into laughter.

Brigitte and I immediately sped up, giving them as wide a berth as possible, but Sying stopped in her tracks, glaring provocatively at the men. I tugged on her arm to urge her along, but she shrugged me off.

"White trash bogans!" she spat at their backs.

Buzz Cut whipped around, closing the distance between him and Sying in two easy strides. Towering above her, he sneered, "What did you say to me?"

She stared up at him, jaw set in an expression of defiance.

By now his friend had joined him, and they were both looking down at her with obvious disgust.

"Well?" He jabbed at her shoulder, causing her to stagger back.

"Don't you touch her!" Brigitte hissed.

Buzz Cut spun around to face her, a cruel smile appearing like a gash on his face. "Hey, this one can talk."

The one with the freckles pounced on Brigitte, one hand gripping her waist, the other cupped over her right breast, squeezing. "She's pretty hot for a chink. Let's get her behind those bushes over there. See what else she can do with that mouth."

"Oh, yeah, baby."

Panicked, I launched myself at Freckles, sinking my teeth into his wrist. He howled with pain, dropping Brigitte. I didn't see the back of his hand until I felt a sharp blow to my face, my head recoiling. In a daze, I touched my cheek, tasting blood in my mouth.

Freckles had his arms around Brigitte again, dragging her

away from the track as she kicked and thrashed. I sprang into action, barreling toward them.

"Hey, what do you think you're doing?" A mother had just come around the bend with a gaggle of kids trailing behind her.

Freckles let go of Brigitte and held up both hands, grinning. "Ah, we were just messing around."

When they were out of sight, Brigitte spun around to face Sying, eyes blazing. "What the heck is wrong with you, Sying? What the hell were you thinking?"

"Don't speak to her like that," I said, coming to Sying's defense, even though I still felt the sting in my cheek.

Ignoring me, Brigitte continued her tirade. "Look at the size of those guys! Do you know the danger you put us in? Those men could have dragged me off into the bush . . . could have easily taken you both as well. Don't think it can't happen in broad daylight or it won't happen to you. Girls get dragged into the bush all the time, and they don't always make it back out. That's why you don't go around provoking creepy guys like that just to make a stupid point."

"They were being racist," I countered, feeling bad for Sying, who stood rooted to the spot, small, puckered lips opening and closing like those of a goldfish out of water, gasping for air.

Brigitte turned to me. "So what? It's nothing new, is it? Sticks and stones, remember? It's not the names we are called that matter but the ones we answer to. Just think about what could have happened if that woman hadn't come along!"

"And what are we supposed to do, ignore it every time it happens? How will anything ever change if we don't stand up to guys like that?"

"Guys like that?" She let out a strangled laugh. "Guys like that are a lost cause. If you want things to change, you need to convince the ones who aren't so fixed in their prejudice."

"And how do we do that?"

"I don't know, Ai. Maybe by breaking down stereotypes, showing them we're no different—"

"That's not going to work, Brigitte—not for us, anyway. Maybe for you."

"What does that mean, Ai? I'm Asian, same as you."

"We're nothing alike, you and me. I don't have everyone bending over backward for me, especially not boys. And certainly not if they're white. Don't you get it? It doesn't matter because you're pretty. That's your 'get out of jail free' card. You're always going to have an easier time than the rest of us."

Her cheeks were flushed now. "How can you say that to me after what just happened? How can you say that to me, Ai?"

In my heart I knew Brigitte was right, but I kept at it, and soon it was clear we weren't arguing about the incident but something else entirely.

Back by the lake, things between me and Brigitte were still tense, but we put on a united front as we always did around the boys. Brigitte began telling them what had happened and, perhaps to temper their indignation, downplayed the whole thing. Soon I began to question if it had been as bad as I thought. Everything calmed down after that, and the conversation turned to the weather. We chatted about how warm it was for this time of year, then moved on to the hour-long drive up when we'd passed by a minor accident involving a motorcycle. Still fresh in our minds was a man, helmet tucked under one arm, talking solemnly to a police officer. Then Tin said he'd always wanted a Ducati, and we all took turns expressing our alarm. He waved us off good-naturedly. "Okay, okay."

"I didn't tell you guys this," Brigitte said, a wicked gleam flashing in her eyes. "You know how we stopped at the station for petrol and I got a bottle of Coke?"

I could recall Brigitte at the counter, regaling the affable attendant with her theories about why Coke tastes better in a glass bottle. Back in the car, we couldn't find a bottle opener, so Tin with some difficulty had got the lid loose with a pocket-knife. The bottle had hissed and fizzed, spilling onto his jeans and T-shirt, causing him to cry out in surprise.

She continued, "My bottle fell off the seat and somehow got stuck behind the brake pad while I was doing over a hundred K's on the highway."

We all looked at her in horror, and she seemed to enjoy our reaction.

"I didn't say anything because then you'd all panic and make it worse. Instead, I just calmly kicked at it with my other foot until I got it loose. Lucky I did."

"Holy shit, Brigitte!" Bowie sounded more impressed than alarmed.

Brigitte grinned at him, but when her eyes met mine, her

smile waned. Sying watched this exchange with interest, giving me a nudge as though to confirm a thought she'd imagined had just crossed my mind. Annoyed by Sying's lack of subtlety, I turned away from her and toward the lake while Brigitte busied herself, unpacking the lunch she had prepared. On the rug appeared an assortment of all my favorite things. Spring rolls, bánh mì sandwiches, and a pack of cream-filled lamington cakes. We wolfed them down with a six-pack of ginger ale. The shadows had grown longer when we ventured to a shed by the lake hiring out Jet Skis by the hour. The guy manning the booth was in his mid-twenties, with sandy-white hair and a cute, roguish smile. Brigitte was flirting with him, and he was reciprocating.

Next thing I knew, Brigitte was stripped down to her swimsuit, bright orange life jacket strapped on, straddling the Jet Ski with an easy confidence. Bowie made a remark of admiration that sent my stomach into knots. Then he said, "Come on, Ai."

It had been decided earlier I'd ride behind Bowie, but now I changed my mind.

"You go ahead. I'll keep Sying company." I gestured toward Sying, who was sitting at a nearby park bench by the river, tossing stale bread at the ducks.

He shot her a look of annoyance. "I don't know why you invited her. She's a real stick-in-the-mud."

"She's my friend," I said defensively.

"Bullshit! You don't even like her all that much. I think you only asked her here to annoy Brigitte."

"You would know," I retorted.

He sighed. "Come on, Ai, please don't start with all that again."

"Whatever you say."

By this time Brigitte and Tin were already zooming across the water, and Bowie seemed eager to join them. He looked at me, conflicted. "Want me to stay here with you?"

"No," I said flatly.

"Are you still upset about what happened at Brigitte's place last night?"

I shrugged in response.

"It's not what you think it is, Ai. We just went to get the pizzas. That's where it starts and ends."

"Why didn't you ask me to come?"

"Jeez, Ai, I don't know what more I can say to convince you. You've got it all wrong."

"It just doesn't make sense to me, that's all. Not after what I heard last night."

"Well, just as I said, it wasn't even about you."

"Then why don't you just tell me what it is? Why can't you and Brigitte just tell me?"

"Why don't you ask Tin?"

"What does Tin have to do with any of this?"

With a sigh, Bowie said, "Just ask him."

"I barely know him. Why should I have to ask him something that my own boyfriend should be telling me himself?"

"I'm not going to say this again, Ai: Just ask Tin."

Something in his tone irked me and I felt the sudden urge

to lash out. Whenever I look back on this moment, I wish with all my heart I could take back what I was about to say. "You do know Brigitte cheated on you, right? She got together with Alex while you were still dating. She was screwing him behind your back."

Bowie looked at me for a moment as though I were a stranger. Then a spark of anger flashed through his eyes, and I couldn't tell if it was a reaction to the news or the fact that I'd said something spiteful purely to hurt him.

Shaking his head at me, he said, "I can't believe you'd stoop that low, Ai. I don't even feel like you're the same person anymore." Reaching into his pocket, he drew out my silver magpie chain. "Here's the necklace you threw in my face last night. I fixed it for you."

As I stared at the silver magpie glinting in the palm of my hand, Bowie roared away to join the others.

When I took a seat next to Sying on the bench, I was almost incandescent with rage.

"Are you okay, Ai?"

"Sure," I said, struggling to level my voice.

"Did you get an explanation from Bowie about what happened last night at Brigitte's? I wish I could have been there so I can help you figure out what was going on."

"Don't worry about it."

"I can't believe Brigitte would wear a swimsuit in this weather. She's such a show-off. No wonder she has guys grabbing her."

I whipped my head around to face Sying and felt a violent urge to slap her. I immediately subdued the impulse but it continued to trouble me. Taking a few deep breaths, I said through gritted teeth, "Let's just forget it, okay? I don't want to talk about Brigitte anymore."

We fell silent, watching Brigitte zigzagging between the boys, daring them to go faster.

Out of nowhere, I saw the two men from earlier, making their way to the shed hiring out Jet Skis, one pointing to Brigitte, who was blissfully unaware. My stomach tightened as they paid for their rentals and joined our friends on the lake.

The one with the buzz cut called out to Brigitte, catching her attention. Her expression darkened with recognition, but only for a moment. Smirking, she revved her engine with a loud, defiant roar. Buzz Cut whistled, standing upright and making lewd gestures with his hips.

In a blatant attempt to ignore him, Brigitte pulled off an impressive wheelie, head thrown back, laughing, spinning around like a ballerina in a music box. This is how I always think of her, inky-black hair whipping around her milky skin, a touch of pink on her cheeks, so light you weren't even sure it was there. To this day, I can't think of anything more radiant or alive than she was right at that moment. The memory is always accompanied by an ache.

The men whooped and cheered as Bowie and Tin, who seemed to have caught on to the situation, moved to position their Jet Skis between Brigitte and the men. This only served to rile them up further as they took turns aggressively speeding toward the boys before changing direction at the last moment, playing chicken. Then, spotting a gap in Brigitte's defense,

Freckles accelerated suddenly, hurtling toward her, gaining traction at a sickening rate.

"Hey, slow down!" cried the guy at the booth, waving both his arms in the air. But Freckles seemed hell-bent on his mission, gunning his engine as the lake frothed and bubbled up around him. Brigitte remained stationary, bobbing on the water, eyes meeting the oncoming vehicle with an expression of steely determination. It was clear neither was willing to give in, so Bowie swerved in front of Brigitte to force Freckles into correcting his path, but either his estimation was off or Freckles took a beat too long to react.

I stood up and screamed, "Bowie, no!"

It was too late. Freckles slammed straight into Bowie and the impact sent them both flying. And then one Jet Ski was pinwheeling wildly in the air straight toward Brigitte.

This is the part in the story where someone I love would only appear again in flashbacks.

Eight

HERE IS THE sequence of events that immediately followed the crash. First there was the Jet Ski sailing in the air toward Brigitte, punctuated by Sying's ear-piercing scream. Next was Freckles clambering onto Buzz Cut's jet ski, the two of them speeding to shore, no doubt eager to extricate themselves from the scene.

Someone pointing at them shouted, "Call triple zero, quick. Don't let those guys get away!"

A little girl said in a hushed voice, "Are they dead, Mama?"

Sying on her hands and knees, retching.

Then, in the distance, I spotted Tin on the water slowed to a standstill and bobbing like a lifeboat. And then I shut my eyes.

Although much of the aftermath has been permanently etched in my mind, there were certain details I found hard to recall. I couldn't name the police officer who wrapped a blanket around my shivering shoulders and pushed a hot chocolate into my hands. But I can still taste the lukewarm liquid, sickly sweet as I took small, tentative sips. I don't know how long it took

for the ambulance to arrive, but I can still hear the exact pitch
of its hysterical wail cutting out abruptly on its approach and
leaving behind a dull, residual silence. I don't know when Bowie's
parents appeared like an apparition, his dad grave and stoic
standing with his wife beside him as Bowie lay on a stretcher,
a white sheet pulled over his face. Or how long Tin had been
circling the water, looking through the wreckage for Brigitte before driving her bent and broken body back to shore, to a wailing
Lucille, who stood with a trio of grim-faced men in white plastic jumpsuits. Tin placing a tentative hand on her shoulder and
Lucille looking at him in shock before her face twisted into an
expression of pure anguish. As he pulled her into his arms, the
surprising closeness between them drew a lump in my throat.
I was just about to make my way over when I caught sight of
Mum barrelling toward me, anxiously patting my body down for
evidence of injury. Yan, blinking back tears, shaking my shoulders in a rare but unmistakable show of brotherly love. "It could
have been you, Ai, do you know that?"

Tin's dad had yelled at him in front of everyone. Head bowed,
he readily accepted his father's abuse as a small rivulet of blood
coursed down his leg, only a superficial wound. Aside from the
story he had told about his mother, Tin had never mentioned his
family. He had kept that part of his life so carefully guarded that
until that moment, I couldn't even imagine him existing outside
the parameters of our group. But there was his dad, screeching
loudly in Vietnamese, bristling with unabashed fury. A female
officer—the one who earlier had handed me the hot chocolate—
felt compelled to step in. "Sir, please be kind to your son. He's

just gone through a traumatic event. Do you know how lucky he is to be standing here?"

Tin's dad paused for barely a moment in his cruel tirade against his son to silence the kind officer with a hard, simmering stare.

There is one other thing I recall about that day. As I stood by the lake moments before the crash, a long-forgotten memory bubbled up, gripping me with such force that one recollection would always underscore the other.

On the twenty-sixth of January in 1988, Australia was celebrating two hundred years since colonization. I was eight years old at the time and could not begin to comprehend the complexity of the day and what it meant to the long-suffering indigenous people of our country. Back then, it was a day viewed as celebratory; the one narrative pushed by the government and media of the time, parroted by our teachers gushing: *What a special day it was! A birthday*, they said. That, my eight-year-old self could understand.

In the city, there would be pomp and pageantry, which included a reenactment of the arrival of the First Fleet from England, glossing over the atrocities unleashed onto a land inhabited by a peaceful and nomadic race, ripped from those whose word for ownership conflicted so wildly with their aggressors.

To encourage the festivities, public transport was free that day. After Mum dressed me and Yan in our best clothes, we set out for the hour-long train to the city, then across on the ferry to Luna Park.

On the ferry, I got separated from my family but wasn't worried. We were on the same vessel, gliding toward a fun park, toward the mouth of a giant, grinning clown and all the sweet incredulities that awaited us there. I stood on the deck of the ferry, one hand tightly gripping the rail, the other waving a tiny Australian flag. I'd never seen crowds like this, jubilant and cheering, saturated in sunlight under the same indiscriminate sky. A communal chant ringing into the warm air, one that would forever be tied to my self-worth in an ever-present, inexplicable way. "*Aussie! Aussie! Aussie! Oi! Oi! Oi!*" To my ears, the mantra had yet to sound like a hateful jeer.

Sydney Harbor on a day such as this sparkled like a jewel as I breathed in the sea salt air, truly believing then it was just as much mine as any other, when suddenly a large glob of spit, sticky and jellylike, sailed past my head, flashed through my periphery, before landing with a satisfied splatter onto my hand. I let go off the railing, reeling with shock, head snapping back to the crowd behind me, searching for the person who had committed this minor atrocity, only to witness a myriad of faces, cruel in their collective defiance. My eyes returned to my hand, forever marred by the puddle of mucus with its colony of tiny bubbles cresting and bursting as though it were a living, breathing thing. Panicked, I wiped it on my dress and was instantly filled with regret. It was the one my mother had lovingly hand-stitched with a thousand iridescent beads all along the collar and hemline, my very best dress. Stunned tears sprung to my eyes as if I had just been handed a riddle that I would not begin to untangle until nearly a decade later when I watched, helpless, as the Jet Ski sliced effortlessly through the air.

In the days that followed the tragedy, I was mostly numb. At first the loss was indistinguishable, a black and broadening plume, one so dense and dark it obscured all the details. It was only when the dust settled that I was able to see the destruction, to gauge what part of me had taken the most damage. I thought of Brigitte and the way my entire being felt tethered to her absence. I agonized over my last words to Bowie.

The loneliness I felt was indescribable. It was as though I had lost everyone in one fell swoop. Losing Brigitte and Bowie meant losing Tin by proximity. Since the tragedy, Sying had been distant, so in a way I lost her too. I didn't even have Pedro to confide in. The timing of his absence was like another punch to the gut. To think we had chatted almost every day for months, yet immediately after the accident he inexplicably went silent.

At school, I had to adjust to a world where all the rules had been rewritten. I didn't know how to behave, where to put my hands. I felt both unseen and painfully visible. My classmates, taking care to avoid my gaze, would go on to whisper about me the moment my back was turned. During my obligatory sessions with the school counselor, I was warned unresolved trauma could fester inside like a rotten apple, sprouting poisonous spores that grew veined and thorny, drilling deep down only to surface further along in ugly and unexpected ways. I approached each new emotion cautiously as though I were entering a dim and un-familiar room, one tentative foot feeling in the dark, the ever-present sense of something lurking in the shadows, waiting to lunge at me. In my present state, it seemed unfathomable that I could function at all, yet somehow I managed.

I kept myself busy with essays and equations, glue sticks and colored sheets of paper. I made paper hearts and experimented with gold leaf. I played Brigitte's favorite song, "Hey Jupiter," by Tori Amos on repeat, until I knew the lyrics by heart.

Tin and I passed each other in the school playground, sat rows apart in classrooms. Sometimes it felt like we were the only two people left in this world, but he could have been on the moon. We hadn't spoken a single word to each other since that day at the park. Sying also kept her distance, using the exhibition as an excuse to busy herself whenever I tried to initiate a conversation with her. Aysum must have sensed how isolated I felt because she barely left me alone. "Nadine's busy with Trevor anyway," she'd say when I told her she didn't need to fuss. During lunch break one day, she sat with me in an empty classroom while I worked on my major art project. Running her hands across the leather texture of the faux passport, she said, "It's coming along so well."

"It took forever to get the gold foil right," I admitted.

On the far side of the room was a mannequin draped in a crudely made cheongsam with a Versace logo outlined in black marker. Pointing to it, Aysum asked, "Is that Sying's work?"

I nodded. "She hasn't spent much time on it because of the exhibition. But she's planning to fill in the logo with sequins."

"Are you still going? To the opening, I mean."

"I guess so. How about you?"

She shook her head. "I tried asking my parents again, but they said no."

"It's weird how Sying's still going ahead with it after everything that's happened, don't you think?"

"Maybe she's just trying to do the decent thing and honor Brigitte's memory."

"The other day I caught her bragging about how the NSW premier might be attending. I just keep thinking back to our lunch at BKK when she was dismissing Brigitte's idea. And now she's happy to take all the credit."

"I guess this exhibition could be her way of coping. I don't know." Aysum shrugged. "Sying's a tough one to read."

"She doesn't seem all that upset to me; that's my honest opinion. Even though she was right next to me when it happened and felt the impact go through her body. She must know how much I need to talk to someone about what happened, someone who was there that day. But when I bring it up, she makes some stupid excuse about being busy with the exhibition. Just like what I did to Brigitte."

"How about Tin? He was there, wasn't he?"

I shook my head. "You'd think it would be easy, wouldn't you? That Tin and I would be there for each other, But, nope—no such luck. It's like Bowie held us together just like the spine of a book, and without him . . ." I paused, swallowing a gulp of air. "Without him, we're just loose pages scattered in the wind. Now what am I supposed to do, Aysum? If it's so hard to get Sying talking, then Tin is a lost cause, isn't he?"

Aysum placed a gentle hand on my shoulder. "Maybe you can try writing him a letter?"

Later that night, I was midway through an essay about the women's suffrage movement in the late 1800s when I thought about what Aysum had said. Turning to a fresh page in my workbook, I began a letter to Tin.

> *There is so much I want to say to you, but I don't know where to start. I guess this is as good a place as any. I keep thinking about that night before the accident when we were all at Brigitte's house. I don't know if I've missed anything. I keep wondering if maybe there was something I got horribly wrong. Not that it matters anymore, but that doesn't stop it from eating away at me. The truth is, I miss Bowie so damn much and I miss Brigitte even more. You're part of that equation too. When the four of us were hanging out, I felt like I didn't need anyone else in the world. All I remember is happiness, only I didn't recognize it at the time. I keep thinking about the last time I spoke to Bowie, when he was on that Jet Ski. We were arguing about what happened at Brigitte's the night before. It's a conversation that will forever haunt me and I wish I can take back the horrible things I said.*
>
> *Bowie said a strange thing to me then when we were arguing about something I had overheard between him and Brigitte. He said, "Ask Tin." I don't know what he meant by that but I was hoping you could tell me? To be honest, it was probably nothing*

anyway and I guess it's kind of pointless writing to you about it. I'm sorry. I thought this would be easy, but it's not. I don't want to upset you. It's just that I feel we are two parts of a page torn in half—we are each other's missing part of the story. Someday maybe we'll be brave enough to piece it all together.

Capping my pen, I neatly tore the lined paper sheet from my workbook. After chem the next day, I walked up to Tin and, with a deep breath, pressed the letter into his hand. He looked surprised, muttered, "Thanks," and slipped it into his pocket.

Nine

DESPITE THE YEAR moving at such a rapid pace, I still thought of my Higher School Certificate exams as something far away, relegated to a time in the distant future. And then it was as though the date in my calendar I was inching my way toward lurched suddenly forward to meet me in the present.

I was spending so much time on my major art project that my other subjects were slipping. But now, standing in my bedroom looking at my completed work, I felt it was worthy of the sacrifice. On my study desk, the vintage-style suitcase I'd found at a junk shop sat open, lined with plush red velvet. From its leather handle dangled the rabbit's foot I had made from felt, an invitation to Wonderland. The case was filled with similar "souvenirs" collected from my literary travels. Among the items were the box of square sweets that look round I imagined to have quietly pocketed from a tour at Willy Wonka's chocolate factory, and a large brass key Mary Lennox had pressed into my hand as we stood at the foot of the walled garden. A single red petal fallen like a tear from a beautiful rose as she wept for lost love, and a pair of silver high heels Dorothy lent me for my precarious return home from Oz.

Placed carefully to appear as though it had been carelessly tossed into the suitcase was a passport, its pages stamped and notarized with dates of my arrival and length of time spent in these fantastical places. Accompanying the passport was a travel journal that held sketches and diary entries documenting my trip. It was a project that gave me the perfect excuse to revisit all the books I loved from my childhood, to hide myself away. The escapism served me well, and I was grateful my mind was able to seek solace in other worlds.

As I examined the work from every angle, I noticed the velvet lining had lifted in one corner. Earlier that day, I had lent Sying my bottle of PVA glue, thinking I wouldn't be needing it. All at once, I was seized by an irrational panic, throwing myself at my tallboy, viciously ransacking its drawers, stuffed to the brim with odds and ends, the top surface overcrowded with books, pencil tins, and stuffed toys, all wobbling precariously like a ship in a storm. I stopped when an old ceramic canister slid off the side and smashed to the ground, spilling its contents. Among the shattered pieces lay a pink strawberry-scented eraser, a Hello Kitty key chain, an assortment of brightly colored paper clips, and a folded-up Post-it Note stuck to a ball of Blu-Tack. I gently peeled the note away from the sticky ball, unfolding it to find an exchange written between Brigitte and me. I had no memory of this note; there had been many others like it scrawled surreptitiously in class to curb our boredom while a teacher droned on. My eyes skimmed over the words, heart racing as I read.

Hello hi, Ai what's new with you?

Nothing Brighetti spaghetti, how are you?

Good thank you, now bye Ai spy, See you later alligator.

OK Brigitte the baguette Don't forget me!!!!

I won't Ai, not until the day I die, die.

I began trembling all over, taking deep breaths to steady myself, desperate to supress the rising panic. Then, driven by a loud, insistent voice in my head, I gathered up the suitcase and marched out to our tiny balcony. The foldout clothesline skidded noisily across the concrete as I pushed it aside, damp socks swaying precariously. Behind were a stack of old newspapers and a metal drum we used for burning ghost money. I nudged it with my foot to hear the satisfying rattle of a lighter bouncing off the sides.

Kneeling, I set the suitcase down beside the drum and went to work. I balled up sheets of newspaper, dropping it into the bin. Then I set it alight, watching as the flames gained momentum. As though in a trance, I took out each item in my suitcase and, one at a time, dropped them into the fire. As I witnessed the bulk of my year's work disintegrate before me, I expected a wave of hysteria to hit. Instead, an inexplicable sense of calm washed over me. The loud, overriding voice that had driven me out here onto the balcony was now subdued. I decided the next day I would submit the work as it was, a suitcase filled with ashes, like an urn. Back in my room, I opened a new page in my VAPD diary and wrote, "The Articulation of Grief." After recording the date and time I added,

I have just now reduced my artwork to ash. The countless hours I've spent writing, drawing, making, are gone. As I was looking at my finished artwork it occurred to me how juvenile it was. More than that, it felt inauthentic, ridiculous even. Suddenly, I just despised it so much. I recently lost someone who meant the world to me. And I don't know who I am without her. All I know is the part of me who created the artwork died along with her. I think I'm starting to understand Picasso when he said, "Every act of creation is first an act of destruction." Maybe that's what it means to be an artist. To chip away parts of yourself, like a lapidarist, cutting away at a stone, until a glittering gem emerges. I don't know if this is true, but I guess I'll find out.

The night before my first High School Certificate exam, I had all my textbooks spread out on the kitchen table. Mum sat beside me even though it was already past midnight, humming over her embroidery hoop, her quick, nimble fingers moving with a quiet confidence, flowers blooming gently under her needle and thread. My pen scratching contentedly away at a past paper.

Suddenly there was a loud banging on the door, followed by an animal howl. Mum stood up, spilling colored yarn from her lap to the floor. She called to my dad, who emerged a few moments later in a sleepy stupor. As the banging continued, his body stiffened with a sudden alertness. A strangled, disembodied voice reached us from the other side of the door. "Please let me in—he'll kill me. Please—he'll kill me . . ."

I moved toward the door, panicked. "We have to let them in."

She pressed a finger to her mouth and shook her head. "No—no open, Ai."

My dad stepped between me and the door, shaking his head. "Ai, no. Listen to mum."

Mum asked him, "You have money?"

Dad nodded.

Home invasions were common in Whitlam, which was why Dad made sure there was an envelope of cash set aside, in case someone broke in. The amount was intended to placate them but not enough to entice them back. Sometimes it would be an act, the person on the other side only pretending to be in distress, while their accomplice stood waiting for the door to open.

"Ai, call police." Dad motioned to the phone.

I picked it up and with shaky fingers dialed triple zero. When I got through to Emergency, I blurted, "There's someone banging on our door. I think they might be trying to break in."

The knocking had now moved across the hallway from us, but the anguished cries continued. The operator asked me for details, her voice warm and soothing. When I gave her my name and address, her tone changed dramatically with the mention of Whitlam. I put down the receiver, feeling inexplicably ashamed.

The person was back at our door again, their howls suddenly intersected by an angry voice, one that shared the same scratchy, guttural intonations as Tin's dad. Then there was a long, tortured wail that sent chills down my spine, followed by another desperate barrage of fists against our door.

"Mum," I sobbed.

"Shhh . . . ," she said softly.

And then, as though to calm me, she spoke one of the only few words in Khmer I recognized, a word that was at once a lamentation and a prayer. *Child.* She repeated this word over and over as she clasped her hands over my ears.

On my last day of school, I was clearing out my locker when I found a letter from Tin. Stowed away in my school bag on the walk home, the weight of it felt more substantial than the heavy textbooks I was carrying.

At home, it was silent, which meant I had the place to myself. I took my time settling in, changing into sweatpants and a T-shirt. I grabbed a cold can of Fanta, taking a long swig before setting it on my bedside table. Sitting on the edge of my bed, I read the letter.

There is a lot I've been wanting to talk to you about too, but I'm kind of weird about stuff like that. As you already know, Bowie was like a crutch for me when it came to conversation. I think this is the hundredth letter I've written you, so I guess this one is

*it. I'm sorry it took so long, but everything is a mess right now,
or maybe that's how it's always been. It's just different degrees
of bad, I guess. It's like we're all cursed, as though we've all been
marked by death and it's only a matter of time before he comes to
collect his dues. Ack, I don't know what I'm saying or what this
has to do with anything. I hope it doesn't freak you out.*

*I had three sisters. And my mum—that makes four. And I
remember all of us crouched in an old, rusty fishing boat, the
way the ocean tossed us around like we were nothing. There was
a plastic tarpaulin sheet that was meant to stop the waves from
hitting us, but I was still gulping mouthfuls of water and it
occurred to me that the sea was trying to drown us. I thought to
myself, "The war is on this boat with us. It's coming with us to
wherever we're going." I feel sorry for the place we were going
to, that lets us in. They don't know we're cursed, that the war is
stuck to us like shit on the bottom of someone's shoe." I was barely
six, but I'd seen horrific things by then. I was haunted even
though I already felt like a ghost. I think we just keep dying
in more cruel and abstract ways. I remember how the pirates
roared when they saw my mother. I knew they would take her.
I knew what they would do with my sisters because I'd seen it
happen before. God, my sisters . . . they were like matryoshka
dolls, clones of my mother, who was so beautiful, my dad loathed
her for it. Punished her all the time because of it.*

*And then it was just me and Dad on the boat with a bunch
of other bewildered strangers who'd had their lives cleaved up*

more than they already were. Dad was more concerned for himself than anything. I don't think he's capable of love, yet he remarried anyway, pretty much as soon as we got to Sydney. My stepmum's okay, I guess. She sometimes sticks up for me when Dad's been drinking and goes to a dark place. But she'll throw me in the fire to protect my little sister, Tri, not that I blame her. I don't know if you know I have a sister. A half sister, but sometimes it feels like she's my only family. She's nine now and, in a weird way, kind of reminds me of you. The other day she gave me a jar full of origami stars, all in different colors. She does all this dumb sister stuff that can be annoying, but the stars really got to me.

I think I know what Bowie meant when he said, "Ask Tin." There is something I have been meaning to tell you, but every time I try, it gets stuck like a fishbone lodged in my throat. Maybe it won't always be there. Your letter put that thought in my head anyway.

I read Tin's letter twice over. The third time I felt something crack inside me, like a burst dam. I buried my face in my hands and howled, the way that nameless person had howled while beating at our door.

Ten

A DAY BEFORE the opening, Sying invited me to preview her exhibition at the Whitlam Library. We met in the foyer, and she led me up the stairs into the large study room, lined with shelves of books and a cluster of desks in the center. Scattered around the room were tall wood easels where black-and-white portraits of refugees were mounted, their hard, lined faces peering at us from the canvas, ravaged but defiant. Suspended beside each portrait with invisible string was an accompanying story printed on thick, letter-sized cards. I gritted my teeth as I took in the scene, feeling like I was betraying Brigitte all over again. It was my expectation that Sying would honor Brigitte's memory, but as we moved through the exhibit, I could see no evidence of this.

Sying seemed oblivious to my darkening mood as she walked by my side with a clipboard in hand, chattering away about how the event would be a red-carpet affair and the NSW premier had sent his RSVP the week before, confirming his attendance. "There'll be a ton of journalists and everything. Have you thought about what you're going to wear?"

"Not yet, but I'll find something," I mumbled as we continued our amble from one portrait to another. Admittedly, I could distinguish between the profiles that had been created by Brigitte and felt a sudden, spiteful urge to comment on this.

Then we came to a picture of my mother, and I froze. Brigitte had captured Mum sitting at her Singer, unaware she was being photographed. Her hands were holding a garment in place, face serene and contemplative, as though she were considering the answer to a question she'd always longed for someone to ask. I drew in a sharp breath at the raw, astonishing beauty of her face in that moment of repose. And suddenly I understood in a whole new way what Brigitte meant when she spoke about love being quantifiable.

Beside the photograph was Mum's name, which translated from Chinese meant "Jewel," followed by an article about her escape from the Khmer Rouge. As I read what Brigitte had written, I felt the resonance of my best friend's spirit pulsing through each line. The care and attention she put into the piece overwhelmed me in such a way that I was unable to move. It seemed Sying wanted to steer me away from the picture, and almost of its own accord my arm shot out and grabbed her wrist.

Trying to keep my tone even, I said, "Why haven't you credited Brigitte for this piece? It's her photo; I was there when she took it. Obviously, she wrote the article. So why is she not mentioned here or anywhere in this entire exhibit?"

Sying stiffened, eyes moving in a daze to my hand clutching her wrist. Shaking her head, she said, "Of course I haven't forgotten Brigitte. I'll be thanking her in my speech tomorrow night."

"Is that all? You're not going to mention anywhere that this exhibition was her idea to begin with? Or at least differentiate between the profiles she did and yours? Or were you hoping to take full credit for everything?" I tightened my grip on her wrist. She winced but made no effort to pull her hand away. It was as though my words had left her paralyzed.

Looking down at her feet now, she said in high, wobbly voice, "I'll talk to the team. Maybe there's still time to design a tribute. We can put it on display by the entrance."

"You mean as an afterthought?"

She began trembling all over then, tears pooling in her eyes, shoulders hunched. I finally let go of her wrist and she rubbed at it gingerly. Then, raising her eyes slowly to meet mine, she said, "Do you remember how I got home after the accident?"

I was taken aback by the bluntness of her question, which left me feeling immediately unsettled. In an uncertain voice, I asked, "What does that have to with anything?"

"Do you remember?" she repeated.

My mind made the reluctant trip back to that late afternoon, the dimming sky. The intermittent headlights beaming through the thicket from the nearby parking lot. Our parents coming to collect us. I tried to recall Sying's mum at the scene but couldn't picture her face. Then I realized I didn't even know what she looked like. There wasn't a single school pickup, award ceremony, or parent-teacher interview where she'd shown up. Sying mentioned her every now and then in passing, but only in vague, incidental terms: "Just have to pick up some meds for my mum" when passing by a chemist. Or during a midday call, she'd say in a hushed tone, "I have to be quiet: Mum's still asleep."

I knew Sying stayed at the library until the last possible moment and this was something I attributed to her overly studious nature, but maybe there was something about her home life she was avoiding. I remember Bowie making an offhand comment once about Sying's mother being estranged from the rest of the family.

Sying nodded at me as though sensing my growing comprehension. "Mum didn't turn up as usual; they couldn't get a hold of her. My bet is she was at the club, glued to a slot machine, high on whatever she picked up at the train station that morning. I had to hitch a ride with Bowie's parents; you probably know he's a distant cousin of mine. Can you imagine what that was like? The way his parents were at each other's throats all the way back to my house. Blaming everyone under the sun—even you got a mention, Ai—yet they didn't even consider me. As far as they were concerned, I was invisible, just like I am to my mother. You know, I almost wanted to tell Bowie's parents the truth: that their son was dead because of me. If I hadn't been there that day, there would have been no confrontation with those guys; they wouldn't have gone after Brigitte on the lake. There, I've said it. Someone had to."

I shook my head vehemently. "That's not true, Sying. The blame lies only on those two guys and no one else. That's the truth."

"If that's the case, then why did the coroner rule it as an

accident? If those guys were to blame, why weren't they charged for manslaughter?"

"I don't know, Sying. I can't speak for the justice system, but if you want to blame yourself, then you might as well blame me for inviting you."

"That's the point, Ai, I do blame you. I blame us both. But at least you tried to stop me from confronting those guys. Both you and Brigitte tried to stop me."

"Is this why you've been avoiding me, Sying?" I felt my own tears now, blurring everything. "Because I really did need you, you know. After the accident, I really needed a friend."

She turned away from me, her face in profile, looking at something far away that wasn't in the room with us. "I'm not the one you need, Ai. I can't give you the answers you want. I'm not the one you should be asking."

Back home in my room, I was busy clearing out some things when I heard our front door open. After a pause, I heard Mum call out for assistance with the groceries.

As we stood in the kitchen, pulling items from the bags, I noticed red welts around her wrists where the plastic had dug into her skin. I clucked my disapproval and said, "You should have waited until I got home. I could have come out to the shops with you."

"Mum not know when you come back."

"Why didn't you take the car?"

Reaching into one of the bags, she pulled out several cans

of condensed milk. "Not much buy today but mum see this one special."

"You should have brought the cart—the one Yan got you."

She clucks her tongue and simulates pulling the cart. "Make too much noisy."

We put away the remaining groceries, a cut of pork belly, packs of vermicelli, and a bouquet of mint and coriander, bunched together with a rubber band.

"I go Lucille bread shop," she said, as I shut the fridge door.

I paused and took a deep breath before turning to face her. "Did you see Lucille?"

Mum had a reproachful look on her face. "Lucille say you not see her. Long time now. Why, Ai? Why you not go see Brigitte mother? Long time!"

I shook my head, turning to avoid her gaze. The last time I had seen Lucille was at Brigitte's funeral, looking surprisingly composed, a picture of strength and dignity. When I finally plucked up the courage to approach her, she folded me up in her arms, breaking down into tears. Squeezing me tight, she said, "You come and see me—you hear?" I meant to honor that request but kept finding excuses to put it off. I was deeply ashamed of how I had treated Brigitte in the months leading up to the tragedy and knew my behavior was unlikely to have gone unnoticed by Lucille. As I opened my mouth to make up another excuse, Mum cut me off. "Lucille say she go away. Moving."

My eyes widened. "Lucille's moving? To where?"

"Far away, she tell me that."

"Did she tell you when she's leaving?"

"She say she go soon. You go see her before she go away. Brigitte like your sister. You go see Brigitte mother."

Late that afternoon, I drove my parents' Cressida over to Brigitte's, taking along a box of her things I'd kept from the picnic.

A girl who looked about nine answered the door. She had on a pinafore dress and a dozen tiny butterflies clipped into her short, silky bob, a smear of glitter across one cheek. Seeing me, she exclaimed, "Hello!"

"Hi. Is Lucille home?"

She cocked her head to the side and asked, "Are you Ai?"

"Yes," I said, mildly taken aback. "How did you know?"

"My brother pointed you out in the class photo," she said cheekily.

I frowned. "Who is your brother?"

She cupped a hand over her mouth and giggled. "Tin, silly!"

"Oh, you must be Tri, then."

Tugging on my hand, she pulled me down the hallway and into the lounge room, calling out to Lucille. I set the box of Brigitte's things on the coffee table and noticed moving boxes strewn all around the place. They were labeled with words such as *Stationery* and *Brigitte's books*. I felt a wave of sadness thinking of Brigitte's possessions, which were as familiar to me as my own. Just as the thought entered my mind, Lucille walked into the room, lifting an apron over her head. Her eyes filled with warmth when they met mine, putting me at ease.

"Honey," she said, arms open. As they enveloped me, the fa-

miliar smell of shortcake and vanilla brought Brigitte back with
a vividness like a punch to the stomach.

I motioned to the box on the coffee table. "I brought back
some of Brigitte's things. Sorry I didn't come sooner."

We settled ourselves on the couch, watching Tri pick through
the items. After fishing out a towel and sunglasses, she found
Brigitte's Nikon and held it up as though it were a long-lost relic.

"Brigitte really loved this camera, didn't she?"

"Oh—you knew Brigitte?" I asked, surprised. I'd only learned
Tin had a sister from his letter, and Brigitte had never mentioned Tri to me. I felt a tinge of sadness wondering what else I
had missed during those months I had wasted, chasing shadows.

"Come here, Tri," said Lucille.

Tri planted herself on Lucille's lap, arms snaking around her
neck. They grinned at each other, and the warmth between them
felt like an unexpected gift.

It was as though Lucille could read my thoughts because she
said, "This little girl has been an absolute godsend."

Tri declared, "Lucille has been teaching me French."

"*Comment vous appelez-vous?*" Lucille prompted Tri.

"*Je m'appelle Tri Nguyen.*"

"*Bonne fille*—good girl."

Tri giggled. "Hey, Ai, Tin says you're good at doing crafts.
Want to make Christmas cards with me?"

I stared at her wide-eyed, reeling from the unexpected insight into Tin's world. It was bewildering how she was able to
divulge with an almost casual indifference what had seemed to
me impenetrable.

"I'd love to make cards with you," I finally answered.

"Oops, I think we might have packed the scissors," Tri said to Lucille. "You know the ones that cut the zigzag pattern?" Tri danced around the room, from box to box, sifting through them. I felt a new wave of sadness, thinking of Brigitte's possessions.

Lucille must have caught my expression because she said, "I'm guessing your mum told you about me moving away?"

I nodded. "Where are you going?"

"I'm moving to Brisbane."

"Brisbane?" I said, surprised. "When?"

"Just over a week from now."

I drew in a deep breath. "That soon?"

"I bought a catering company—one where I previously worked. The opportunity came out of the blue, so I jumped at it. I think it's a good excuse to get out of Whitlam. There are too many memories here . . ."

"But what about the bakery?"

"I'm going to sell Paris. It's getting too dangerous here anyway. You know we got broken into twice last month? It's just not worth it anymore."

"We're coming too!" Tri declared, a pair of bright orange scissors in her hands. She held them up triumphantly.

It took a moment for me to digest what she was saying. "You mean you're going with Lucille?"

"Yes. So's my brother. He's going to help Lucille with the new business, and we begged Mum to let me come as well. At first she said no, but then she said yes." A sad look crossed her face, like a cloud passing over the sun. "I hope Mum doesn't get into trouble with Dad for letting me go. She told me not to tell him, so I won't even get to say goodbye."

"It's only for the summer," Lucille reminded her. "Like a holiday."

Tri brightened at this. "I've never been on a holiday before."

"You'll love it, sweetheart. We'll have a swimming pool in the backyard, and if you ever get bored splashing around in that, the beach is only minutes away. You'll have lots of ice cream in your belly, not to mention all the new friends you're going to make."

Tri beamed at Lucille, then turned to grin at me. Snipping the air above her head, she said, "Come on, Ai, let's get started."

We settled at the coffee table, laden with colored paper, glue, and scissors. A timer went off, calling Lucille back into the kitchen.

"She's making strawberry shortcake," Tri said happily.

"That's my favorite."

"Lucky you came, then."

Shaking out a tube of silver glitter, Tri said, "I was just wondering about something."

"What's that?"

"Do merry-go-rounds only go in one direction?"

"I've never thought about it, but it's an interesting question."

"I think you'd have to visit a whole load of them just to see. All over the world as well."

"Next time I go on a merry-go-round, I'll make a note of which way it's going."

She seemed really pleased about this, toothy grin widening.

Then, squinting up at me, she said, "You're kind of pretty, you know. Maybe not as pretty as Brigitte was, but I can see why my brother likes you."

I went to join Lucille in the kitchen to see if I could help, and she put me to work slicing strawberries. A comfortable silence fell between us, punctuated by the dull thud of my knife hitting the cutting board as my mind tried to process everything I had learned in the past few minutes. It felt like I was bombarded with so much new information, I was struggling to make sense of everything. First, I was wondering why Tin and Tri were going to stay with Lucille, and this thought was immediately followed by a hollowed-out feeling in my chest. It was then I realized how much I wanted Tin to stay here, even if we never spoke again, just to know he was close. Until now, I hadn't realized how much that meant to me. Then my thoughts turned to what Tri had said about Tin liking me. The words reverberated through my entire body in an entirely unexpected way, rousing emotions that were bittersweet. It was as though Tri had unwittingly answered a question I had never dared to ask. But now that she had spoken the words, I could no longer deny how much I had longed to hear them. I was still mulling over this when Lucille interrupted my thoughts.

"How are you, sweetheart?" she asked, cutting through a round sponge and spreading a thin layer of cream onto the bottom half.

"I've been okay, I guess."

"I've missed having you around, you know."

"Sorry . . . I was busy with exams."

"Everything went well?"

"I think so."

"How are you planning to spend the summer?"

"I'll be back working at Pepe's, saving every cent I earn for college next year."

"What do you plan on studying?"

"Textiles design at the College of Fine Arts. I got an early offer."

"Good girl," she said, pleased.

"Mum has always talked about opening a bridal shop in town, which means I can help her out when I graduate."

"Is that your real passion, Ai? Don't get me wrong: you'd be great at it and all. But you know what this town is like. I wouldn't want to see you stuck here."

I shrugged. "It seems like a good plan. The best one I've got so far."

"It's funny, but the other day I got up the courage to finally sort through Brigitte's things. I was putting it off, but the move has forced me to deal with it. Anyway, I found the dress you made for her birthday last year. You know the red strapless one?"

"Oh, yes. Mum helped me with that."

"She was saving it for a special occasion. Maybe you can find somewhere to wear it."

A short silence fell between us as we focused on our individual tasks. By now I was done with the strawberries and, with a smile of approval, Lucille cupped them in her hands. "If fashion doesn't work out for you, I think you may have a future in hospitality. Look how uniform these are."

I grinned. "Anytime you need an extra pair of hands, let me know."

Lucille went to work arranging the strawberries and piping the cream as I had seen her do with Brigitte so many times before. Unexpectedly, I felt a tear run down my cheek, followed by another. And then I just couldn't stop crying.

"Oh, honey!" Lucille turned to me, her face falling as she set down her piping tool, drawing me into her. I pressed my face against the rough linen of her apron while she stroked my hair, letting me cry it out until my sobs gradually subsided. Then she tore a piece of paper towel from a roll and handed it to me, and I blew my nose.

"It's okay. Tin will be back again before you know it."

I looked at her, surprised, and she gave me a knowing smile. "You know, when I suggested he come to Brisbane, he was reluctant to go. He wouldn't say why at first, but eventually I got the truth out of him. Just like I suspected, it was because he didn't want to leave you behind."

"Really? He's barely spoken to me since the accident."

"It's still too raw for him, Ai. Tin has a hard time expressing his emotions at the best of times, but I get the feeling there's a lot he needs to get off his chest. I know it won't be easy being in different states, but I sense a bond between you that will always be there. I don't know how two people can go through what you have and not have that connection. The four of you were so close; anyone could see that. For months you spent almost every moment together, and to have that suddenly ripped away would be a shock to your system. One morning I had an early start at the bakery and got up just before dawn was about to break. In my lounge room I stumbled on the four of you, cuddled up under a pile of cushions and blankets, fast asleep like a litter of puppies."

I smiled softly at the memory. "It *was* special, wasn't it? What the four of us had."

"When you're young, you tend to think it's easy to meet people with whom you feel a connection. As you go through your life, you learn it only happens a handful of times. That's something I wish I had known when I was your age."

"I would give anything to go back only a few months, for a chance to be a better friend to Brigitte. We hadn't been getting on so well."

"I know, sweetheart. It made me sad to see the two of you grow apart. She couldn't figure out what she'd done wrong."

"Nothing—she did nothing wrong. I wish I could tell her that. I'll never forget what she said one time when she confronted me about the way I was acting. She said, 'The worst thing is not knowing.'"

For a few moments Lucille seemed to busy herself pulling things out of the drawer and putting them back. Then she stopped and turned to face me, a pleading look in her eyes. "Ai, do you think you can tell me the reason why you distanced yourself from Brigitte? I think it would really help me to know."

"Yes," I said, nodding slowly. "Of course I should tell you."

"Only if you want to, I don't mean to pry . . ."

I paused, taking the time to gather my thoughts. Then, letting out a deep breath, I said, "The reason why I pulled away from Brigitte was because I thought maybe she and Bowie were getting close again."

Lucille raised her eyebrows, looking genuinely surprised. "Whatever gave you that idea?"

I walked back through the corridors of my memory, past the night before the picnic, the shock of finding the shorts on Brigitte's bed, past the moment when Bowie stood up with a forced nonchalance and said, "I'm going to pick up the pizzas," and Brigitte responded a beat too quickly, "I'll tag along." Past the innocuous comment Bowie made about Brigitte's legs and the look of abject terror on Sying's face when Brigitte whispered in her ear, until finally I found the exact moment the seed of mistrust was sown. I took a deep breath. "I guess it started right here in this kitchen, with a conversation I overheard between you and Brigitte . . ."

Lucille furrowed her brow. "Between me and Brigitte?"

"Do you remember that birthday party she threw for me?" Lucille nodded and I continued. "Well at the time, I'd just started seeing Bowie, and you said something like, 'You can have him back anytime you want because you're the pretty one.' I just assumed you were talking about Bowie and me."

"Oh, sweetheart, why would I ever say such a thing about you?"

"At the time, I'd only been dating Bowie for just over a month, so I figured you thought he was more Brigitte's boyfriend than mine . . ."

While looking intently at me, Lucille's expression suddenly changed as though something had just occurred to her. "Did you say this was on your birthday, Ai?"

I nodded.

"Oh, I think I know what this is about. That morning, we went to pick up supplies for your party, and Brigitte was so excited, chattering about how surprised you were going to be. You know what she was like when she had a project: everything had to be perfect. On the drive back home, she asked to stop by Alex's house because he'd found a T-shirt she'd left there. It was her favorite; you know the Chicago Bulls one?"

I nodded, recalling the exchange between Brigitte and Alex during our school excursion to see Art Express, just days before my birthday.

Lucille continued, "Brigitte had accused me several times of misplacing the shirt or throwing it out by mistake. Anyway, the whole way there, I was gloating about the fact that she had been the one to lose the shirt and not me. You know how we used to have these silly fights all the time. And it's weird, but that's what I miss the most. The way we used to get on each other's nerves. I think only people you really love can get under your skin like that."

"So we got to Alex's house, and Brigitte must have told him she was dropping by, because he'd set up an inflatable pool on his front lawn. He was in the pool, wearing only trunks, with a bikini-clad girl draped all over him. It was clear to me he'd arranged the whole thing just to upset Brigitte. The scene reeked of desperation, but it worked. We left without even getting the shirt. For the rest of the day she put on a brave face because she didn't want to ruin your birthday, but I could tell she was crestfallen. I must have been comparing her to the other girl when I told Brigitte she was the pretty one. It was just a stupid, immature comment that meant absolutely nothing. I hate the idea that you've been carrying this for such a long time. I just wished you had asked me about it back then. I would have set the record straight."

I digested Lucille's words slowly as they stripped away the accusations I had long held against Brigitte.

"B-but," I stammered, "why didn't she tell me she went to see him? I understand she didn't want to ruin my birthday, but what about the day after? If she had told me what had happened, I would have naturally assumed that's what the two of you were referring to. It fits now, but without the context of that scene it sounded like you were talking about me and Bowie. You can understand how I can make that mistake . . . can't you?" There was a hysterical note to my voice, as though I had just uncovered the exact point in time where everything could have gone in a different direction. "Why didn't she tell me?"

Lucille pursed her lips and shook her head. "She was embarrassed; it's as simple as that. How many times had she promised us she was done with Alex? But for some reason, she just couldn't let him go."

My mind staggered through all the instances when I had

chastised her about Alex, rolled my eyes at the mention of his name, told her to get over him as though her heart were a switch she could turn off. I couldn't figure out why she kept falling for his tricks. With a startling realization, I knew my lack of empathy was because I had yet to experience loss the way she had. "Oh, God," I said, as the full realization of Lucille's words sunk in. "Oh, everything could have been so different . . . Bowie warned me not to let Sying get in my head, and that's exactly what I did."

"Brigitte told me all about the exhibition, how she was forced to give it up because Sying seemed hell-bent on ruining her life."

"Everyone tried to warn me about Sying, but I wouldn't listen. It seems obvious to me now, but at the time I just couldn't see it."

"She's a strange fish, isn't she? You and Brigitte tried so hard to include her, but it was never enough. I didn't know her all that well, but I sense she is a deeply unhappy person."

"It's my own fault: she couldn't convince me of anything I hadn't already talked myself into. When you make your mind up about someone, everything they do becomes a confirmation of your bias. That's how you start to lose your ability to judge what's real. One minor preconception after another. If you don't pay attention, it can set you on a completely different path. And if I'd kept a watch on it, maybe I wouldn't have let it go as far as I did. I would have resisted going down that road of suspicion when it came to Brigitte and Bowie. Then maybe I wouldn't have invited Sying that day to the picnic and our paths might have never crossed with those two men and maybe . . . just maybe . . ."

I shook my head, seized by a feeling of utter helplessness, by an irrational anger at how fixed we were to the past. "It's like an ugly jigsaw puzzle I keep constructing repeatedly in my mind."

"Just like you, I spend every waking moment trying to piece it all together. I keep asking why. Why was my sweet, precious girl taken instead of those two jerks? And Bowie: Why did they take Bowie, who was only trying to protect his friend? I know how much you loved her, Ai—more than anyone. I know. And she loved you, too, so very much. If she were still with us, I just know the two of you would have worked things out."

I nodded, a fresh spring of tears welling up. "Thank you for saying that."

We were silent for a few moments, lost in our own thoughts. Then Lucille said, "You know, there are days when I can't even get out of bed. I wonder, 'What's the point? What does it matter?' But then, out of nowhere, a little bird will sing, drawing my eyes to the window. I'd look over and think, 'Doesn't the sunlight seem just a little prettier than usual today?'" Half turning from me, she nodded in the direction of the lounge room, where we heard Tri humming softly to herself. "I think, 'Isn't there a brilliant little girl who still needs me?' And then I am—almost against my will—overwhelmed with the notion, 'Well, I guess it's not so bad today, after all.'" One last, lonely tear ran down my cheek as Lucille cupped my face in her hands. "Today is a good day."

As I left, I heard the patter of footsteps behind me. "Ai! Wait!" I turned to see Tri, arm extended out to me with Brigitte's Nikon in her hand. "Lucille told me to give you this. There's only one shot left on the roll. Maybe you can take a picture with my brother." Her mischievous grin was infectious, and I found myself smiling back.

"Thanks, Tri."

"Will you stop by to visit here again—before we leave?"

"Of course."

"Good," she said with a firm nod. "Lucille says it was almost as though she had Brigitte back for a while."

Eleven

IT WAS THE opening night of Sying's exhibition, and I had now circled twice around the block where the Whitlam Library was positioned, looking for a place to park. The entire street was abuzz with locals who had gathered to watch the commotion, gawking at the out-of-towners dressed in their slick attire, segregated like oil from water when they stepped out of their chauffeured cars and pushed their way into the throng. The intermittent flash of cameras added to the surreal atmosphere, reminding me of my first date with Bowie, the incongruence of the scene.

I had to drive several streets up before I finally found a space, mumbling to myself that I should have just walked, since I was now halfway between our flat and the library. I stepped into the warm night air, glancing skyward to the scattering of stars, high heels treading the same old familiar pavement, feeling as though it were leading me somewhere new.

Coming up to the slate-gray building, I noticed how the yellowish light glowing from the glass doors appeared especially vibrant, as though blushing from all the attention. Slipping into the crowd, I immersed myself in the lively chatter, absorbing snippets of conversation in accents I rarely heard except on television, the context of which felt entirely abstract to me.

"Oh, you must simply try it, darling! They only take twelve guests on the island. Wonderfully private. Get away from it all, you know? You're assigned your own nanny and chef—the whole kit and caboodle. Ours made the most divine ceviche; he was a friendly chap too. Anyway, you don't have to lift a finger: everything's just done for you and always with an air of cheeriness. John felt like a grilled cheese in the middle of the night, and it was no trouble at all. Oh, and they bring you champagne in a wicker basket. Champagne in a wicker basket—isn't that a lark? Stan and the kids would love it, darling. You must try to tear him away from all those dreary boardroom meetings. John was like a new man by the end of it, weren't you, dear?"

"Ai!" Sying appeared before me like an apparition holding out her hand. I grabbed at it, eager to reorient myself back to reality. But after seeing her kohl-rimmed eyes and red puckered lips, I felt even more removed.

"I don't know anyone here," she laughed. "Do you?"

I shook my head, opening my mouth to speak, when her attention was turned elsewhere and she shot away.

Watching her flitting through the crowd hummingbird-like—air-kissing, shaking hands, never lingering for a moment longer than was necessary—I felt an intense urge to describe this fevered dream to Brigitte. Gulping back waves of nausea, I pushed the thought away.

Jolted by a tap on my shoulder, I spun around to see Tri in

a white lace dress with a blue satin sash. Like the opening of a music box, the melody from *The Sound of Music* burst into my mind. I'd only seen the ending of that movie days ago and had felt, alongside the Von Trapp children, a crushing loss of innocence.

Smoothing out her skirt, Tri said matter-of-factly, "I was a flower girl at my cousin's wedding last year and really wanted to wear this dress again."

Her presence had a calming effect on me, and I smiled. "You look lovely, Tri."

She looked me up and down. "Is that Brigitte's red dress you're wearing?"

I nodded.

"You look beautiful." She beamed. "Wait until my brother sees you."

"Is he here?"

"I think he's on his way now. I came earlier with Lucille." She tucked her little hand in mine, and together we stepped through the glass door of the library. "Check out all the TV vans here. Do you think we'll be on television?"

"Maybe."

"And it will be for something good this time?"

"I think so."

She seemed pleased about this. "Because there are a lot of good things here, aren't there? Not just all the yucky stuff they show on the news." She looked sad suddenly. "There are a lot of bad people, for sure, but there are good people too. Like you and Lucille."

I squeezed her hand as we walked up the stairs to the exhibit.

"There's a picture of my dad up, you know. Sying interviewed him last week. I was the translator. At first she asked my brother if he would do it, but he said no. But after he left our house, Sying came back to ask me." Her face glowed with pride. "Do you know anyone in the show?"

"My mum's been featured too."

"That means she must have lived a pretty interesting life."

In the room upstairs were clusters of people migrating from one easel to another in a slow, methodical dance. Their expressions appropriately serious as they studied each photograph, mouths moving along silently to their accompanying stories. There was no change to the setup Sying had showed me the previous day, no tribute to Brigitte as she had half-heartedly considered. The only difference was an addition of a lectern at the far end of the wall where projected footage from the Vietnam War played on a loop. I spotted Lucille across the room in deep conversation with a friend and she waved at us, smiling. Tri guided me to the photo of her dad, which I hadn't yet seen. Sying must have been heavy-handed with the zoom when she took the picture. The portrait of Tin's dad felt uncomfortably close, his features caricature-like. Course, wiry hair ran unkempt along his jawline, nose speckled with dirty, enlarged pores, every blemish and rough patch of skin magnified in a way that was intensely unflattering. I observed the same hint of menace in his eyes I had witnessed the day he came to collect his son from the Royal National Park.

The story about Tin's dad was unusually brief when compared with the others, as though it had been written in a hurry. Still, I read through line by line, hoping I could glean some new insight into Tin's other life. When I was on the last paragraph, I was interrupted by an angry growl.

"Why the fuck is he part of this exhibit?"

At first, I didn't recognize the voice, and when I turned around it was almost impossible to reconcile it with the boy standing there, dressed in a neat button-up tuxedo.

"Tin—" I began, spun out by the way the suit had transformed him, adding new bulk and broadness to his usually slight frame.

He looked past me, at the large square canvas plastered with his dad's face. The room, which had begun to fill up, paused to observe the scene. Louder, Tin repeated, "Why the fuck is this man part of the exhibit?" He pointed an accusatory finger at the canvas.

Tri grabbed at his arm, but he shook it off impatiently. His body was trembling with a rage that I had never seen in him— could not have imagined he possessed until this moment.

"It's Daddy," Tri said dumbly. "He's our dad."

"He's a piece of shit!" spat Tin as a hush went around the room.

More people were gathering now.

"Tin," I cajoled, my hand reaching for his shoulder. He shrugged me off, eyes fixed to the canvas, jaw tightly clenched.

Sying came barreling in, asking anxiously, "Is everything okay?"

Jabbing a finger at the canvas, Tin said, "I want this lowlife removed from the exhibit." When she didn't move, he yelled, "Now!"

She jumped from the unexpected ferocity of his voice. "Your dad?" she gasped. "But . . . but . . . he's a refugee. That's why he's been featured in this exhibition. He has every right to be here, Tin."

Through gritted teeth, Tin said, "I told you I didn't want him in it, Sying. Why didn't you respect my wishes? You knew how I felt about this, but you still went ahead anyway. What the hell is wrong with you?" Clearly it was taking all his strength to remain in control, but I could sense the anger bubbling away underneath, on the cusp of erupting.

"Tri wanted him in," Sying retorted. "He's her dad as well, you know."

"You stay the fuck away from my sister," he spat.

Tri started to cry. "But he's our dad, Tin . . . He's our dad."

Sying spoke to Tin slowly, as though explaining to a child. "He came to this country with nothing, Tin, and he's built a whole new life here—" She stopped in the face of his mounting fury.

"He's built nothing. He's achieved nothing. Don't tell me about my own dad, okay, Sying? You've got no idea what you're talking about. Are you going to get rid of it? Are you?"

She shook her head slowly.

"No?" he goaded, moving toward the canvas. Sying quickly stepped between Tin and the easel, arms comically splayed in a protective stance.

"Get out of the way, Sying."

She shook her head again, resolute.

He took a step toward her and said through clenched teeth, "Sying, I am warning you."

Sying stumbled backward as though she had been struck, her foot knocking against the leg of the easel, the canvas rocking unsteadily. Tin pounced on it and there was a collective intake of breath in the room, people muttering their prejudices out aloud.

". . . these youth gangs . . ."

". . . probably on drugs . . ."

". . . better suited to the jungle . . ."

A woman wailed, "Someone, call security—quick!"

Tin held the canvas in his tightly clenched fists, raising it high above his head before smashing it to the ground. It hit hard, emitting a loud crack as the wood splintered, compressing the square frame into a loose diamond. Everyone watched in horror as he stomped on the canvas repeatedly, causing a tear to rip down the middle. Still not satisfied, he continued attacking the broken canvas in a frenzy, scratching and clawing until it was left scattered in pieces on the floor. Then he stopped, breathing hard from the rampage, his intense glare met by looks of shock and repulsion. I wanted to scream out loud, *This is not Tin. This is not who he is.* But this brutal version was all that most of the onlookers would ever see.

Tri covered her eyes with her hands. "No! No!"

Sying looked on, red, puckered lips mumbling something inaudible, eyes darting from side to side. As she stood, stupefied, there was sudden movement all around the room. A pair of vigilantes took it upon themselves to restrain Tin, their arms hooked under his as he struggled, kicking and swearing at them. I caught sight of a hysterical Tri pitching herself into Lucille's arms. Over the top of Tri's head, I met Lucille's gaze, and she nodded at me with intent. Tin broke away from the men, bolting from the room. Whipping off my high heels, I chased after him.

Outside, I spotted him racing down the street. "Tin!" I called. "Tin!"

He stopped running and turned toward me, breathing hard. When I caught up to him, he looked at me as though it was the first he'd seen me all night. "Ai."

I was about to respond when someone barked, "You! Come back here." I swiveled around to see a guard standing outside the library, pointing a baton in our direction. "You're in big trouble, boy. You get back here now!"

We stood frozen for a moment, trying to anticipate what the guard would do next. The instant he made a motion toward us, I grabbed Tin's hand and cried, "Come on!"

We ran as fast as we could into the night, not daring to look back once—not even when the heavy pounding of feet behind us had stopped giving chase; not when my ankle twisted painfully underneath me and I stumbled, skinning my knee on the pavement; not until we finally collapsed against the door of my car, clinging to each other as we fought to catch our breath.

It got darker as we drove away from Whitlam, as though the trees growing in their density were swallowing the light. I had the strangest sensation that the entire world had turned into something loose and undefined, blurring like shadows, ready to be shaped into something new. Tin, who had been an enigma to me for so long, was now the only thing that seemed to possess depth and substance. I was heading in the direction of the Royal National Park, drawn there by invisible strings, by an impulse that felt strangely familiar. The whole way there, I snuck a few glances at Tin, but he remained silent, lost in thought. He didn't ask me where we were going, but somehow I sensed he knew.

By the entrance, I parked next to the tall carved wood sign and cut the engine. The lot was deserted this time of night, and the fog settling over the shrubbery gave the place a haunted feel, reminding me this was where we had last left Bowie and Brigitte. I unhooked my seat belt and looked over at Tin, who was staring straight ahead, unblinking. I could tell he was about to speak, and I braced myself for the deluge, sensing when the words came, they would hurt.

Breaking the hour-long silence between us, he began. "A couple of days before the picnic, Dad arrived home in the early hours of the morning, blind drunk and in a foul mood. I think he'd lost a lot of money at the casino again. It got worse as the day wore on. He kept harassing my stepmum, Hua—about the money she was keeping aside for rent—but she wouldn't give it to him. Finally, he snapped and started breaking shit: vases, the television, a ceramic pigeon Tri had made him, all shattered to pieces on the ground. Tri was hiding behind me, arms around my waist. She was so scared. Then Dad grabbed Hua by the hair and dragged her into their bedroom. We begged him to let her go, but he wouldn't. Instead, he locked the door behind him. Tri and I threw ourselves at the door, pounding with our fists. I knew from the sounds coming from behind the door that Dad was raping her. Tri was screaming, 'Mum, Mum!' but Dad wouldn't stop. In the chaos, I heard Hua wailing, 'Get Tri out of the house, Tin! Get her out! Get her out now!' So I grabbed Tri around the waist and she began shrieking, scratching at me, gripping on to the door handle. Somehow I managed to get her in the car and we drove.

"She was a mess because she adores Dad, won't ever acknowledge the shit that he is. I didn't know where to go, so we went to Bowie's. He didn't want his mum to know what was happening, so he got in the car with us. We went to Brigitte's place and that's when I told them what had happened that night. Lucille was there, too, and she was so good with Tri. Brigitte made her a hot chocolate with marshmallows. Then Lucille said we were welcome to stay whenever we liked. Just like that, she said we could stay. It was surreal. Ever since I was a kid, there was nowhere else to go. I had to keep this horrible secret to myself. I had no other choice. But suddenly that wasn't the case anymore. I felt such a tremendous relief because I didn't want to go on that way. Tri was getting older, and I didn't want to live with that dread in the pit of my stomach. I didn't want to stay quiet."

"Oh, Tin," I whispered, reeling from the shock of what he had just told me. I took his hand in mine, pressed it to my cheek.

"I wish I had known . . . I wish you had told me. All this time, I didn't know . . . and oh God—Tri . . ." I trailed off, not wanting to finish the sentence.

He squeezed my hand. "I wanted to tell you, Ai; I really did. Bowie thought it was best I tell you myself, rather than hear it secondhand from him or Brigitte. I meant to tell you the night before the picnic. But then you got upset about something and Bowie took you home. Why were you upset that night, Ai? What happened?"

I went deathly silent as my mind shot back to the night of the picnic. Then I started piecing everything together. The strange mood the group was in, the dark circles under Tin's eyes. Bowie and Brigitte using the pizza trip as an excuse for me to be alone with Tin, to give him a chance to tell me the same terrible truth they had learned the night before. Tin and Tri had been staying at Lucille's, which explained the shorts on Brigitte's bed. Then there was the conversation I caught between Bowie and Brigitte on their return. *My heart breaks for her.* Of course they had been talking about Tri and not myself—just as Bowie had kept insisting.

"Ai?" Tin gently prompted. "What happened that night? Why were you upset?"

I took a long shaky breath. "It was a conversation I caught between Bowie and Brigitte after they came back with the pizzas. They were talking about Tri and what the two of you had gone through—everything you told me just now—but for some reason my mind twisted it into something else. I thought they were talking about me."

His brows furrowed, perplexed. "Why did you think they were talking about you?"

I cast my eyes down, feeling deeply ashamed of the way I had behaved that night at Brigitte's. "For a while I thought Bowie and Brigitte were falling for each other again. I thought they were planning to break the news to me that night. That's what I took the conversation to mean at the time."

The look on Tin's face showed me just how far off the mark I was. "You didn't have to worry about that, Ai. There was nothing between them. Believe me, I would know. The only real thing Brigitte and Bowie had in common was how much they loved you. But maybe if I had just told you about my dad that night, this could have all been avoided. I don't know why I didn't just tell you, Ai . . . I'm sorry."

"No," I said firmly. "You don't need to apologize. What you went through is—" I stopped, unable to find the appropriate word. With a shake of my head, I continued, "And Tri . . . she's so wonderful. I've only just met her and all I want to do is protect her. I can only imagine how you feel . . ." I broke down then, feeling winded by my grief, by the way it had shown the depth of my love for Brigitte only when it was too late. A love for which I had no other comparison, not even with Bowie.

And then Tin was kissing me, softly brushing away my tears.

I pulled away, shaking my head. "No, no. We can't—"

"Don't say that, Ai."

I covered my face with my hands. "Tin . . ."

Gently peeling my fingers away from my face, he kissed me again.

I made a sound in my throat that was halfway between a sob and a sigh. My fingers went to the delicate chain around my neck and I thought of the callous way I had ripped it off and thrown it in Bowie's face. I thought of how he had fixed it for me. "You don't understand, Tin. I said something horrible to Bowie when he was on that Jet Ski. I told him Brigitte had cheated on him, that she had been screwing Alex behind his back. That's the last thing I ever said to him. Can you imagine? I was still going on about my meltdown at Brigitte's the night before and he kept telling me the conversation I overheard was about someone else. But I wouldn't believe him. I couldn't understand why he kept telling me to ask you."

Tin pulled me into him, gently rubbing my back. "You know, if those bastards hadn't showed up, this would have all been straightened out by now. It's not your fault. What happened to Bowie and Brigitte had nothing to do with you. None of that has anything to do with us and how we've wound up here." Despite my initial resistance, I found myself entangled in him, as though my limbs had been making small incremental movements toward him the whole time. His mouth found mine again and I couldn't stop him. I didn't want to.

His hand gripped my thigh and I let out an involuntary whimper. He sighed deeply, tucking his head into my neck. I stroked the back of his head as he looked up at me.

In a trembling voice I asked, "How could you want me after all of this?"

"When I look at you, I can't think of anything else I could ever want."

I cupped his face in my hands, looking into eyes that felt centuries old. "Sometimes I feel like you're the last person left in the entire world."

"That's how I feel about you. Only I've always felt it, even before Bowie. Way before then. I just wish I'd had the courage to tell you."

"I wish you didn't have to go."

He gathered my hands like a bouquet, burying his face in them and breathing deeply. "You understand why I have to, don't you?"

"Of course I do."

"I need to get Tri away from my dad before something bad happens to her. Even Hua knows that. Tri loves him so much and he'll use that against her. Dad's always threatening to kick me out, and when that day comes, Tri's at his mercy. I'd rather die than let him hurt her."

"I know, Tin. You don't need to convince me. I already know."

"If there was any other way to stay here with you, I would."

My lips were wet on his cheek, wet with tears that were a mixture of his and my own. It felt as though we'd finally found each other and we were already saying goodbye.

"Tin," I whispered.

"Ai," he replied.

I went to kiss him again, fingers fumbling at the pearlescent buttons dotting their way down his crisp white shirt. I got the first one loose, and then the second. I kissed the hollow of his neck. A low growl sounded at the back of his throat as I whispered, "We should stop . . ."

"No . . . don't . . ."

I untucked his shirt, slid a hand underneath to rest my palm against the rise of his chest. He touched my cheek, then drew me into his arms. We were both crying now, wading through our grief to snatch at this one morsel of joy. I felt like I could have died then and there. Through my tears, I whispered, "Even if this is all we have, it's enough for me, Tin."

"It's enough for me too . . ."

He brought my hand to his lips, kissed the tips of my trembling fingers. I unzipped my dress and guided his hands toward my body, to all the places where I ached for him. Over and over, I felt myself clutching at each moment, bittersweet and tremulous, before it slipped out of my grasp and into memory. Over and over, I said to myself, *Remember this. Remember everything.*

Afterward, we lay in the back seat of the car, skin to skin under his tuxedo jacket, my chin resting on his shoulder, his fingers drawing concentric circles on my bare arms. Time seemed to slow almost to a standstill. Outside, the night sky resembled dusk, but it had already been hours since we got here. Pressed against his body, I felt the soft hum of his words, as though they were reverberating through me. We hadn't stopped talking since we got here; now he was confessing his greatest fear. "What if the bad thing inside my dad is also in me?"

"It's not."

"That day on the lake, I was ready to kill those guys. And if Bowie hadn't swerved in front of Brigitte, maybe that's what I would have done. There is so much rage inside me, it takes all my strength to keep it under control. If I take my eyes off it for a second, I'm scared I'll no longer be myself."

"The thing you're talking about, Tin—that darkness—we all have it. It's in all of us."

"But I think there's too much of it in me. If I could go back in time, I'd probably do it, you know: I'd ram my Jet Ski into those bastards. I'd do it regardless of whether it would bring Brigitte and Bowie back."

"I'd do it, too, Tin, in a heartbeat. It kills me every time I think about those guys walking around free."

"I can't believe how easily they got away with it—not because of who they are, but because of who *we* are. The way the papers twisted everything somehow made us the bad guys. And tonight I proved them right, didn't I? All those posers will run back to their posh neighborhoods and tell everyone they witnessed a Viet thug in his natural habitat. They'll spread the word around while sipping their expensive wine, give themselves another reason to turn the other way when we're being screwed over by the government, the media, the police, the justice system. It makes me sick to my stomach. And that's the part of me I'm afraid of, Ai. I've just got so much rage inside me, sometimes I can't separate myself from it."

"You do know, given the circumstances, it was perfectly understandable how you behaved tonight. You know that, right?"

"I just felt so out of control, so out of my body. I mean, what if it happens again? What if next time it happens and it's not warranted?"

"Why do you think that, Tin? It's never happened before, has it?"

He swallowed hard. "Just one other time, but I was only a kid then."

"What happened?"

Beneath me, I felt him tense, and I ran my hand gently across his brow. It was damp with sweat.

In a quiet voice he said, "The last time I was angry, someone got seriously hurt. I've never told anyone about this."

"You can tell me."

He was trembling and I wrapped my arms tighter around him, pressing my mouth against his warm neck. "Tell me, Tin . . ."

He spoke in a monotone voice, as though giving any emotion to this memory would make it too difficult to tell. "When I was seven, I lost my temper—just went completely off the rails. I don't know what had set off the tantrum, but it was late at night and neither Dad nor Hua could get through to me. Dad got so fed up, he bundled me into the car, drove me to a sports field, and left me there. I didn't think he'd drive away, and even after he did, I thought he would come straight back. So, I waited by a lamppost. I waited and waited. Then I walked around the field in my pajamas, bewildered and crying, the wet grass soaking through my socks. I was cold and scared. I wanted to head home, but I wasn't sure which way to go. To me, the street names all looked unfamiliar.

"I heard some voices nearby and hid behind a dumpster. Then I walked for what seemed like a long time until I was startled by a dog hurtling toward me. I ran as fast as I could, not daring to look back until the barking finally stopped. By then I had found myself in a dark alleyway and saw, at the end, the orange glow from the tip of a cigarette. A man was leaning against the brick wall, smoking. He looked at me, unsmiling. I was afraid to ask him for help, but I had no other choice. Luckily for me, he took me to the nearest police station. There, I was given a mug of hot chocolate by a nice officer who tried to coax me into telling her what had happened. What was I doing out this time of night? Where did I live? Who were my parents? I was too frightened to speak, but I wrote down my phone number on a notepad."

Taking a deep, shuddering breath, he continued, "When Dad finally came to get me, he was questioned by the officer. She made every attempt to reason with Dad, but he just kept getting more agitated. She tried me again, but I kept my mouth shut. I think Dad was pleased with me for not telling on him. It was morning by the time we left the police station. He took me to McDonald's and got me a Happy Meal, smiling, ruffling my hair as I devoured my cheeseburger. It was such a rare treat for me, both the Happy Meal and Dad's kindness. I remember thinking that it almost made the terrible night worthwhile. The toy from the Happy Meal was one of those musical key chains with buttons you press to play a little tune. Even though the mood had lightened, I was still afraid to press the buttons. When he got home, Hua was sitting on the bottom step of our porch, still in her nightdress. When she saw me, her shoulders sagged with relief. Dad started blaming her for what had happened, really laying into her. Tri was still a baby then and Hua hadn't been getting all that much sleep. I guess she'd complained about my tantrum the night before, worried that I would wake Tri. Now she seemed to regret bothering Dad about it in the first place. As his fury escalated, Hua started crying. Dad hated it when she cried. He couldn't stand it. She ended up in hospital that day. After that, I learned it was safer to stay quiet."

"Oh, Tin," I said, feeling unbearably sad for his child self. I understood then why he was so reserved, so reluctant to express any emotion, and how this had shaped his entire way of being.

"That was the last time I let my temper get the better of me—at least, until tonight. I couldn't stand the way Tri was looking at me, like I was a stranger. I didn't feel like I was in control of myself, didn't think about the havoc my actions could wreak on those around me. Just like my dad. Exactly like my dad."

I let his words rise and fall like breath and then disperse into the silence. After a pause I said, "Do you remember the time when the four of us were together and you were telling everyone about how you could make a sentence with my name? That it means 'Whom I Love.' Do you remember?"

He nodded.

I placed my hand on his chest, over his heart. "That can only come from somewhere beautiful, you know—somewhere good. That was a gift that you gave me. Now I can't see my name without thinking of that sentence. It's such a gift, Tin. Don't you see? That's the essence of who you truly are."

"Ai," he said, voice hoarse with emotion. "You don't know what that means to me, hearing you say that. I feel like there is so much good in you, and it makes me want to be a better person."

Tin's words were far from what I believed to be true about myself. All the good he saw in me was an illusion, even though I wanted so badly to be the person he imagined me to be. But so far in my young life I had already caused so much pain to the ones I loved most. I felt the need to set the record straight, once and for all.

Quietly, I said, "The darkness is in me, too, Tin. You know that, don't you? Maybe it's not explosive like yours was tonight, but it's insidious and can be just as destructive. Perhaps even more so. Look at the way I treated my best friend leading up to the accident. And what I said to Bowie just before he died . . ." I shook my head. "There's no excusing my behavior, no matter what anyone says. Everything would have been different if I hadn't given in to that dark impulse, if only I'd gone the other way instead."

"Do you remember the drive up to the picnic? We passed by a motorcycle accident. If we hadn't doubled back for Brigitte's Nikon, we could have been caught up in that. And you heard what Brigitte said, about her bottle of Coke getting caught behind the brake pedal when we were speeding down the highway. My point is, even if you had done everything right, things could have still ended up the same. Maybe even worse. You just don't know."

I smiled sadly. "No, but I'd take the risk. I'd go back and do it all over if I could. Even if it doesn't bring them back. I'd take my chances."

The next morning I caught a train out to the city, wandering the busy streets on my own, my head buzzing from the lack of sleep. The sunlight appeared unusually vibrant to me, illuminating. Down a quiet side street, I paused outside a medical clinic with a sign in its window stating a female doctor was on duty.

Inside, the receptionist wrote down my name and asked me to take a seat. A television mounted on a bracket overhead played an infomercial advertising the ThighMaster, starring a grinning, spandex-clad blonde ecstatically utilizing the contraption. Across from me sat a young mother bouncing a crying baby on her knee, cooing in his ear while a toddler tugged insistently at her arm. In the corner sat an old woman, tired and shrunken, clothed from head to toe in black. My eyes were drawn to the small, jerky movements of her fingers, and on closer examination I realized she was counting a string of rosary beads. Soon I was ushered into a room by a nurse who introduced herself to me as Julie.

The room was small and neutral. The only distinguishing feature was a framed print of a lighthouse stuck above an examination bed. There was a desk and a couple of chairs by a floor-to-ceiling shelf stocked with medical paraphernalia. Julie picked up a clipboard from the desk and motioned for me to sit.

"'Ai'? Is that how you pronounce your name?"

I nodded and she asked why I was there.

Casting my eyes down, I mumbled, "I need a prescription for the morning-after pill."

When I looked up, her eyes had widened fractionally, showing a flicker of concern. When she spoke, her manner remained professional. "Can I ask how old you are, Ai?"

"I'm seventeen, even though I may look younger."

"And when did you last have sex?"

"Last night, for the first time."

"And you're feeling okay?"

"I'm fine. A little emotional, maybe, but perfectly fine."

"Do you need to ask me any questions—about contraception or STDs?"

I shook my head. "It was his first time, too, and he's leaving soon anyway." My voice cracked at the word "soon" and Julie seemed to register this.

"In that case, I just have to take down some details before you see the doctor." She rattled off a list of questions, which I answered to the best of my knowledge. When she asked me about my family history, I shook my head again.

"I'm sorry, but I can't give you my family history."

"Oh? Why is that?"

"It's because I don't have one." Taking a deep breath, I launched into a brief retelling of my family's past, about the Khmer Rouge, the systematic genocide of my ancestors, my subsequent birth in a Thai refugee camp, and our immigration to Australia. "I don't even have a birth certificate," I finished.

Putting down her clipboard and pen, Julie gazed past me, a

distant look in her eyes. "In the late seventies I was stationed with the Red Cross at Khao I Dang. I will never forget my first day as a young nurse. At the base of the camp, my colleagues and I were watching a wall of refugees walking toward us, and what struck me most—what has stayed with me all these years—is the silence. Not a baby crying, not a single word uttered among them, it was like a silent movie, so profoundly haunting." She shuddered as though the memory chilled her. Then, looking at me, she said, "I'm glad you and your family made it here safe."

"Thank you," I said, tears piercing my eyes, spilling down my cheeks. "Thank you for helping us."

"Oh, darling, that's okay. It was my job, after all." She handed me a tissue, and the small act of kindness induced a fresh spring of tears.

"We're good people, you know . . . there are a lot of problems in our community, but most of us are trying, really we are."

She put a hand on my shoulder and smiled kindly. "I know there's been a lot of negative talk about immigrants, and I understand how upsetting it must be for you. But I want you to know I'm glad you're here and there are so many others like me who feel the same."

There was a knock at the door, and Julie was called to attend to another patient. I thanked her again and she hugged me warmly. "You take care of yourself, okay?"

At the exit of the clinic, I paused for a moment. I thought of Mum and the fish she stole, a bridge between her old life and new. I thought of Tin's mother and sisters, forever lost at sea. I thought of Tri walking the tightrope from the wreckage of her home to the safe haven of Lucille's. I thought of Brigitte and Bowie, the day that came and left without them. Here in front of me was a door, the rest of my life shimmering on the other side. I looked once to the left for Brigitte, once to the right for Bowie. With the same reverence and care as someone about to step into traffic, I walked through the door.

Part Two

✦

Twelve

MY FIRST YEAR at the College of Fine Arts in Sydney came and went with little fanfare as I grappled with the challenge of starting anew in an unfamiliar environment. Living in the city was a culture shock, with its sheer noise and busyness, the constant onslaught of crowds swarming the pavement, learning to navigate my way through. I found a job working as a waitress at a tapas bar for minimum wage while I learned to adapt to the new college routine of classes, guidelines, and politics, down to the grading system, where anything over a credit was admirable and the high of a distinction was like a drug I rabidly chased. I lived for the thrill of a lecturer calling out my score, followed by the hush that went around the classroom, and then my peers congratulating me after class. Mum, who was used to seeing straight As from me in school, was flummoxed by all the credits and distinctions, which appeared as Cs and Ds on my college report. I had to explain that, in college, Cs and Ds were a good thing. Not that I saw my family much during that year. In fact, when I look back on that time now, I can barely recall anything but the daily struggle to balance my workload and finances.

Still, there were moments that stood out, like enrollment day when I lined up for my student card, the flash of the camera going off before I was ready, or a challenging exercise where we were tasked with building a bridge out of paper that could support a single brick but would buckle at two. I was overzealous with my design, and when my bridge still didn't give way by the third brick, the class fell about in hysterics. I went crazy over a particular grilled sandwich at the cafeteria, even though most days I had to settle for a plain naan sold in a take-out joint across the road. There was a social experiment I carried out with some classmates where I had to block a busy doorway to gauge people's reaction. Most stepped around me as best as they could, but there was one guy who growled, "Get out of my way, bitch." Of course, this story was immediately shared around my class, and soon everyone was parroting the line back at me. "Get out of my way, bitch" became something of a catchphrase that year, with everyone delighting at the in-joke whenever it came into play.

Although everyone was friendly, I didn't make any firm friends. There was only one other Asian girl in my class; her parents lived in a town bordering Whitlam. I thought sharing that commonality would mean we'd get along, but she kept giving me the cold shoulder. At first, I just assumed she didn't like me until the afternoon we bumped into each other at the train station, after classes had finished for the day. We were both heading back to visit our parents, taking the same hour-long train ride. I dreaded the trip, thinking she'd be standoffish the whole way. But to my surprise she was suddenly a different person, chatting away as though we were old friends. The next day I spotted her on campus, calling out her name, and she pretended she hadn't heard me, even though it was obvious she had. I figured her strange behavior stemmed from a deep-seated desire to fit in, and she must have felt her proximity to me would lessen her chances of this. It was as though her being Asian was enough of a social handicap without having me complicate things for her. It was a kind of prejudice that I'd never experienced before, but I understood how growing up as a minority could skew your sense of self in a myriad of ways. I knew not to take it personally.

There was also the transient nature of that first year, with kids trying on the new curriculum like an outfit before deciding if it was truly for them. The sheer number of projects assigned and the pressure to create work of a standard that was expected of us was too much for many. Which meant by the time second year came around, there were hardly any familiar faces left. By then, I felt well and truly settled in, ready to take on the next year.

The first week, a lace specialist named Catherine came to visit our textiles class. It was fast becoming my favorite subject, with experts dropping by to teach us things from hand-stitching to working with a loom.

Catherine spoke to our class about a competition she was running in conjunction with the Art & Technology Centre that was open to entries worldwide, and she invited us to submit our work. She defined "lace" as any type of weave that showed up negative spaces and was looking for new techniques that could translate into wearable fashion. Handing out information booklets, she promised to be back in a couple of weeks to review our progress.

I spent that time playing with paper, which was a medium I felt the most confident working in. Then I remembered the paper swan that Sharon, the interviewer, had been so impressed with. A week later, I had made a decent start on a new sculpture and it appeared to be at once structural and delicate, as was specified in the brief.

On Catherine's return, she walked from desk to desk, surveying the work, offering words of encouragement. When she got to mine, she stopped, pressing a hand to her chest. "Oh," she said, picking up my piece and staring at it in wonder. The other students began to gather around my table as she passed the piece between them. When it was in her hands again, she looked intently at me. "Where did you learn to do this?"

"Back in my hometown, all the girls just started making these origami sculptures. I'm not sure why, but it was something we just did."

"And where is your hometown?"

"Whitlam," I said, before launching into a quick description of the infamous settlement.

"That's remarkable. My sister is a human rights activist who lives in the States and back in the early nineties, a cargo ship known as the *Golden Venture* ran aground on the coast of New York. On the ship were hundreds of undocumented Chinese immigrants, illegally smuggled into the country, who had been living in unspeakable conditions. Many of them wound up in detention centers and then were sent to prison for years on end. During their time in incarceration, they started making paper sculptures that got more and more complex until, with only bits of scrap paper and old magazines, they invented a new method of paper crafting known as '*Golden Venture* folding.' The sculptures were given as gifts to the activists and lawyers who assisted them in gaining their freedom. In fact, I have one of those beautiful swans my sister sent to me, along with photographs documenting the process. Knowing my background in lace, she knew I'd appreciate it. Someone on that ship must have somehow wound up in the settlement where you're from and passed on that skill. How utterly profound."

A hush went around the classroom, mesmerized by the emotional richness of the story, the idea that an artistic technique could be traced back to its origin, born in the depths of despair, to flourish and appear in the most unlikely places. I was just as awed by the cultural significance of something that had once seemed so ordinary to me.

Rubbing at her bare arms, my lecturer Libby said, "I have goose bumps. What a gorgeous story, Catherine. You must tell your sister about Whitlam."

"Oh, for sure, I'll call her tonight. She'd be blown away." Then, turning her attention to me, Catherine continued, "I've never seen this technique adapted to fabric. I'm not sure if it's even possible, but I'd really love to see it."

"What do you think, Ai?" Libby asked, smiling widely at me.

I bit my lip. "It sounds really tricky . . ." Even though it was my second year at college, I still found it strange calling teachers by their first names.

Turning to Catherine, Libby said with a lot more assurance than I felt, "Ai's one of our most promising students here, so if anyone can do it, she can."

With their attention on me now, I raised my hands in a shrug and said with a small, hesitant smile, "I'll give it a try."

After class, I made my way over to the nearest pay phone and called Mum. "Have you got any spare fabric?" I asked when she answered.

"Which one you want?"

"Anything that's lightweight. It can't be too heavy."

"Netting okay?"

"What color?" I asked.

"Pink. Very strong this color."

I cringed inwardly, vaguely recalling the hot pink netting sitting among her rolls of fabric. Netting was a scratchy nylon fabric and hard to work with at the best of times. It certainly wasn't ideal for the ambitious nature of the project I had in mind, and the bright pink would further emphasize the tackiness of the material. And yet, to complete the design I had planned, I would need at least a full roll of fabric, which I couldn't afford to buy.

"I make delivery to city later," Mum said. She must have sensed my hesitation because she added, "Ai, you want this one?"

"Yes, I do."

"I take to you then."

"Thanks, Mum."

• • •

I was inspecting the roll of hot pink netting while Mum surveyed my cluttered room, clucking her disapproval. Her eyes roamed from the tired mannequin draped with a peach-colored chiffon to the pictures torn from fashion magazines and fabric swatches stuck haphazardly wall-to-wall. A sad-looking single bed was tucked into one corner, dressed in the same worn Winnie-the-Pooh bedspread I'd had since childhood. When I was considering this place, the landlord offered me a choice between a cupboard-sized room in the main house or the converted garage out back. Needing the space, I chose the latter. It had a solid workbench and several shelves where I could store rolls of brown butcher's paper and plastic containers filled with assorted beads, sequins, and buttons. It had the added benefit of being only a short bus ride away from my campus and I was offered a small discount if I paid in cash. Although it only had a toilet and sink, I was free to shower and do my cooking and laundry in the main house. My flatmates who lived there were quiet and studious, and days often passed before I ran into anyone. They were pleasant enough, with the exception of Beth, an English major with mousy brown hair and a dense smattering of freckles across her nose and cheeks. She was highly religious and often asked me for old books that she'd package and send to missionaries in East Timor. She must have known about the flowerpot under which I'd tuck my key, because once I came home stunned to find my room tidy when it had been left in a state of disarray as I rushed out that morning for an early class. In the center of my immaculately made-up bed was placed—with obvious deliberation—a pack of condoms that I had kept in the top drawer of my bedside table. When I confronted her about entering my room without permission, she was nonplussed. "We ran out of milk and I thought there might be a spare carton in your minifridge. I didn't think you'd mind." From then on, I made sure to carry my key with me.

"You have money?" Mum asked, reeling me back into the present.

I didn't want to tell her there was never enough money, so I nodded.

"Why look too skinny? You not eating?"

Financially, I got through my first year of college by the skin of my teeth. I hadn't anticipated how much everything would cost. At the tapas bar where I waitressed, I earned barely enough to cover the constant flood of supplies that demanded replenishment for my course: sticks of lead to feed my mechanical pencil, art diaries, paints, pencils, fabric, volatile sawblades prone to snapping that cost over a dollar each. Too many times to count, I had to make the hard choice between a meal or a sheet of Perspex. This did not go unnoticed by my classmates; once I shook out a couple of Tic Tacs from the box and someone remarked, "Oh, look, Ai's having her lunch." But somehow I got through with the aid of government subsidies along with the money I'd saved working at Pepe's over the summer before college, doing the odd delivery when we were short-staffed. I made sure to let everyone know I would be happy to cover their shifts, even at short notice. Once I overheard a conversation between two of my coworkers. One girl said, "My dad doesn't want me to do the late shift anymore because it's just me and the manager here and it's only a matter of time before there's a stickup."

The other girl had responded, "Just ask Ai to do it: she's desperate for anything."

At night I would double-check the back door, and the times I had to take out the trash on my own I'd do so with a set of keys tucked between my fingers. One week a delivery driver returned battered and bruised. Someone had hit him with a baseball bat before snatching the pouch around his waist that drivers used to carry change.

"Dude, you should go the hospital," the manager said. Then, sending a pointed look my way, he added, "No more deliveries for you, Ai. It's too dangerous for a girl."

After a while we fell back into complacency, and I took on the risk for the hourly rate and tips.

By orientation week I had thousands saved up and, buzzing with naïve optimism, dived headfirst into my new life, vowing never to return to Whitlam. Mum resisted the idea of me moving out, and I didn't want to prove her right. Now she was gesturing at a dirty mug, soup stains congealed along the rim. Shaking her head, she said, "Maybe better you come home."

"I'll think about it," I said, as a way to placate her. In my mind I was adamant that I would never return to Whitlam.

Patting her pocket, she said, " Daddy give you tea. This one, he say you like."

One of the small comforts from home was Dad's parting gift, his precious Yixing clay teapot, which was known to enhance the flavor of tea, having seasoned over many years. I brightened at this unexpected luxury, tucking my nose into the paper packet and breathing in the fragrant green pearls of rolled-up leaves from the high mountains of Taiwan. Tucking it away safely inside my Yixing pot, I decided to make a start on the project. "Let's try out a sample of netting."

We went to work, measuring and cutting out strips of netting. The color was garish, almost fluorescent, reminding me of a fly screen. It wouldn't behave the way I wanted.

Pointing to the iron, Mum urged, "Try this one."

We played around with the settings and figured it worked best on a high heat with a sheet of cheesecloth placed in between to keep the nylon from scorching. It was extremely finicky, with both of us holding down each fold and then immediately stitching them into place. There were six folds in one piece alone, and this step would have to be repeated hundreds of times.

Soon we had a few pieces ready and I assembled them just like the paper versions, inserting each triangular module into the other and then stitching it in place. I was pleased to see how well it worked, but when I showed Mum the sketch of the ball gown I planned to make, she blanched. "Ai, long time to make."

"I don't need to hand it in until July. Don't worry."

"You do this one for school?"

"Yes," I lied, not wanting to worry her.

From her expression, I could tell she wasn't convinced. "Mum busy now. Can't help Ai with this one. You do by self. Okay?"

"That's okay. I can do it myself," I insisted.

Tutting, she repeated, "Long time to make."

• • •

As always, Mum was right. By the following week I had barely made any progress. I underestimated the workload, finding that even after hours of folding, crimping, and sewing I only had a handful of the triangular modules to show for it. It was far easier with an extra pair of hands, like the night Mum helped out. On my own, I had to work using my feet to position the netting as I sewed it into place. My back hurt from the ironing, so I borrowed a steamer from my lecturer Libby. After the first session, I was disheartened to discover that it not only made the task more difficult but the chemical smell made me ill. So I went back to the convoluted method I had established from the beginning.

One night I was sitting on my floor, working away. I had just gotten the netting in place, ready to sew, when I was startled by a knock on my door. My foot lifted and the netting escaped. I dissolved into a flood of tears, kicking at the netting before getting up to answer my door. It was Beth, the last person I wanted to see.

"Hey, Ai. I'm just about to send a package off. Do you have any old books you can spare?" She stopped when she saw my face. "Hey, why are you crying?"

"This fucking project," I said through gritted teeth, then covered my mouth with my hands. "Oops, sorry."

She looked past me into the mess of nylon netting on my floor. "Do you need help?"

• • •

Beth became something of a substitute for Mum. Not only was she an extra pair of hands, for which I was immensely grateful, but she fussed over things like the state of my room and how much sleep I had been getting. Even though she was only a few years older than me, she had the mannerisms of a woman in her forties, matter-of-fact and opinionated. She was the oldest of seven siblings, which could explain her overtly bossy nature. Her father was an analyst, her mother an architect. She always spoke about them with disdain. "They're always moaning about putting us kids through private school, yet they manage to find the money to keep up a country club membership they never use."

Beth was insatiably curious, asking me pointed questions that were direct and at times lacking in sensitivity. She was brutally honest, and I could see how this could rub people the wrong way. Contrary to these odd character traits, she was also kind and generous, often appearing at my door with plates of sandwiches stuffed with pot chicken and gravy.

Once, she was tidying up my room in her usual bullish way, when she came across my stash of oolong. Thinking it was weed, she dropped it, recoiling with horror. Laughing, I brewed us a pot of tea, Gong Fu–style, in an informal ceremony. She watched, fascinated.

"What's that?" she asked, pointing to a scaly, toadlike figurine which I had just drenched in tea.

"That's my tea pet," I answered.

Crinkling her nose, she asked, "What's a tea pet?"

"You're not meant to drink the first infusion of tea. The purpose is to heat the teapot and unfurl the leaves. So you use that excess tea to 'feed' your tea pet. It's meant to bring you luck."

"Are you superstitious?"

"If you're talking about black cats and things, yeah, a little."

"Is that the reason why you're always touching your necklace?" She pointed at the silver magpie hanging around my neck. "It's almost like you keep checking that it's still there, but it can't be that valuable."

"It's not, but it's very special to me. It was a gift from my boyfriend at the time."

"Are you still in love with him?"

Quietly, I said, "He passed away back when I was still at school."

Without missing a beat, she asked, "How did he die?"

"It was a Jet Ski accident. I lost my best friend, Brigitte, the same way." I launched into a quick retelling of that day, bracing myself for the emotional toll it always took on me. But I never missed an opportunity to tell this story, for a chance to highlight the terrible injustice Bowie and Brigitte had suffered.

When I was done, Beth said in her usual, straightforward way, "And those two guys got away with it? That's wrong. If it had been up to me, I would have banged them up in prison."

The following day, my rent was due, so I went to get cash from a nearby ATM. On my way there, I walked by Tessuto, a boutique that sold quality fabrics. On impulse, I stepped into the cool, air-conditioned store, where rolls of fabric were displayed horizontally on wrought-iron racks. I walked along the neat rows of racks, gazing in awe at the exquisite lace, pashmina wool, and mulberry silk. My mind was spinning with all the things I could create with them. Then my eyes landed on a roll of French tulle in dove gray. I reached out to touch its feathery-soft texture, captivated by the sheer beauty of the fabric, picturing the potential of the ball gown if only I could have used this instead of the netting.

I turned to see a well-dressed woman watching me from behind the counter, a sudden forced smile appearing on her face. "Can I help you?"

"How much is this?" I asked

In a blunt tone, she said, "Seventy-five per yard." She must have seen the look on my face because she added, "It's a hundred percent silk."

I calculated the amount I would need in relation to the cost and at once felt deflated.

"Would you like me to cut you a yard?"

I shook my head no before hurrying out of the store.

By April the gown was taking shape, thanks to Beth's assistance. But she had to vacate her room due to the damage caused by a freak hailstorm that had come out of nowhere, hitting isolated areas on the outskirts of the city. Hailstones the size of cricket balls rained down at random, causing severe damage to some buildings and sparing others. In affluent suburbs like Paddington, luxury cars were crushed beyond repair and boutique windows smashed, the pavements scattered with broken glass. Among the debris of leaves and branches lay the broken bodies of dead birds. Our college library had its roof caved in, damaging equipment and wiping away records of overdue fines. Like many others, I hadn't been initially warned about the exorbitant fees that were incurred each day a book was brought back late. At a dollar per day, the rate was ten times what I was used to, and I'd unknowingly racked up an eye-watering debt, one which had still been outstanding until the storm hit.

Overnight, the cityscape turned into a sea of tarpaulins as roofing companies struggled to keep up with the unprecedented demand. I happened to be visiting Whitlam on the night of the storm and had missed the whole thing.

Now Beth was living back at home with her parents, all the way out in Avalon Beach. Before she left, she gave me a comprehensive list of instructions detailing which cleaning products worked best and the importance of getting enough vitamin D, since my room lacked a window. She signed off with a verse from the Bible: *Now to him who is able to do immeasurably more than all we ask or imagine, according to his power that is at work within us . . .* Ephesians 3:20. As I read the verse, I felt a strange connection to the words.

Back on campus, I had just picked up a coffee in the main square and was heading to the computer room to work on a CAD project. Finding a free Mac G4, I settled in, loading up the software and inserting my Zip disk. I spent some time setting up the file, then clicked together complex shapes, zooming in to make sure the lines were connected. In our first year, our lecturer got us to join two lines, which seemed like a deceptively simple task. Upon zooming in, we all realized with a collective gasp that the lines weren't attached. Then we were taught how to link them using a simple command. The software could be used to design virtually anything, both in 2D and 3D. I enjoyed working in 3D the most, but my preference was only marginal.

My current project was to create a toy car. I'd sketched out a rough design for a Jeep, Barbie Pink and decorated with sticker motifs. I was about a quarter way through, drawing in the axles, when I decided to take a break. Clicking out of CAD, I logged onto my email. As usual, I scanned my inbox hoping to see a message from Tin. As my eyes waded through the list of junk and college-related news, I felt an emptiness in the pit of my stomach.

After Sying's exhibition, I'd had only had a few precious days to spend with Tin. Our time was cut short when Mum had to deliver a wedding dress to Canberra and wanted company on the four-hour-long drive. The plan was to stay overnight with some distant relatives, but then we came down with a terrible stomach bug and our visit ended up stretching out for almost a week. By the time I got back, Tin had already left for Brisbane and I had missed my chance to say a proper goodbye. Over that summer, we spoke on the phone, racking up interstate bills we couldn't afford, making plans for when he returned to Sydney. When Tin told me they were staying with Lucille indefinitely, I was gutted. At the same time, I was relieved that Tri would remain a safe distance from her abusive father.

Gradually, my conversations with Tin grew less frequent

when I moved to the city and was difficult to reach. We became entrenched in our separate lives, exchanging the occasional email. In the end, the distance wore us down and we lost touch altogether.

Thinking of all this now, I searched for the last email he'd sent me. The time stamp read 3:45 p.m. on July 17, 1998. Almost a year had passed since then.

I keep thinking about what you said on the phone last night, about seeing other people, and I guess there's someone you already have in mind. To be honest, I've been expecting it for a while. And I'm okay with it, Ai— you don't owe me anything. You have a lot going on and you need to focus on that. I don't think you have room for me in your life right now and I get it. I could blame the distance between us, but that's only circumstantial. It's okay to just not be ready.

I know you want to stay friends and part of me thinks that I'd rather have that than nothing at all. But I don't think I can be friends, Ai. Not with you. But that doesn't mean I won't be here when you need me. I just can't do all that day-to-day-friend stuff knowing what you are to me, what you will always be to me. I'm not exactly sure who I am to you but that's something you need to figure out on your own.

For what must be the hundredth time, I clicked the reply button and then clicked out again. As I stared blankly at the screen,

I thought of the way our lives had taken shape, independent of each other. I thought of the few times something had sparked with someone else, the thrill of new beginnings. But nothing had ever come close to the connection I shared with Tin. Still, it was a period in my life when I felt insatiable, wanting everything I could have and all the things I couldn't. Wishing I could live my life many times over and choose a different path each time. I didn't know to explain that feeling to Tin without making more of a mess than I already had.

I sighed, making a conscious effort to leave the past where it was. Refreshing my screen, I spotted a new email from Aysum with the subject line "Call me." It seemed important, so I packed up my things and made my way down the corridor to the pay phone, punching in her number.

"Why are you so hard to get a hold off?" she asked.

"I did give you the number for the main house."

"There's no point if you're never there. I called five times and some guy named Ben said you weren't home and to call back later. Did he pass on my message?"

"Nope, he didn't mention anything to me."

"That damn landline doesn't even have an answering machine."

"What's so important anyway?"

"My cousin Ahmed runs a fabric cutting business that services a bunch of fashion labels. Anyway, he desperately needs someone to draw up patterns and I thought you'd be perfect. Are you looking for a job?"

"Ah . . . ," I said, trailing off. I should be saying no, since I was falling so far behind in my subjects, but then my mind turned reflexively to that luscious French tulle.

Aysum prompted, "So, are you interested in the job?"

"Yes, I am."

Ahmed's factory was situated in an industrial zone just outside the city and a short walk from the train station. He was there to greet me outside in the parking lot with a warm, welcoming smile. "Find this place okay?" he asked.

"No problems at all."

He took me through the cutting floor with its hum of machinery and intermittent chatter from the busy workers. A woman paused to give me a curious look, then called out to Ahmed, "Is that the new girl, boss?" to which he responded with a thumbs-up. I waved an awkward hello and got a friendly smile back.

Compared to most cutting houses I'd seen, this one was particularly neat and orderly, with piles of fabric lined symmetrically on the large rows of cutting benches, offcuts neatly set to one side. "I run a tight ship," said Ahmed proudly as he led me up a flight of stairs to the office area, where there was a large, open-plan space with a handful of desks and a reception area where a girl had just answered a ringing phone. The windows in the room took up the length of an entire wall, stretching from floor to ceiling, saturating the place in sunlight. In the center was a kitchenette where someone was making a coffee, the aroma rich and inviting.

"Over here, Ai," said Ahmed, gesturing to a desk in the far

corner of the room, tucked beside a floor-to-ceiling shelf stacked with boxes. Pulling out chairs, he sat me down. "My usual girl's still on maternity leave and won't be back for six weeks," he said, explaining the nature of the role. "I have a freelancer on, but I've got some big jobs coming in and need someone to work weekends. Are you okay with that?" He was a large teddy bear of a guy with rosy cheeks and a cheery, playful disposition. Aysum said he was the loveliest person she knew and I could see why.

"Weekends are perfect," I said, eyes roaming over the desk near where I was sitting. I figured it must belong to Ahmed's regular employee, the wall above the PC laptop plastered with pictures torn from magazines similar to the ones stuck up in my room. Ahmed caught me looking at the wall and said, "Kate, our regular girl, runs a small fashion label." He got out of his chair and strolled over to the shelves adjacent to the desk. Reaching into a box, he pulled out a pair of blue denim cutoffs adorned with white, red, and green beading on the pockets in a kaleidoscopic pattern of dollar signs. "Three hundred bucks they retail for." He shook his head at the exorbitant price tag. "But everything is hand-stitched."

"Oh, I love them," I gushed when he handed me the shorts. I was impressed with Kate's attention to detail, from the label embroidered with her brand name, Money for Jam, to the swing tags fixed to the shorts with rivets and candy-cane string. Fascinated, I turned a pocket inside out and on the insert was a print of Scrooge McDuck counting golds coins. "Gosh, I would kill for a pair of these." Reluctantly, I handed them back.

"I'll tell Kate you said that; she'll be thrilled. She's been picked up by a handful of boutiques, but she started as a fashion student, just like you." Then, settling back into the chair across from me, he said, "Now, Ai, Aysum thinks you're the bee's knees, so the only question I really need to ask is: Do you know CAD?"

"Sure do. We learned it back in first year."

"Did you pass?"

"Top of the class."

"Okay, you're hired, then."

As he was filling in the forms, he asked for a contact number.

"Oh, I do have a number, but it's in the main house, which makes it tricky . . ." I explained my living situation to him.

He looked at me, aghast. "You're living in a garage?"

"Well, it's a converted garage and only temporary until I find something else."

"And you don't have a mobile phone? Ai, we're practically in the twenty-first century." Shaking his head, he said, "You wait here."

After a few minutes he came back with a clamshell flip phone. "It's brand-new," he said, handing it to me. "Bought it for my wife but she won't touch it. Thinks technology is the work of the devil."

I looked at the phone in my hand. It was the color of red wine, with diamantés bordering the front window. "I can't take this," I said.

"Don't worry, I'm not going to dock your pay or anything. It's just sitting in my drawer, collecting dust, so you might as well put it to good use."

"That's really generous," I said, still hesitant.

"It's going to change your life, Ai."

I went to my bank with proof of my new employment and applied for a personal loan. The teller went through my options, which I weighed up before making a decision. "The interest is high, which does add up if you don't keep up with the repayments," she warned.

"I'll be fine," I said, with a lot more confidence than I felt.

When I left the bank, I marched a few doors down to Tessuto before I could change my mind. Inside, the same lady was behind the counter. "Oh, it's you again."

My eyes scanned the racks of fabric, but I couldn't find the French tulle. Panic rose in my chest. Turning back to the lady, I said, "The French tulle in the dove gray—do you still have it?"

She stared at me for a moment as I held my breath.

"The French tulle? I believe it's in the storeroom out back. Would you like me to cut a yard for you?"

"I'll take the entire roll, thanks."

Thirteen

MUM EXAMINED THE completed ball gown on my mannequin, which I had earlier dressed for her visit. She seemed surprised I'd completed it with plenty of time to spare. I told her about the unexpected assistance I had received from my previous flatmate and she nodded knowingly. "That lucky she help. Mum say it take long time. This one finish so you study now. Okay?"

I nodded, thinking of the French tulle I'd hidden away under my bed, not wanting to worry her. I still hadn't decided if I would start over and make a new ball gown. At this point I could still sell the tulle or keep it for another project. The task of completing a new ball gown seemed insurmountable to me, like spinning straw into gold—impossible without the intervention of magic. But I had already had a miracle the first time around, thanks to Beth. Thinking of her now, I glanced at the quote she had left, which I'd stuck to my wall: *Now to him who is able to do immeasurably more than all we ask or imagine, according to his power that is at work within us* . . . Ephesians 3:20

As Mum further scrutinized the gown, she seemed to be

thinking about something. "Ai, you know we go to Canberra before? When finish your school?"

I nodded, recalling the ill-fated trip to deliver the wedding gown. "Yes, I remember that trip," I said. "What about it?"

Pointing at the netting she said, "This one for that."

"You mean the wedding dress we delivered? But it was French tulle, remember?"

"She buy this one first. Then she no want," Mum explained.

"Oh," I said. "So she bought the netting at first then decided to swap it out for the tulle?"

Mum nodded. "Big difference, netting and tulle. Big difference, you know?"

"Big difference," I repeated under my breath.

It was a striking coincidence, the bride moving from the netting to the tulle, and I wondered if there was some deeper meaning to it. My eyes shifted involuntarily to the space under my bed.

"Why you looking that?" Mum asked, narrowing her eyes. She made a move toward my bed and in a panic I stepped forward, blocking her path. But then we were interrupted by a knock on the door. When I opened it, there stood Yan, a slightly peeved look on his face. "How much longer are you guys going to be? Dad's been waiting in the car for ages."

It was rare for Dad to make a trip out to the city, but he'd won a crossword competition run by the Chinese newspaper *Sing Tao Daily*. We were going to collect his winnings from their office in Chinatown and then he wanted to treat us to a yum cha lunch.

At a loud, bustling eatery, Dad was surreptitiously pouring us each a cup of tea from a thermos that he'd brought from home, which was against restaurant rules. "Taste better, this one," he rationalized. In the jungles of Cambodia, while on the verge of starvation, he'd promised himself that if by some miracle he escaped the clutches of the Khmer Rouge, he would never again drink bad tea.

We all chatted away as cart after cart rattled to a stop at our table and we feasted our eyes on their delicious offerings: bamboo baskets filled with steaming dumplings, sticky rice wrapped in banana leaves, cheong fun, char siu bao, and custard egg tarts. I couldn't remember the last time I'd stuffed myself like this.

Rolling his eyes at me, Yan said, "God, sis, when was the last time you ate?"

"Easy for you to say, moneybags," I retorted. Yan, who was now working at a brokerage firm, chose to live at home, funneling the money he would have spent on rent toward a deposit for a house.

"Eating too fast, Ai. Make tummy hurt." Mum chastised me as I went to grab a char siu bao before finishing the one already in my hand. I grinned, rubbing my belly and making exaggerated "Mmmm" sounds, much to my family's consternation. When the waitress asked if anyone wanted a container for leftovers, I put my hand up.

The factory was empty on weekends, when I'd walk quickly past the cutting floor with its stilled machinery and ghostly silence, making my way upstairs into the office, where the sunlight streaming through the windows made it feel less lonely. Most days, I was the only one there. Sometimes Ahmed dropped by to pick up a set of keys left behind or the odd jacket. Often his little girl would be attached to his hip, a toddler named Samira with glossy, ebony locks and wide, curious eyes. While he was there, we'd banter a little and then he'd say something philosophical such as, "You know, Ai, in this world there are more glasses than there are eyes."

I finally met Kate midway through my contract when she came in to check on a pattern I was drawing up for a fussy client. She was tall and stylish, shoulder-length honey-blond hair worn in a blunt cut, tight skinny jeans tucked into ankle boots with gold studs. It was hard to believe she'd recently had a baby as she strutted around in her fitted outfits, looking footloose and fancy-free. We immediately struck up a rapport and she happily showed me more of her designs, which I found inspiring. "Where did you get these buttons?" I asked as I tugged on one of her fine bolero jackets, its amber-colored buttons shimmering iridescently as though lit from within.

"Where I get all my buttons," she answered, a mischievous smile playing on her lips.

"And where is that?"

With a wink she said, "I steal them from teddy bears, of course. They have such pretty eyes."

Aysum came to hang out with me one Sunday. She had recently gotten engaged to her boyfriend, Tuncay, whom she had met at a market stall where her family sold leather goods. Now she was showing off her ring, a solitaire diamond that was so large, I gasped.

"Two whole carats," she said with satisfaction. "My future husband happens to be a diamond merchant."

"Way to go," I laughed as we high-fived, our hands suspended in the air, clamped tightly together. If anyone deserved a happy ending, it was Aysum.

"I can't stop looking at it," she gushed, hands splayed and fingers wiggling so the ring shimmered like a disco ball. "On my way here, it caught the sun and blinded me for a second. Damn thing almost got me into a car wreck."

She brought a plastic container filled with her mum's vine leaves. "Oh, God, I've missed these," I moaned, popping one in my mouth.

Then she watched as I worked the software, connecting lines with quick clicks of my mouse, adding pleats and darts where they were required.

"Sheesh, that looks really complicated."

"I'm Asian; we're naturally good at this stuff."

She laughed. "Hey, I heard you've got an actual phone now."

I sighed happily. "Your cousin is an angel, just like you said." I took out my shiny new phone, to which I'd grown very attached, showing her all the features. "So when you click this, the screen turns into a mirror, in case you need to touch up your lipstick. You can text a number and it sends your horoscope, and, oh, there's even a program that keeps track of your period."

Aysum looked me up and down. "Are you even getting your period? You look really skinny."

"Why does everyone keep saying that?"

"Because it's true. You're all skin and bones and your hair looks like it's falling out."

"Well, I've learned the hard way that food requires either huge amounts of energy or money. Both things I'm always short on. I never thought about it when I was at home because Mum took care of all that. It's been a real mission to keep myself fed."

Aysum must have mentioned our conversation to Ahmed, because after that day I would find meals in the communal kitchen stuck with Post-it Notes, my name scrawled beside a bracket-and-semicolon smiley face. There were plates of garlic pita bread, bowls of pilaf and tomato salad, plastic containers filled with hummus, falafel, olives, and baklava. I remembered that conversation years ago in chem class when Brigitte talked about capturing instances of parental love. When I was in that small kitchenette, knowing Ahmed had gone out of his way to make sure I didn't go hungry that day, I thought about that a lot.

As the weeks wore on, I knew my contract was coming to an end. I dreaded the idea of this and tried not to count down the days because I loved my job and the hours suited me perfectly. Twelve days altogether I had spent here, spread over six week-ends, but, thanks to Ahmed, this place had felt a little like home.

"You're the best boss ever," I said truthfully when the time came to pack up my desk.

Squeezing my arm, he said, "You're a pretty good employee, yourself. Couldn't have made it through these weeks without you."

I grinned. "If you ever need my help again . . . well, you've got my number."

Fourteen

BY THE SECOND week of May, just as the first term was coming to an end, the dean called me into his office.

"As you're probably well aware, Ai, your grades are slipping. It's a dramatic change from your marks last year, when you were topping most of your classes. Is everything okay?"

I lowered my eyes, feeling deeply ashamed. Until now, I had managed to delude myself that there was time to catch up on all my work. But the crushing weight of reality was fast bearing down on me. "Everything's fine; I just got really caught up in the lace project, that's all."

"Libby mentioned that to me. I believe it's been completed?"

I settled on a half-truth: "Almost."

"Good. I've heard great things about your gown, but it's a personal project that doesn't count toward your credits. And if you don't make them up soon, you might want to consider summer school."

"That's always an option," I said, even though I had been planning to work the following summer in a meatpacking plant just outside of Whitlam. Despite the grueling nature of the job,

I heard it paid well and they were always keen to take on new workers. I couldn't afford another year living in the city otherwise.

"You may prove me wrong, of course," the dean said. "If anyone can do it, Ai, it'll be you."

I was touched by the dean's faith in me, but even he wasn't fully aware of how far behind I really was. The entire semester was dedicated to constructing the ball gown, like a whirlpool that dragged everything into its center. The warning bells Mum had sounded at the start of the project were getting louder by the minute. I went to visit Admin to check my options for summer school.

"I'm going to fail Measured Drawing for sure," I said in a hushed voice to Linda, who was manning the counter and assessing my current situation on the college computer. She was everyone's favorite, helpful and efficient, and I was glad she was the one assisting me today.

"Looks like the first installment of your tuition fee is still outstanding. When do you think you can pay it?"

I felt a sense of dread. "God, I completely forgot about that. I'm just stuck in this terrible cycle where I need a job to pay for things, but I can't focus on my studies while I'm working."

"Most students are in that position, Ai."

I gave her a wry smile. "Actually, most kids I know here have their parents covering everything."

"Have you thought about deferring your studies?" she asked, eyes flickering away from the screen to meet mine.

Curious, I asked, "How would that work?"

"Well, you can take a year off, but you do need a solid reason. In your case, you can claim financial hardship."

"And I can come back?"

"You can: as long as you make up the credits on your return, you'd still be on track to graduate, albeit a year later."

It was as though Linda had opened a door for me, wide and inviting, showing me a way out. Beyond the confines of the mess I had created was a pathway leading straight to the ball gown I had always envisioned. In my mind's eye I saw it blooming to life like a rare and delicate flower, the dove-gray tulle, the inconceivable lightness of it. I didn't have to hand it in until July. There was still time.

"Is it a hard process to defer? Like, do I need to consult anyone?" I asked, trying to contain the feeling of glee that was bubbling below the surface. From the moment my eyes landed on the tulle, I had barely thought of anything else.

"Not if you're over eighteen, which you are. But it's a big decision, Ai: you might want to speak with someone first, like a family member or a mentor."

I wondered if I should give Yan a call, maybe sound it out with him. But I'd already made up my mind, and instinctively I knew he would try to talk me out of it. Worse still, he might even get Mum involved, and she was already suspicious that something was up.

"Most students don't come back when they defer, you know," Linda warned, cutting into my thoughts.

"What?" I said, taken aback by her comment.

"It's weird, I know, but most students never come back."

I let out a nervous laugh. "Oh, that would never happen to me, I love it here. It's just hard at the moment to get on top of everything. But once I sort myself out, I'll be back for sure."

"Uh-huh. Yeah. They all say that."

I stumbled out of the office in a daze, feeling at once fearful and giddy. Everything I had been working toward had shifted, like a roller coaster jerked unexpectedly off the rails. I was free-falling without a safety net, with nothing but the air underneath.

Back in my room, I considered what I had done, the reckless-ness of it. The silence was deafening and I wished Beth would come striding in, scolding me for making such a rash, foolish de-cision, putting my entire future on the line. But the decision had been made, taking me down the only conceivable path. Tugging the French tulle out from under my bed, I got straight to work.

For the next month I locked myself in my room, eating pot noo-dles when I was hungry or cookies pilfered from the pantry in the main house. There was also the odd slice of pizza left out on the counter, or a lone chicken drumstick someone forgot to discard, sitting cold in the oven. If anyone noticed, they didn't say anything. I bought a sack of jasmine rice at a discount and made myself a small bowl whenever I was hungry, although I could never get the consistency right. Before I drowned my bowl of rice in soy sauce, I'd pick out the weevils with my fingers when I spotted their pale yellow bodies hiding among the sticky, bloated grains. Meals were haphazard and I treated them as a form of sustenance and nothing more. I craved Mum's dumplings and Phnom Penh noodle soup, but there was no time to hop on a train back home to Whitlam for a homecooked meal. Every hour to me was precious.

Despite the constant hunger pains, I fell into the rhythm of constructing the new ball gown and found myself engrossed in the single-mindedness of the goal. It felt almost meditative, the repetition of cutting, setting, and sewing. The silk tulle was more yielding but the workload was still immense.

I sat day after day, night after night, folding the tulle, crimping and sewing the fabric into triangular modules. My back ached and my hands kept cramping up. Still, with dogged determination, I kept going. I started talking to myself. I started talking to Brigitte, and on some late nights when I was delirious with hunger and sleep deprived, she spoke back.

You're putting way too much effort into this, Ai. Seriously, you're putting everything at stake, and for what?

I don't know.

What if you don't win?

It's not about winning.

Yes it is. With you, it's always about winning.

No it isn't.

Yes it is.

The imaginary conversation with Brigitte sparked up memories of my final year at high school when I was working just as feverishly on another project and, in a moment of madness, set the whole thing alight. When the letter from Art Express arrived, no one was more surprised than me. It never occurred to me that such a thing could be fit to exhibit. The pile of ash in an old, vintage-style suitcase showed burnt remnants of my major work in melted plastic and scorched leather—a scattering of tiny, nondescript fragments glinting gold. Hung above was a framed photograph of the suitcase when it had been entirely intact. My family came to see the display in the Art Gallery of New South Wales, their faces shining. Like me, they never imagined that such a thing was possible for people like us. Yan nudged his approval, grinning at me the whole time we were there. My dad made a rare trip into the city, his head held high as he showered me with praise. My parents stood next to my work for a photograph, their faces aglow in a way I had never seen. The emotion it roused in me was one I was desperate to experience again.

Slowly the ball gown took shape, and it was just as beautiful as I had imagined, layers and layers of tulle cascading like a multi-tiered cake, rich and decadent. I had never seen anything like it. When it was finally completed, I stood back in awe, casting a furtive glance at the pink netted gown shoved into the corner, the one Beth had helped me to construct. Although the new design was similar, there was no question the two garments were worlds apart. One looked as though it belonged in a tacky costume shop, the other on the catwalks of Milan. I took a deep breath, allowing my hand to brush the silky surface of the dove-gray tulle as it stirred lightly beneath my fingertips as though it were coming to life. Suddenly I was painfully aware of how this project had solidified a certain path for me, cementing a creative process in which I would give myself over to inspiration, throw myself at its mercy even if it meant sleepwalking into certain disaster. I didn't know what was next for me, but right now I was standing in front of the best work I had created and that was enough. I was past the point of exhaustion but it was done and I was happy. The next day I carefully packed my gown in a large box and addressed it to Catherine at the Art & Technology Centre, making sure to include my artist statement and contact number. Although I wasn't at all religious, I sent it off with a prayer.

Each day, I waited with bated breath for a call from Catherine. I had been on pins and needles from the moment I handed the package over to the courier, biting my nails, waiting for my verdict. One day went by, and then two.

On the third day, her voice came through on my flip phone, breathless and full of wonder. "Oh, Ai, it is absolutely stunning, I'm speechless. We were just discussing how we'd photograph the gown and were keen to honor its *Golden Venture* roots and surprising connection to Whitlam. Would you be interested in modeling your gown for us?"

Mum tagged along with me to the photography studio, where I sat in a director's chair while being made up. In the mirror before me, our eyes met briefly before she looked away, a soft, conciliatory smile on her lips. She learned about the switch-up days earlier and had at once assaulted me with a flurry of questions I didn't want to answer. For now, though, I had a reprieve, as she was distracted by the unexpected attention the ball gown had garnered.

As I was tweezered and plucked beyond recognition, false lashes glued to the tips of my eyelids, lips lined and colored in a bright, fairy-tale red, cheeks lightly rouged and dewy, I thought of Sying and the night of the exhibition. Before the altercation with Tin, she had been on top of the world. I wondered idly about the trajectory of her life extending from that evening to now—if there had been anything else for her which compared to that experience.

Against a stark white background, a cute, trendy-looking photographer introduced himself to me as Luke. He snapped my picture, suggesting poses that could further emphasize the lusciousness of the French tulle. He said, "That's the best piece I've seen today," at which point I casually mentioned that I was the maker of the gown.

"Really? You made this?" Luke said, with a look of genuine surprise. "I thought you were just the model."

After the shoot, I changed into a T-shirt and jeans, examining myself in the mirror. I still had on a face full of makeup as I blinked at my reflection, eyelashes fluttering prettily. I grinned happily at myself. My braces had been removed a few months before and I was still getting used to seeing my teeth without them: startling white and perfectly aligned. For the first time ever, I felt comfortable in my own skin.

On the way out to meet up with Mum, I spotted Luke standing by a set of studio lights, loading a roll of film onto his camera. I felt a sudden jolt of attraction that had taken root earlier while he was photographing me. His words *I thought you were just the model* had been playing on my mind ever since he said them. I couldn't help but wonder if it was more than just a passing comment.

Heart hammering loudly in my chest, I tried to channel Brigitte and the easy confidence she had had with members of the opposite sex. Taking a deep breath, I tapped him on the shoulder. "Hey, Luke."

"Hi," Luke said, looking up from his camera.

"Um, I was just wondering if you're doing anything later?"

"Later?" His forehead creased in confusion.

"Would you like to have a coffee with me?" I blurted, then cringed inwardly.

In a dismissive tone, he said, "I'm busy, sorry."

I felt my cheeks redden, humiliated by his response. It wasn't that I couldn't handle rejection, but it was the way he had said it, as though I had insulted him by asking.

"No, I didn't mean—" I started, but it only made things worse. It was so out of my character to ask someone out like this, but all the attention and praise that day must have gone to my head. During my first year of college, I dated a couple of guys, but in those instances I was the one being pursued. Although I never felt a deep enough connection to either one of them, they did help to fill a void while it lasted. Which was never more than a few weeks.

Luke turned his attention back to the camera in his hand as I continued to stand there, not realizing our conversation was over.

He shot an odd look my way and in that moment I caught something in his expression that made me want to curl up and die.

A photograph from that shoot appeared in *Good Weekend*, the lifestyle magazine attached to *The Sydney Morning Herald*. There I was, an entire page all to myself, the headlining piece in the exhibition.

Earlier that morning I had walked to the corner store to purchase the publication. Back in my room, I sat on the empty floor with its threadbare carpet and dirty walls, staring at myself as though peering through the Looking Glass. In the picture, I was facing away from the camera, bow-shaped lips turned down, eyes closed as though deep in reverie. It appeared as though I had been possessed by the moody temperament of the gown, its dove-gray hue sucking away all color from its surroundings. My makeup seemed pared down from what I remembered that day, with the exception of my shut eyes, which, dark and feathered, felt like a precursor to something ominous, like the weight of a shadow falling.

On the opening night of the *Modern Lace* exhibition, Mum and Yan came to support me, wearing their best clothes, trying not to look out of place. Beth showed up, looking as stern and serious as I remember. "This is a very different dress to the one I was helping you with, Ai."

I grinned at her. "I know."

"Although it is by far the loveliest piece here. I think you might have a shot at winning."

"Oh, I don't know," I laughed.

Mum and Beth hit it off right away, their conversation robust and animated, with Yan acting as translator. They bonded over their shared concerns about my living habits and ability to take adequate care of myself. Their conversation then moved on to the other entries, at which point I gladly joined in. There was a minidress made with the pull tabs from soda cans, an intricate blouse constructed entirely of buttons, and work by a bevy of skilled artisans who spun magic with their bobbins and pins.

Several people came up to congratulate me for my piece. My lecturer Libby gushed, "Did you see the feature in *Good Weekend*? I passed it around the table at a dinner party and made sure everyone knew you were my student."

When it came time to announce the winners, I stood with Mum, Yan, and Beth, a fluted champagne glass in one hand, the other fingering the sharp edges of the silver magpie hanging around my neck. The judge was an industry heavyweight; everyone knew who she was even before she introduced herself. After a dramatic pause, she called out the name of the runner-up and then, in a loud, resounding voice, announced the winner. There was clapping and cheering as I stood there frozen, stunned it was all over. Then it all came crashing down on me: the debt I had gotten myself into, the way I had gambled my entire future on this project without once considering the grim reality that it wasn't worth it. Even if I had won, it wouldn't have been worth it. All that time, all that money, only to have my life veer in a direction over which I was no longer in control. I was staring at the champagne flute in my hand. My eyes were seeing my hand right there, holding the glass, but for some strange reason I couldn't feel any sensation, no pressure against my thumb or fingers to assure me I was actually holding the glass. My hand shook, then loosened involuntarily. The glass slipped out of my grasp, smashing onto the ground, sending a tiny shock wave through the crowd. Out of the corner of my eye, I registered a waiter hurrying over with a dustpan and broom. And then I discovered to my horror I could no longer breathe. I sucked at the air but it was so dense, I might as well have been underwater. *I'm dying*, I thought. Then the room started spinning and everything faded to black.

Fifteen

I WAS GIVEN a few days' grace before the rapid-fire questions came from Mum, harsh and relentless, wearing me down. In my vulnerable state, there was no choice but to divulge the truth, which previously I had gone to great lengths to conceal. Then it all came out, one awful revelation after another. I had deferred my studies and taken out a loan to purchase the French tulle, the high interest trapping me in a cycle of debt that I didn't have a hope of repaying.

My family banded together around me, tackling each problem one at a time. Yan dug into his savings to pay off my debt with the understanding I would replenish those funds as soon as I was able. He also paid off the lease on my room, which was only a few weeks away from renewal; the removal of what few possessions I had stored there took one measly car trip. As for my studies, I would pick up where I had left off the following year. This way I could spend the time until then working, building myself back up financially to where I once had been. Linda from Admin had said that most students who deferred never returned. At the time it seemed preposterous that it could happen to me. Now I wasn't so sure. Despite everything being squared off, there was a heaviness I just couldn't shake. I didn't know what was wrong with me, only that it had something to do with being back in my room, stacked almost ceiling-high with boxes of my old possessions and rolls of Mum's fabrics moved up from the garage, a sore reminder of her simple bridal shop dream that had never transpired. My own life echoed the same sentiment of wasted potential as I drifted into a kind of limbo.

Most days I found it hard to get out of bed. Between long periods of fitful sleep, I researched my symptoms on the family computer, which only served to confuse me further. Was I having a nervous breakdown, or was it an anxiety disorder? Was it burn-out, malnutrition, or Chronic Fatigue Syndrome? Whatever it was, it seemed the only antidote was time.

One day I was riffling through the bottom drawer of my tallboy when I discovered a stack of my old journals. The urge to write came back to me like muscle memory, strong and visceral. I began composing poem after poem, in a fanatical yet methodical way. They began as long-winded, self-indulgent vestiges exploring my identity, and then in an organic arch they grew into love poems. As I condensed the poems, their intensity grew. It occurred to me with every stroke of my pen that writing was an act of self-love. Mum chastised me for my idleness. Yan kept niggling me about my employment status, understandably anxious about the risk he'd taken on my behalf. But in a strange way Dad seemed to understand what I was going through, bringing me cups of bitter tea and motivational quotes scrawled on scraps of paper, painstakingly translated using a Chinese-to-English dictionary.

Despite my family's reservations, I was possessed with an inexplicable sense that this was what I had to do and that it would all make sense to me someday. I must have spent months this way, cocooned in a haze of self-pity and regret, senselessly writing poem after poem. The Moon Festival came around, reminding me spring was now here and I had barely left my room since moving back. Mum tried to lure me out with pretty paper lanterns and an array of moon cakes filled with red bean paste, salted egg yolk, and mixed nuts. You could only get them during the month of September, a sweet, uniquely dense dessert stamped with intricate, swirling designs bearing messages of luck and prosperity. Coinciding with the period when the moon was at its biggest and brightest, it was a time to embrace the joy of family and togetherness, yet I had never felt more detached from everyone, including myself.

Each day, Dad tore a page from the graphic calendar that was affixed to the wall in our living room, marking the end of another day. The date printed up large and bold in grass green was bordered by goddesses and mythical creatures, hexagrams depicting forecasts from the I Ching. Every night, I would listen for the tearing of another page, knowing another day had been discarded and I had slept most of it away. On television, there were news stories about the world ending, hysteria over Y2K, talk of nuclear bombs launching themselves, planes falling out of the sky as soon as the clock struck twelve on the last day of the year. None of which transpired. And still I barely left my room.

The Lunar New Year arrived, welcoming in the Year of the Dragon with firecrackers and merriment, signaling for me the end of my college dream. Friends and distant relatives came by, cheerfully asking after me as I hid in my room, ashamed of my present situation. They left red envelopes for me, which I passed on to Yan. It wasn't much, but it was something. Mum, who had grown increasingly worried about my inertia, my unwillingness to move forward, tried to coax me back to my former industrious self by cooking all my favorite comfort foods, but even then I couldn't muster up an appetite.

I continued in this fugue-like state for months, believing it would be this way for the rest of my life, until late one afternoon, in the midst of a long nap, I was gripped by a dream so vivid that it felt indistinguishable from reality. In this dream I was an omnipresent being watching everything unfold from a distance, like in a movie. It was late at night when Lucille called Brigitte to let her know she was stuck in the middle of nowhere, her car veering off the road after she'd blown a tire. The weather was torrential, yet Brigitte dutifully got in her car and set out into the night, headlights on high beam, windshield wipers furiously batting away the downpour. She kept getting lost, taking the wrong turns over and over, winding up in dead ends. Just when she was about to give up, she saw Lucille's car parked ahead by the side of the road. Pulling up, she got out of her car and was immediately drenched by the rain. She threw up her hands at

Lucille as though to say, *How did you get yourself into this situation?* They began bellowing at each other in French, their frantic voices interrupted by the crash of a thunderclap, long silky locks tousled by the howling wind, holding on to each other as though they were on a ship about to capsize. I couldn't understand what they were yelling to one another over the storm but I sensed an urgency in what they were trying to communicate. Then Lucille cried loudly in English, "Tell Ai what you've just told me." Brigitte turned to me, hair whipping around her face, lips slightly parted, eyes looking intently into mine. Eerily, everything grew quiet as she addressed me in a voice that was lucid and affecting, "You've been asleep for a long time, Ai. But it's time to wake up."

My eyes fluttered open to the sun setting outside my window, a feeling of calm and well-being settling over me. For the first time in months, I felt fully rested. The old, familiar noises of home seeped through the walls of my bedroom, the television blaring a Coca-Cola commercial, the clatter of a teacup, kids playing downstairs, one yelling their indignation. Suddenly I felt like a child again, curled up in my bed, warm and safe. The phone rang in the hallway, followed by gentle footsteps padding by. After a few moments, Mum called, "Ai, telephone for you."

When I answered the phone, it took a few moments for me to register that it was Lucille on the other end. In a daze, I said, "I just had a dream about you and Brigitte. It felt so real." I launched into the details of the dream, describing it as accurately as I could remember. When I was done, I was alarmed to hear Lucille quietly crying on the other end.

"I'm sorry. It was only a dream. I didn't mean to upset you."

"No . . . no, you didn't upset me. I'm crying because last night I found myself stranded in the middle of nowhere with a flat tire."

"Are you serious?" Goose bumps rose all along my arms.

"As I was waiting for roadside assistance, you suddenly popped into my mind. I've been thinking about you all day long, wondering what you're up to. How have you been, sweetheart?"

"I've been going through some heavy stuff," I admitted, giving her a brief recap of my year, detailing the *Modern Lace* exhibition, how constructing the ball gowns had spiraled into a meltdown, forcing me to quit my studies and move back to Whitlam.

"I'm glad I called, then," said Lucille. "I think, in a way, Brigitte wanted me to check up on you."

I felt myself dissolving into tears. "I think I really needed to hear from you today."

We spoke for a long time about Brigitte, our joint recollections adding new and surprising insights to long-established memories. I regaled her with stories of the night we stopped for dinner at a restaurant in Chinatown. On impulse we ordered an entire lobster, neither of us being sure how much money was in our accounts. When it came time to pay, we held our breaths as we took turns at the counter, praying one of our cards would go through. Or the time we went to get Lucille a Mother's Day gift and ended up spending all our money on matching friendship bracelets sold to us outside a cinema complex by a dubious man in a trench coat. Scrambling for a gift, we spent the next few hours feverishly constructing a photo frame out of twigs and leaves collected at a park nearby. I spoke about that day on our way back home from school when we took a shortcut by going through a patch of woods. To our delight, we stumbled on a wild blackberry shrub, its branches abundant with fruit. Delighted, we'd dropped our schoolbags, hands reaching eagerly, only to be scratched up by the thorns as we gorged ourselves on the sweet, ripe berries, our mouths stained an ugly purple, Brigitte laughing as we wrestled with the spiky branches, our sweaters catching and tearing. We dangled blackberries from our ears like jewelry, scooping what we could into an empty lunchbox. As Lucille and I reminisced, we laughed and cried, wading in and out of memories, talking about anything that came to the surface. Until now, I hadn't realized how necessary it was for me to talk about Brigitte in this all-embracing, nuanced way with someone who had loved her just as much as I had. Then Lucille told me she was planning a visit to Sydney in a few weeks' time. "I'd love to see you," she said.

It was well into the evening by the time I placed the phone back on the cradle. I caught sight of my parents in the lounge, talking quietly to the hum of the nightly news. Dad was sitting on the couch with Mum plonked down on the floor by his feet. He was pummeling gently at her shoulders, working out the knots that had accumulated from another long day bent over her Singer. That old, familiar act was so laden with tenderness, it brought tears to my eyes. In that moment, I loved them so much that it already felt like loss.

"Mum, Dad," I said. They turned their heads in unison, faces fixed in mild curiosity at my unanticipated appearance.

"Something wrong, Ai?" asked Mum, face creased with concern.

Taking a deep breath, I said, "Everything's fine, Mum. I know I've been sad for a long time and you've both been so worried about me. But I think I'm going to be okay now."

Sixteen

A FEW WEEKS later, Lucille and Tri were in Sydney, and I met them in an old-fashioned burger joint on the city fringes. The last time I had seen them was the night of Sying's exhibition, which felt like a lifetime ago. Tri, now twelve years of age, tanned and rosy-cheeked, had shot up in height, coming up past my shoulders, which she cheerfully pointed out to me. "I'll be taller than you in a year. Taller than Tin, even."

"How is he?" I asked, trying not to sound eager.

Lucille and Tri exchanged a look.

"He's good. Still single," Tri said, a note of mischief to her voice. "Oh, and he's coming back to Sydney soon."

I felt a lurch in my stomach. "Tin's coming back here?"

"I'm expanding my catering business," Lucille explained. "He'll be overseeing the Sydney arm."

"You must be doing really well, Lucille," I said, impressed.

"Lucille has seven employees now," said Tri, beaming with pride. "But it was really hard work in the beginning. Lucky my brother was there to help."

"You did your part, too, missy," said Lucille.

Tri giggled. "I was in charge of napkin folding. You want to see?" Securing a nearby napkin, her hands worked at lightning speed, shaping it into a swan.

I clapped my hands. "So clever!"

"I can do a French pleat, a fan, and a tulip."

Lucille beamed at her. "And she's doing really well in school."

"I won the spelling bee tournament," she blurted. "Best in State."

"That's absolutely right, you clever girl," said Lucille.

"I love my school," she gushed, rattling off a list of friends, regaling me with stories of their popcorn movie nights and slumber parties, days spent scouring the beach for seashells and patting the odd dog who was out for a walk. "You have to come and visit us, Ai. When Tin comes down to Sydney in a few months, he can bring you back up with him to Brisbane. I'll take you to my favorite ice cream shop, okay? They have every flavor you can imagine. Go on, say a flavor, the first thing that pops into your head."

"Um, bubble gum?"

"Yes—they have that!" she declared, triumphant. "They have Hubba Bubba and Goody Goody Gumdrops, which is kind of a bubble gum flavor."

"I love Goody Goody Gumdrops," I laughed. "In fact, Brigitte and I once ate an entire tub all at once, lollies and all. We got terrible bellyaches."

Tri's eyes widened. "Really? That's impressive."

Lucille smiled at me. "I remember that."

The waiter came with our burgers and milkshakes. I wolfed mine right down while Tri showed me her Tamagotchi pet she was gifted for her last birthday. "You can feed him if you want."

I watched as the tiny creature gobbled down the pixel of food offered, feeling an immediate affinity with him. My appetite had come back over the last few weeks, much to Mum's relief. As I was munching on the last of my fries, Lucille said to me, "I'm planning to rebrand my catering business. Something fresh and modern. I would also like uniforms designed for my waitstaff. At the moment they're in the standard black pants and white shirt, but it'll be great to have a point of difference, even if it's subtle. My clientele appreciates that sort of thing. Anyway, Ai, I was wondering if you'd like to do it—if you're available."

I swallowed. "Me?"

"I can't think of a better person." Then, with a meaningful look, she added, "It's quite a big job but could be just what you need at the moment."

"I can look at it, I suppose . . ."

"That's my girl," Lucille said, pleased. Reaching into her large tote bag, she pulled out a booklet. "Here's the brief I put together along with the budget, if you want to have a look."

I leafed through the document, which appeared straightforward. Even though I hadn't taken on a creative project in a while, my mind immediately locked into gear, composing shapes and fonts, assembling pleats, collars, and cuffs. When I got to the budget, I saw that my design fee would cover most of the debt I owed to Yan.

"I think I can do this," I said, feeling energized for the first time in months. "I'll need access to software, so let me check with my old boss. He's really nice, so I don't think it'll be an issue." I whipped my phone out, sending a quick text to Ahmed.

"Hey, what phone is that?" Tri asked, eyes widening.

"It's cute, isn't it? My boss, Ahmed, gave it to me."

"Are they real diamonds?"

I laughed, "No, but it's very precious to me nonetheless."

"Can I see?"

I handed my phone to her and she started tapping away at the keys like a pro, pointing out features even I hadn't discovered. Lucille smiled at her fondly. "This one is already learning how to code."

"I know some HTML," she said proudly. "Tin's teaching me. He's really good at all that kind of stuff."

"Your brother is a pretty clever guy," I agreed.

When we said our goodbyes, it felt almost like hello. Afterward, I checked my phone and saw a new number had been saved in my contacts under the name "Tin."

Ahmed called me later that day. "You know, it's weird you texted, because I was going to call you . . . I swear, Ai," he insisted when I expressed my skepticism. He was so nice that I was worried he'd give me work just for the sake of it—not because I was needed. He went on to explain, "Kate wants to spend more time with her baby, so if you're free, we can go back to the same arrangement. And as long as you make the deadlines, you can use the software all you want."

"As long as you're sure," I said.

"Please, Ai, you'll be doing me a favor. Honest."

"Okay. If you say so."

Being back at the office gave me the feeling I was finally moving forward with my life. Even though things hadn't turned out as I'd planned, I was beginning to feel hopeful about my future. It took me no time at all to design the logo and uniforms. I'd already had most of it sketched up with a pad and pencil, which Lucille had approved. We opted for a simple but elegant pin-tuck shirt with a notched collar and pearl buttons on the cuff. As for the trousers, we went with a sharp tuxedo cut that tapered at the hem. The logo I designed was a graphic bow tie set above a modern serif font. Then I applied the logo to the garments as well as stationery items such as menus, invoices, business cards, and letterheads.

When I was done with the uniforms, I sent the designs off to the maker Lucille had lined up in Brisbane. She called me up as soon as they were completed. "They're perfect, Ai," she gushed. Within a few days I was able to pay most of my debt to Yan, feeling as though a huge weight had been lifted. Lucille had been right: the project was exactly the thing I needed. But I found I couldn't stop there. It was as though, during my time in purgatory, I'd been unwittingly storing away inspiration, and from the moment my eyes roamed over Lucille's brief, the floodgates opened. I began designing blouses and pinafore skirts inspired by my mother's wedding dresses, with whimsical and quirky details such as hearts hand-embroidered onto sleeves or buttons sewn in poetic and meaningful places. It was exhilarating to feel a sense of purpose again, my limbs racing to keep pace with all the ideas that were rushing into my head.

Seeing my progress, Kate cheerfully imparted all the knowledge she'd gained so far as the founder and operator of a small, independent label. She wrote down lists of suppliers who would be helpful, industry grants for which I could apply, and names of buyers who could exert the most influence. She suggested I cut my teeth on the designer market circuit, pointing out the ones that took lower commissions. "It's like being part of a traveling circus," she explained. "We all help each other out where we can. It's a real family and I think you'll fit right in. Have you thought of a name for your label?"

"I'm going to call it 'Maggie.' It's a tribute to my magpie necklace."

"I've noticed how you always have that on; it must be really special to you."

Without feeling like I had to go into further details, I smiled and said, "It is."

Kate wasn't the only one eager to see my designs. Ahmed would hold each new creation against his considerable bulk, posing playfully. Wagging his finger at me, he'd say, "You won't forget me when you're famous, okay, Ai?"

For the last couple years, Mum had been asking me to sort through the pile of boxes in my bedroom stuffed full of schoolbooks and memories, to keep what was precious and throw out the rest. I'd make attempts on my sporadic and fleeting visits home, only to feel overwhelmed by the sheer enormity of the task. There never seemed to be enough time.

I attacked the job with a new sense of purpose, driven by a niggling sense that there was something I was looking for, but I wouldn't know what it was until I held it in the palm of my hand. That day finally came when I stumbled on an old shoebox and its contents that had lived inside like a time capsule, alive and pulsing. I took out each item one at a time, carefully laying them out like treasures from an archaeological dig, feeling as though something precious had been unearthed.

The first item was the note from Tin with which he'd included a key to his locker, offering me the extra space to store my art supplies. I held the key now in my hand, knowing it had once been in his. I thought about the kindness in that gesture, how much it had meant to me at the time. How much more it meant to me now. I ran my fingers over his signature script, the strange tilt of his *r*'s, the familiar blue ink on notepaper, its creases held together with tape from the sheer number of times it had been read. My mind floated to those few precious days we had before I left on that road trip to Canberra with Mum, thinking I would be back in time to say goodbye. Then those long conversations we shared when he was in Brisbane, how the phrase "whom I love" would linger every time he said my name. "Just a few more minutes . . . ," we'd whisper, but there were never enough minutes. We could spend our whole lives together and it wouldn't be enough. And I missed him then, so much that I felt my teeth ache. I reached for my phone, clutching it tightly to my chest, knowing there was a set of numbers waiting among my contacts that belonged to him, like the combination code for a safe containing something unimaginably precious. Anticipation swelled in my chest, but for now it was enough just to have the possibility of him. He would be back in Sydney soon. Maybe I would be brave enough to call him then.

The second item was an old journal I'd furnished with quotes, song lyrics, and the odd recipe. I turned a page and was confronted with a list of accusations I'd collected against Brigitte. I stopped, drawing in a deep breath, bracing myself.

Lucille says, "You're the pretty one"
Bowie—Road trip with Brigitte to get necklace
Brigitte teaching Bowie guitar
Valentine rose—two x's?
Sying says bullying . . .
What did Brigitte whisper in Sying's ear?
Shorts on Brigitte's bed . . .
"My heart breaks for her"
"At least she's got Tin"
"And us—she's got us too . . ."

I grabbed a pen from my bedside table, furiously crossing out each perceived offense that I had gotten so terribly wrong, the pen tip scratching so hard that it tore the paper underneath . . . until I got to the last item on the list and my pen stopped, hovering over the words:

Who is Pedro?

Next to it, I scribbled my answer:

I don't care if it was you, Brigitte, I miss you so much. I don't care.

With a heavy sigh, I picked up the third and last item: Brigitte's old Nikon I had packed away in those preparatory weeks before college, when, like a rocket ship, every ounce of my energy was devoted to leaving. I popped out the film canister, closing my fist around it like a prize.

Mum was in the kitchen, hands steeped in mince and coriander, working their magic. The familiar scene drew an ache in my chest. I went over and put my arms around her waist, squeezing a little too hard.

"Stop this, Ai," she scolded.

"Are you making dumplings?"

She mumbled a distracted yes.

I kissed her cheek and asked, "When will they be ready?"

"Long time."

"I'm going out to the shops now. Do you want anything?"

"Buy mango for mum; green one."

"Sure," I replied, setting out.

She called after me, "Buy nice one, okay? Not many bruise this time."

Being away from Whitlam for so long, I saw it with new eyes. Walking down the bustling main strip, I was reminded of all the things I'd forgotten to miss. The stalls I once saw as tacky and dilapidated now beckoned with their vast array of offerings in luscious, mouthwatering displays. Sago pudding in plastic cups, barbecue char siu strung up behind glass, sweetheart cakes on scratched silver trays, and bowls of steaming-hot pho. The aroma, the noise, and the sheer busyness of the streets felt like a homecoming.

The rise of digital photography meant photo shops were fast becoming obsolete, but it was comforting to see one still standing, stubbornly fixed to the corner of the town plaza. I went in and dropped off the film canister. Outside, I caught the small, square shape of someone familiar.

"Sying!" I called, surprised by my eagerness to see her. The last time we spoke was the night of her exhibition, and we hadn't left on good terms. But the years must have tempered the animosity I had once felt toward her. She turned and waved before walking over. We hugged awkwardly.

"How are you, Ai?" She grinned, doing a little excited skip. "I saw that photograph of you in *Good Weekend* . . ."

"Oh, I've been okay. Just staying with my parents for a bit while I figure things out."

"You're living the dream . . . aren't you? I'm stuck in a boring office job and living vicariously through you!"

I smiled. "How about a coffee?"

We went to a quiet café and ordered our drinks. Sying then launched into details about her administration role at Centrelink, a government organization in charge of welfare payments and wage subsidies. She lamented the long hours, the mind-numbing boredom, and being verbally abused on a daily basis. "People get upset with me when their applications aren't approved. It's got nothing to do with me, but I get all the blame because I'm the one fronting up . . ."

I nodded politely and let her continue. She was going a mile a minute and I wondered if she was nervous. Her eyes had a furtive look to them, darting around the room while she spoke as though looking for a safe place to land. When our iced coffees came, she took a sip and asked, "Tell me, Ai, what it's like, being famous and all?"

I laughed, but there was a bitterness to it I hadn't meant. "I wouldn't say that."

"Is everything okay, Ai? You seem kind of sad."

"Lately, I've been thinking a lot about Brigitte. Living away from Whitlam, I was able to push those thoughts aside, but now she's returned with a vengeance. I don't know if it's to do with this place or whether she's the reason why I'm back here."

Sying spooned some whipped cream into her mouth, and I noticed her hand was shaking a little. She put the spoon down with an awkward clatter and met my gaze briefly before looking away. "You know, I was never all that close to Brigitte, but I get the feeling she's haunting me too."

"I keep thinking back to that day after our moderating session with Mrs. Parker—the one with the three of us. Do you remember?" Sying took a deep breath and nodded as I continued. "In my mind, things went on a dark tangent after that day. And I have this piercing memory of Brigitte whispering something in your ear. You had a look of terror on your face, and I wonder what she said that caused you such distress."

Sying looked away. "I don't know what you mean, Ai. I don't remember." Something in her expression told me otherwise.

"You must remember," I insisted, describing the scene for her again.

Sying fidgeted, shifting in her seat. "I don't want to talk about it, Ai."

I reached over, touching her arm, and she pulled away as though she had just been scalded.

"Please," I pleaded. "I have to know what she said to you that day. I sense it's important somehow."

Sying's hands moved to cover her face and I noticed she had started trembling all over. "I just want to forget all about that time, Ai, I really do. It's taken me so long to get past it and I don't want to go back there again."

"I'm sorry, Sying. I don't mean to open up old wounds, but I really need you to tell me what Brigitte said to you. I believe, at the very least, you owe me that."

She was crying now, and I thought about changing the topic, but I was so close to the truth.

"Sying, please," I said, more forcefully this time.

She pulled her hands away from her face and I watched as tear after tear rolled down her cheeks.

"Please be straight with me, Sying. For once, be straight. Surely it can't be that bad, not after all this time . . ."

Sying seemed to be looking into the distance now. In a voice so soft it was barely audible, she said, "It was just a word, Ai."

I leaned in, "What was it?"

"Pedro."

I furrowed my brow. "Pedro? Do you mean the kid I was chatting to online—the one from Spain? What does Pedro have to do with anything?"

"It was me, Ai," Sying blurted out, a note of hysteria to her voice. "I was Pedro."

My eyes widened. "That was you?"

She nodded, head bobbing miserably.

"But—" I sputtered. My mind was racing, reconfiguring everything. "I thought Brigitte was the one masquerading as Pedro because all he wanted to talk about was Bowie, and I thought—"

Cutting me off, she said, "All *you* wanted to talk about was Bowie . . . I just wanted to talk to you."

I shook my head, feeling as though it just wasn't sinking in. "But he went silent—right after the accident . . ."

"I couldn't continue after what happened to Brigitte," Sying said, her voice now high-pitched and defensive. "I kept seeing her everywhere, felt like she was watching me. Sometimes I'd come across someone who looked like her and my heart would explode in my chest. It terrifies me so much and I don't like to think about it."

"But how did she know you were Pedro?"

"I used to stay back late at the library; maybe I left a window open on the share computer or something . . ."

"Then why wouldn't she tell me?"

"To be honest, I think she was saving it as a last resort. She knew exactly how you'd feel about me if you found out at the time."

"I would have hated you," I said, truthfully.

She blanched at my words and then nodded. "Exactly . . ."

"You did it to manipulate me—to turn me against Brigitte."

"I'm not proud of it, Ai."

"Then why did you do it?"

"I wanted you to like me as much as you liked Brigitte, but I knew it was only a matter of time before she'd rat me out. I lived in fear of that every day. I'm not completely coldhearted, you know. Sometimes the guilt got to me and I wanted to tell you myself, but you have no idea how much that connection with you meant to me, even if it was under false pretenses. Some days, it was all I had to cling to. You shared things with Pedro that you never did with me. Back at school, I never felt like I belonged; for me, it was such a lonely place. Yet everyone around me seemed to be having a ball. Aysum had Nadine; you had Brigitte. And when you got together with Bowie, you suddenly became part of a foursome, and I felt completely shut out."

"I'm sorry for what you felt, but that's no excuse. We made every effort to include you, but most times you were difficult. Even you have to admit that, Sying. You always had to have it your way."

"I know, I know . . . ," she whispered. "I keep hearing voices in my head and they're not kind. I keep thinking it would have been better if I never existed in the first place." To my ears, her words sounded genuine. I felt myself soften against her.

"It's all done and dusted now," I said, feeling suddenly tired. "That's how things went and we can only move on from that. So let's just move on, okay? I think we've already established that it was those two men at fault that day. I don't blame anyone else now. Things could have been different, but the truth is no one knows. I just wish I had been better to Brigitte in the months leading up to the accident, to have that time back again, you know? Even if it doesn't change a thing, just to have that time . . ."

"I think that's what I robbed you of, more than anything."

"We were just kids, Sying. Maybe you did cast a shadow over Brigitte, but I was the one who chose to go down that garden path with you. You didn't convince me of anything that I didn't already believe."

"All I want to do is make amends now. I want to make up for what I did."

"Did you ever apologize to Tin for putting his dad in the exhibition? You know his father was abusive, don't you? You saw what he was like when he came to get Tin after the accident . . . A part of you must have known."

"I tried to reach out to him but Tin's not an easy guy to track down."

"He left for Brisbane a few weeks after the exhibition. He's living there with Lucille."

"You're still in contact with him?"

I shook my head. "Not with Tin, but I did catch up with Lucille and Tri not long ago."

Sying winced at the mention of Tri's name. "I shouldn't have put Tin's dad in the show, not when Tin was dead set against it. But I was short on a profile and just wanted to fill the space. I'll always feel bad about that . . . I still remember the way his dad was yelling at him after the accident. I had tried to feel sorry for him that day, but all I could think was 'At least he showed up.'" She shuddered, as though attempting to shake off her past transgressions. "But I am really sorry for what I did. It was wrong and I see that now. We keep going on about the way this country treats us, but we're not always kind to each other, are we?"

We paused to look out the window at the people passing by, carrying on with their lives. The mood between us seemed to shift without us doing anything to affect this change. Sying looked suddenly wistful. "Still . . . despite all our problems, there is something special about Whitlam, isn't there? For a long time, I would never admit to anyone this was where I grew up. I was so ashamed of my roots. But now I have such a fierce, unapologetic love for this place. Do you know what I mean?"

"I do."

Perhaps sensing the softening of my mood, Sying brightened just a little. "Anyway, things aren't all doom and gloom with me, you know. I was sad for a long time after the exhibition. It felt like the pinnacle of my life, and it will only be downhill from there . . ."

"There will be other things in your life, Sying, I'm sure. You have to believe there are still good things in front of you." I realized that I truly meant it. Our conversation may have veered into unexpected territory, dredging up long-buried emotions, but it did help me to understand the true depth of her loneliness during those cruel adolescent years.

"How about you, Ai? Your life must be amazing, considering how glamorous it seems, especially your love life."

"I've dated a little here and there, but nothing serious. I guess I have a lot of unresolved issues of my own."

We parted ways, promising to keep in touch. As I watched Sying walk away, I caught a flash of her in my mind's eye still in her school uniform, proud and irrepressible, bustling from one group to another in search of the next captive audience.

I thought back to the morning of the picnic when Brigitte had picked me up in her car with its faint scent of flour, the little hula girl dancing on her dashboard, a tiny disco ball dangling from her rearview mirror. Her pretty, tear-streaked face a hailstorm of emotion.

"How can you think that about me, Ai?"

I had sat tight-lipped, staring straight ahead, refusing to answer.

"Bowie would never, ever do that to you—not in a million years." She pressed a hand to my cheek. "More importantly, *I* would never do that to you."

The memory swept in and out like a tide. "Brigitte," I whispered under my breath.

Like an incantation willed against a curse, I felt something lift.

I went to pick up the photographs and found a seat on one of the dull red benches that dotted the plaza. Laughter and chatter swirled all around me in a medley of languages, intermittent words bursting into comprehension. "You." "Me." "Yes." "Good." "How much?" "Thank you." "Where?" "Here." Lifting the tab of the envelope, I slid out the pile of photographs, flipping through them one by one. I drew a sudden, sharp breath. Every picture Brigitte had captured was of Tin, every shot unaware he was being photographed. And in all of them Tin was looking directly at me, the expression on his face unbearably soft, ending in the last picture of the ocean I had taken with the two of us behind the camera, waiting for the sun. And there it was. A story that was never meant to be told any other way.

I silently thanked Brigitte as tears welled up in my eyes. She knew, even then. Suddenly the trauma and grief I had carried since the day of the accident manifested into a dark, malevolent tide, swelling up so fast, I felt like I was drowning. Then, just as abruptly, it popped like an overblown bubble, receding all the way back. I took a deep breath and let the feeling settle into me, into its new home. And now, looking at the pictures of Tin, there came the simple, astounding realization that I loved him. That I'd always loved him.

I fumbled for my flip phone, scrolling through my contacts until I came across his number. I pictured Tri sitting across the table from me with the phone in her hand, a mischievous smile on her face, discreetly punching in Tin's digits. And now, here it was on my screen, staring back at me. How many times had my thumb hovered over this place? How many times had my heart? I pressed down on the call button and held the phone to my ear.

"Hello?" he answered.

"Tin," I said.

There was a brief pause. And then he said my name.

Acknowledgments

I WANT TO thank Alex Nahlous for her expertise and friendship during the early rewrites of this manuscript. Alec Shane for his faith in this book. Amy Baker and the amazing team at Harper Perennial for trusting in my vision and allowing me the creative freedom to bring it to fruition. Thank you to Sophia Kaufman, who has made this book so much more than what I imagined. Jemma Birrell, whose insights have been so helpful to me. My dear friend Aleks, whose recollections of our youth would often spark my own memories. Doug and Brenda for their love and support during the weeks I spent writing in their beautiful house. Michael and Ollie for the happiest years of my life. Mum and Dad for their stories.